P...

Nig...

Readers gave *Night Shift*

★★★★★

'I was not prepared for this to be the
best romance I've ever read'

'I'd give this ten stars if I could'

'OH. MY. GOD. I absolutely love this book'

'A cute and spicy read'

'I am so utterly IN LOVE with this book and
BOTH main characters'

'Absolutely loved it and I couldn't stop reading!'

'Beautifully romantic and thoughtful'

'I read this so fast, I couldn't get enough'

'Who gave NIGHT SHIFT permission to
be so cute and fantastic?!'

'I read it in one sitting and loved every minute of it.
It was so cute and had me laughing out loud so many times'

'I adored it, it was exquisite'

'Full of laughter and heart-warming romance that
it made me giddy with that first love happiness!'

ABOUT THE AUTHOR

Annie Crown is an author of new adult and contemporary romance full of humor, heart and spice. A born-and-raised California girl, she holds a bachelor's in English from USC and enjoys iced coffee in the morning and frozen margaritas in the afternoon. When she isn't writing, she's probably rewatching her comfort shows, adding more romance novels to her ever-growing TBR or daydreaming about fictional men who say things that make you melt.

Night Shift

ANNIE CROWN

PENGUIN BOOKS

PENGUIN BOOKS

UK | USA | Canada | Ireland | Australia
India | New Zealand | South Africa

Penguin Books is part of the Penguin Random House group of companies
whose addresses can be found at global.penguinrandomhouse.com

First published in Canada by Wattpad Books,
an imprint of Wattpad WEBTOON Book Group 2023
First published in Great Britain by Penguin Books 2024
001

Typesetting by Delaney Anderson
Printed and bound in Great Britain by Clays Ltd, Elcograf S.p.A.

The authorized representative in the EEA is Penguin Random House Ireland,
Morrison Chambers, 32 Nassau Street, Dublin D02 YH68

A CIP catalogue record for this book is available from the British Library

ISBN: 978–1–405–96868–3

www.greenpenguin.co.uk

For the daydreamers.

One

I've always loved libraries after dark.

This one—the only twenty-four-hour library at Clement University—may not have the marble floors and cathedral ceilings that adorn Pinterest boards and travel Instagrams, but it's still one of my favorite places on campus. And despite the outdated furniture, questionable carpet stains, fake ferns, and lingering stench of old coffee, there's something magical about the way moonlight floods the central atrium through the glass ceiling overhead, casting the mostly empty tables far below in a soft blue glow.

There's nowhere else I'd rather be at ten o'clock on a Friday night.

It helps, of course, that I'm getting paid to do nothing.

At the beginning of my shift, I did a lap around the second and third floors to collect stray books, which took me all of fifteen minutes. Now I'm wrapped up in my biggest knit cardigan and seated behind the circulation desk. It's the end of October—just past the usual midterm rush—so there are only a few people still scattered around the tables in the atrium: five or six students who seem deeply engrossed in their laptops, a group of girls who are currently packing up to leave, and a boy who's walking back and forth between one of the desktop computers and the old copy machine that never seems to print what you want it to on the first try.

Soon the library will be a ghost town, but outside, campus is buzzing with students. Some of them are trudging back to the dorms from their night classes, but most are leaving pregames in search of house parties. Their drunken laughter and shouts echo in the quad and drift in through the glass front doors of the library. I watch them stumble past from my seat at the circulation desk with a sense of detached curiosity, like I'm on one side of the glass at a zoo exhibit.

I can't figure out if I'm the visitor or the captive animal.

Maybe I should feel lonely during these long and quiet night shifts, but I don't. Not when I'm surrounded by books. And *definitely* not when the rest of my life feels so loud and bright and inescapably hectic.

Besides, I'm not totally on my own. I have Margie, my supervisor and the resident overnight librarian at Clement— who, right on cue, appears at my side and drops a stack of heavy tomes on the desk. Margie might be a foot shorter than me and three times my age, but she's got the arm strength and no-nonsense attitude of a drill sergeant.

"These were on the floor outside the drop box," she says. "Apparently, putting them *into* the box is too much work."

"People are the worst. Here—I'll log them."

The circulation desk is long enough to hold five stations for processing checkouts and returns. During the day, there are enough student workers to staff the entire desk, but tonight, it's only me and Margie. I boot up a computer to log in to the library's record-keeping system, sighing and propping my chin in my palm when it gives me the dreaded loading screen.

Clement University might have a billion-dollar endowment, but our wireless network is notoriously unreliable.

The atrium girls finally walk past my desk on their way to the doors, some of them stopping next to me to toss their empty coffee cups in the trash. I catch bits and pieces of their conversation.

"—professor wants us to read the whole book by Monday."

"You can always drop the class—"

"Oh, fuck, my phone died."

"Guys, Georgia just texted me. She says there's a party at the basketball team's house. Do we want to pregame at her place? She has tequila."

"Aren't they not supposed to be throwing parties this close to the start of the season?"

"Yeah, it's top secret. Invite only. I might still have some chaser in my—"

"Seriously, though, can I borrow someone's charger?"

The door swings shut behind the girls, their now-muffled voices fading until all is quiet again. My eyes slide from the loading screen in front of me to my phone. If the basketball team is having a secret party, that's where Harper and Nina— my roommates—will end up. Which means I'm sure to get some drunk texts over the next few hours.

The three of us have been inseparable since we got shoved into a triple in the freshman dorms. Now that we're juniors, we've gotten good at respecting one another's differences. Harper can't stand theatrical productions or discussions of three-act structure. Nina can't stand anything that involves workout clothes and braving the crowd of sweaty bodies at Clement's gym. And I can't stand college parties—too many people, lukewarm beer, shitty music played at eardrum-rupturing volumes. So, on Fridays, while Harper and Nina go out and get shit-faced, I work the night shift at the library and get a few hours of peace and quiet.

It's the perfect arrangement.

Once I get past the loading screen and into the library's record-keeping system, it takes all of five minutes to process the stack of returns Margie gave me. With nothing else immediately on my agenda, I push back my chair and reach for my backpack. It contains all the things I usually bring for the night shift: a full Hydro Flask, my lanyard with the keys to my apartment and a copy of the key to the library's front door, a plastic baggie of assorted snacks (in case the vending machine by the elevators is out of order again), and—most importantly—my book of the week.

With one last look to make sure no one's watching, I discreetly retrieve *The Mafia's Princess* from the depths of my backpack.

The cover is humiliating. I don't know who made the executive decision to put naked male torsos on romance novels, but I have a sneaking suspicion that some big-shot marketing executive wanted to shame me into buying an e-reader so I wouldn't have to be seen holding this in public. My face heats as I flip it open, press my thumb down the crease, and dive back into the third chapter of yet another story about a bookish young woman and the brooding, smart-ass alpha male who adores her.

My roommates call me a hopeless romantic. I let them. It's nicer than being called a lonely hermit.

"Kendall."

I jolt and shove my book into my lap, hiding it under the desk. Margie is standing between me and the front doors, too busy sorting through her master ring of keys to notice how awkward my arms look and how red my face is. Behind her is the poor kid who's been pacing back and forth between the computer and the copier. From the way his hair is standing on end and the look of utter defeat on his face, I'd guess it isn't going well.

"What's up?" I ask.

"The printer's acting up again," Margie explains. "I'm going to take this young man over to the engineering library to let him use one of their machines. I'll be back in fifteen minutes."

Margie leads the suffering undergrad out through the front doors. As soon as they're gone, I whip out my book and slide down in my chair, giddy with anticipation.

I can't believe I'm getting fifteen minutes of uninterrupted reading time this early in the night—usually I have to wait until after midnight before I can kick my feet up and relax.

The Mafia's Princess isn't groundbreaking literature, but it's exactly what I want out of a romance novel. The heroine, a quick-witted attorney, isn't whiny or too stupid to live, and the hero, a former street fighter and Mafia renegade, isn't so possessive that he's a walking red flag. They're both clever. They're both driven. Also, it's only the third chapter, and there've been two very well-written fight scenes. This is a good sign. Authors who write brilliant fight scenes tend to be good at *other* physical scenes—and if the banter and heated glances between the leads are any indication, I'm fast approaching what might be one of the hottest sex scenes I've ever read.

I'm so absorbed, I barely hear it when one of the student ID–operated turnstiles at the front door beeps and swings open. Maybe it's one of the girls who just left, come to reclaim a forgotten water bottle or phone charger. Or maybe it's Margie and the boy who needed to print. I should look up. But the attorney and her renegade are alone in an elevator, the sexual tension between them crackling like electricity, their breathing heavy and—

A shadow falls over my desk.

I lift my eyes reluctantly.

The guy standing on the other side of the circulation desk is tall. Really, really tall. I tip my head back to look at him properly—and oh. *Oh.* He's equal parts menacing and beautiful. He has dark hair cropped close to his head and eyes the color of ground coffee. Eyes that are watching me with a look I can only describe as hostile.

My heart hiccups with recognition before sinking to my stomach.

Because I know him. We've never spoken, but I've seen him from a distance on campus and, occasionally, on screens. He's the star of Clement's basketball team. The player all the sports broadcasters and basketball fanatics predict is going to be a first-round draft pick. The one who got ejected from last year's big game for breaking our rival point guard's nose with a hard right-handed uppercut.

Vincent Knight.

Two

I'm huddled in my oversized cardigan with half of my blond hair pulled up in a messy knot and a romance novel in my hands. It goes without saying that I'm in no way prepared, mentally or physically, to face the most notorious member of Clement University's beloved basketball team.

Vincent Knight is fearsome. He looks far more like the ex-Mafia romantic lead in my novel than a college athlete—except, maybe, for the sling supporting his left arm and the bulky brace wrapped around his wrist.

"Hi," I blurt. "Can I help you?"

A muscle in Vincent's jaw ticks. His right hand—the one *not* cradled in a sling—is clenched so tightly around his student ID it must be carving into his palm.

"I need some nineteenth-century British poetry."

The timbre of his voice, lowered to a library-appropriate volume, cuts through the quiet and hits me square in the chest. I suppress a shiver.

"Sure. That'll be on the second floor. If you take a right

when you get out of the elevator and follow the signs, it's all the way back by the—"

Vincent cuts me off. "Can you give me any *specific* books?"

It's a totally standard request. The tinge of annoyance dripping from the words is nothing new either. It pales in comparison to what I see during finals, when a combination of sleep deprivation and desperation brings out the worst in humanity. There's really no reason that one brooding basketball player should make me feel like I'm melting with embarrassment in my seat because he needs a reading recommendation.

Abruptly, I remember the romance novel in my hands.

My face burns as I roll my chair forward and shut the book, pressing it cover-down into my lap and praying that Vincent Knight can't read upside down.

"Our overnight librarian is actually out right now," I tell him in my most polite customer service voice. "Do you want to wait for her to get back, or—"

"Are you not qualified?"

My mouth shuts abruptly at his curt tone. Vincent Knight must be used to getting what he wants when he whips out the condescending remarks and the steely glare I've only ever seen him use on the court. I'll admit that I'm intimidated—by the size of him, by the weight of who he is and how everyone at Clement knows his name, by the cool intelligence glinting in his dark eyes—but I'm not about to let him push me around.

"I'm in the honors English program. If anything, I'm *overqualified.*"

"Great," Vincent says, unmoved. "Lead the way."

"Unfortunately, leaving this desk to help cranky kids with their homework isn't in my job description."

Vincent's eyebrows shoot up with surprise. He cuts a glance at the tables in the atrium, where two or three of the late-night studiers have looked up from their laptops and are staring at the star of our school's basketball team like this is the last place in the world they expected to see him on a Friday night. Which leads me to wonder why, exactly, he's here with one arm in a sling and a pressing need for British poetry. Especially since the rest of his team is supposedly throwing a forbidden party at the basketball house.

Vincent turns to face me again and presses his lips together, chastened.

"Do you think you could make an exception for someone who's only got one good arm and is having a really shitty night?"

It's a small surrender of his pride, but he's clearly not used to having to ask for help or apologize for his surliness. But Vincent looks, for a moment, like he knows he's being an asshole and wishes he could stop. Something about that softens the edge on my anger.

We stare each other down. I'm the one who cracks.

"Fine," I say begrudgingly. "I guess I'll just . . . come with you, then."

It'll only be five minutes of my life, and it's not like I have much else to do besides reading about Lorenzo taking Natalie up against an elevator wall. I set *The Mafia's Princess* face down on the circulation desk and flip up the little sign that tells people I'll be back in fifteen minutes.

It's not until I stand up from my chair that I realize how enormous Vincent is. It makes sense that he's tall—he's a Division I basketball player, after all—but I'm nearly five foot eleven, so it's not often that I'm towered over. It throws me off. I snatch my lanyard, keys clanking against my water bottle in my haste, and loop the strap tight around my fist as I march around the desk and brush past Vincent. I catch the scent of laundry detergent and something warm and spiced—and then I absolutely do not think about how good he smells, or how small he makes me feel, or how much I like it.

The stairs are on the far side of the atrium, but considering I was just a few paragraphs from reading about passionate sex in elevators, I'd rather not trap myself in one with Vincent. He trails behind me as we climb to the second floor and plunge into the maze of books, weaving through the stacks like animals on the hunt. I've always been a fast walker. Harper and Nina bitch and moan about it when they fall behind, but Vincent—with his long strides—keeps up without complaint.

He might have his head stuck in his ass, but at least he's not slow.

The British literature is tucked deep in a corner. One of the fluorescents overhead has burned out, leaving this nook of the library dim and oddly intimate. If anyone were to go looking for a private place on campus to make out, this would be the best spot. Not that Vincent and I are going to make out.

Jesus Christ, I scold. *Pull yourself together.*

This is what I get for reading smut on the job.

"Here we go," I huff. "British poetry. It's all sort of thrown together, but I can help you pick out some from the century you need, if you don't know how to work Google."

Vincent rolls his eyes. "Just hand me whatever."

I tilt my head to the side and scan the spines on the shelf, reading off the titles and authors under my breath.

Nineteenth-century British poetry is fairly broad, as far as requests go. I'll need some more specific parameters if we're going to hurry this up so I can get back to my book.

"What class is this for?"

"I'm taking a GE on classic British literature," Vincent says. "We're supposed to analyze a poem by Monday. The professor didn't specify what kind."

So, no pressing midnight deadline, but he's still here instead of at the party with the rest of his team. Why couldn't he wait until tomorrow morning and just come in with a hangover, like every other undergrad at Clement?

I regard Vincent carefully, my eyes dancing over his disheveled hair and the slight shadows beneath his dark eyes. He looks like he could use eight hours of sleep and a good laugh. Maybe he's more anxious about this paper than he wants to let on. Or maybe the sling around his arm and the impending start of basketball season is to blame for his sour attitude. If I had my phone on me, I could send a covert text to Harper and Nina to see if they've got their hands on any intel.

But my phone is downstairs, and Vincent is standing next to me, tall and brooding and visibly agitated as he glares at the books surrounding us.

I stifle a sigh. *One problem at a time.*

"What are you in the mood for?" I pluck a few off the shelf—Byron, Wordsworth, Blake—and stack them in the crook of my arm for his approval. "Some poetry by an old white man, or some poetry by an old white man?"

Vincent doesn't laugh at my joke. Instead, he takes the Byron off the top and flips it over to scrutinize the back cover.

My eyes catch on Vincent's hand. It's nearly twice as

large as mine and moves with a confidence and agility that is, unfortunately, deeply attractive. If this were a romance novel, Vincent Knight would be the hero. There's no argument. He's tall, broad-shouldered, dark-haired, and handsome in the most wicked of ways. He could be the Mafia hit man, the alpha of the pack, the cutthroat billionaire with daddy issues—he could scoop me up with his good arm, pin my back to a bookshelf deep in the stacks, and fill me. He'd whisper dirty things to me too. Not lines out of a bad porno, but *poetry*. Words of passion.

But this isn't a romance novel. And if the way Vincent is frowning down at Lord Byron's compiled works is any indication, I don't think I should expect any poetry from him.

Stop thinking about sex, you miserable little shit.

"That was a joke, by the way," I say, eager to fill the silence. "Everyone knows the best poets of the nineteenth century are women."

Vincent hands the Byron back to me.

"Do you have anything"—he hesitates—"*simpler* than this?"

"I'm afraid Dr. Seuss is twentieth-century American."

Vincent cuts me an annoyed look. I tip my chin up, refusing to apologize.

"Look," he grumbles, "I'm sorry. My wrist is killing me, I haven't slept right all week, and I'm way out of my comfort zone with this—this poetry shit." Twin spots of pink bloom on his cheeks, but surely it's only a trick of the light. "English was never my best subject."

I slot the three books back on the shelf.

"A lot of people struggle with it," I admit. "Especially

poetry. Which honestly isn't surprising, given the way it's taught."

Vincent snorts bitterly. "I *hated* high school English. I was shit at it. I almost had to sit out basketball my freshman year because my teacher was going to fail me for not memorizing a Shakespeare poem." He cuts another sideways glance at me. "I got my grades up, obviously. I was smart enough to graduate high school."

"Just because poetry never clicked for you doesn't mean you're not smart. Poetry is—it's almost like another language. It doesn't matter if you can recite every word from memory. Learning a bunch of vocabulary won't do you any good if you don't learn the grammar and cultural context too."

If Vincent finds my monologue embarrassingly pretentious, he doesn't say anything. His eyes are patient. Locked in. His attentiveness gives me the confidence to keep going. I run my eyes over the rows of books in front of us, then I pluck a familiar and very thick tome—*Engman's Anthology, Twelfth Edition with Extended Prologue*—off the shelf and flick through it until I find the section on Elizabeth Barrett Browning.

"Okay, this one's good," I say, tapping the page with my fingertip.

Vincent shifts closer to read over my shoulder. I hold myself very still, determined to neither flinch away nor lean into the heat of his large body.

"If thou must love me," he reads, warm breath ghosting over my collarbone and the back of my outstretched hand.

"It's a sonnet," I say, pulling my hand into a fist. "Fourteen lines, iambic pentameter. Very easy to spot. The trick with sonnets is usually to watch for a turn toward the end. Sometimes it's in the last couplet—the last two lines—if the rest of the poem is split into three quatrains—"

"That's four lines, right?"

I glance up at Vincent. It's a mistake. He's so close I can see freckles on the bridge of his nose and a little white scar just under his right eyebrow. His eyes aren't on the poem. They're on me.

"Um, yes." I clear my throat and consult the book again. "Four lines. But see, this is a Petrarchan sonnet. One octave and a sestet. So, the turn is in the sestet—those last six lines."

"If thou must love me, let it be for nought." Vincent reads the first line.

"Except for love's sake only," I continue.

The air around us slows, and the world narrows to this one corner of the library. I read the rest of the sonnet out loud, tripping over a few words as I go, but Vincent doesn't snicker or correct me. He's silent. Reverent. It feels sacred, somehow, to read the work of a woman long dead in a chapel built to honor words and their makers.

". . . But love me for love's sake, that evermore thou mayst love on, through love's eternity."

There is a moment of silence—a shared breath—after I read the last line.

Then Vincent asks, "What does it mean, Professor?"

I laugh in a quiet exhalation, thankful he's the one who's broken the tension.

"Elizabeth wrote this for her husband. She doesn't like the idea that he might love her for her intelligence or her beauty. *I love her for her smile—her look—her way of speaking gently.* She doesn't want that. Those things can change. She'll get old.

She might get sick. She could just . . . change. And she doesn't want his love to be conditional."

Vincent steps back, the heat of his body lingering for a moment before I'm cold again. I shut the anthology and turn to face him.

"Shit," he says, a genuinely stunned smile tugging at his lips. "You're good."

His words send a flood of heat through my body. I think I'm damp between my legs. It's humiliating—that one silly little compliment can have such a strong effect on me. That one kind word said in a quiet corner of the library can make me feel like I'm on fire.

"That's why they pay me the big bucks," I joke, my voice weak as I shove the book at Vincent. "Well, actually, I make minimum wage. Although we get an extra buck an hour for the night shift, which is pretty sweet."

Vincent weighs *Engman's Anthology* in his good hand like he's considering something. "How late do you work?"

For the life of me, I can't tell why he's asking.

"Um, I should get out of here by five. I mean, assuming whoever has the morning shift isn't a total dick and actually gets here on time."

Vincent lets out a low whistle. "Jesus. That's rough. How often do you have to work nights?"

"I usually volunteer to take Fridays," I say with a shrug.

"Why would you do that?" He sounds almost affronted. "Everyone knows all the best parties are on Friday."

"I'm not a big fan of parties. I mean, I definitely like drinking with friends, but I'm more low-key about it. Crowds make me—I don't know." I shiver at the thought of deafening music and dark rooms packed tight with strangers. "But I have a social life. I party, in my own way. My roommates and I do wine and movie nights every Thursday and boozy brunches on Sundays."

The corner of Vincent's mouth tugs up in a knowing smile.

"So," he says, "Thursdays and Sundays, you party."

"Yep."

"And on Fridays, you sit behind that front desk reading porn."

Three

My mouth falls open in shock.

"I don't read—it wasn't—it's not *porn*."

Vincent holds his hands up, palms out in surrender. "Hey, there's nothing wrong with a little self-indulgence. I won't judge. And I promise I won't report you for reading on the job, either, if that's what you're worried about."

He's teasing me. My blind panic is replaced with exasperation. I lift my chin and glare at him with unbridled fury, but rather than looking intimidated, Vincent simply presses his lips together to hold in a laugh.

"Fiction," I snarl, "is a healthy way to exercise the imagination—"

"Come on. You don't *need* an imagination. You could walk into the nearest house party and find a line of guys willing to do whatever you want." As soon as the words leave his mouth, Vincent's nose crinkles, like the idea sounded better in his head.

I fold my arms over my chest. My lack of experience with sexual intimacy is a sore spot, and he's prodded it like a fresh bruise.

"I'm fully capable of hooking up, if I wanted to," I say. "But I don't, because college boys are immature little gremlins who play video games in dingy basements and say misogynistic shit for laughs and can't find the clitoris. The men in my novels are passionate and accomplished and—"

"Fictional."

At the sight of my withering glare, Vincent raises an eyebrow, daring me to say he's wrong.

Instead, I say, "So, you admit that college boys are trash?"

Vincent laughs. I refuse to be proud of myself for drawing the sound out of him and instead turn to one of the shelves, my eyes dancing over the spines but not really catching any of the author names or titles.

When I risk another look at Vincent, he's smiling at me like he's found the last corner piece of an elaborate jigsaw puzzle.

"I get it now," he says.

"Get what?" I demand.

Vincent lifts the book in his hand. "There's a reason you love that poem so much."

"And why's that?"

"Because you're scared too."

I laugh, more with bitterness than with humor. "Scared of what?"

"It's Friday night. You're young and pr—pretty smart, and you've got your head buried so deep in a romance novel I practically had to drag you out of it. So, either you think you're above it all or you're scared of putting yourself out there. You don't want to give up control, and you don't want to do anything if you can't look up spoilers for the end. *But love me for love's sake*. Books don't change. People do. You"—he points at me with *Engman's Anthology*—"are a coward."

Rage floods my veins like wildfire, so hot and horrible it makes my eyes sting.

"You're wrong."

"Am I?"

No, a voice in my head whispers. "Abso-fucking-lutely."

I stare at him. He stares back. And then, just once—so quick I could blink and miss it—Vincent's self-assured gaze flickers to my mouth.

"Prove it."

It's like the world tilts beneath my feet. Like suddenly I'm Alice down the rabbit hole or Lucy Pevensie through the wardrobe—a girl stumbling headfirst into a fantasy.

Maybe it's the challenge sparkling in Vincent's dark eyes, or maybe it's my anger that makes me so brave, so determined to show him that he doesn't know shit. Because one moment I'm glaring at him, chest heaving and heart hammering, and the next moment I'm up on my tiptoes with my hands braced on his shoulders and my fingernails digging deep into the cotton of his black T-shirt. Like I can punish him for being so utterly infuriating, so full of himself that he had the nerve to psychoanalyze me in my own sacred space.

I kiss him. *Hard*.

Vincent groans against my mouth, his lips parting against mine and his chest rumbling beneath my palms. For a moment I'm proud, because I think I've surprised him, but then I feel the Velcro of his wrist brace snag my shirt and realize his injured arm is trapped between us.

I peel myself off him and stumble back a step.

Did I really just do that?

"Oh, fuck, I'm sorry," I say, breathless and mortified. "Is your arm—"

I don't even get to finish the question.

Vincent drops *Engman's Anthology*. The moment it lands at our feet with a heavy thud, his now-unoccupied hand circles the back of my neck. Vincent may be built like a brick wall, but there's a gentleness in the way his hand anchors me. It's not demanding. It's a patient, supportive touch.

He gives my neck a soft squeeze, silently asking me to meet his eyes. I do. There's a fire burning in them that matches the fire in me.

"Stop apologizing," he says, very seriously, "and try that again."

This is *wild*.

How is he making me feel like I'm the one in charge here? Like I'm the one calling the shots? Because by all accounts, Vincent is the one holding me together in one hand while my body threatens to shatter.

"I've never kissed anyone sober," I admit, my entire face flushing with heat.

Vincent's face softens.

"Then practice on me," he offers. "I'm here. I'm all yours."

He doesn't try to press the matter or talk me into it. Instead, he holds still and steady for me—like a rock I can cling to in the crashing waves of my anxieties—and gives me the time I need to collect my thoughts.

I want to kiss him. That's a given. And unless Vincent is the world's most convincing liar, he's definitely open to the idea of kissing me too. But my scrambled brain can't make sense of the equation. Normal people don't make out within ten minutes of meeting each other unless they're drunk off their asses—even if those ten minutes include some heated banter and reading sonnets in a dark corner of a nearly empty library.

Real life is never like the novels.

What's the catch?

Vincent misreads my hesitation. "If you're not into this, you can go back to your book. My ego can take the hit, I promise. But don't hold out on me because you're scared."

The fire in me reignites. "I'm *not*—"

Vincent's hand squeezes my neck again, more urgently. "Then come here," he murmurs.

Fuck it, I tell myself. Yes, my hair is a mess and my makeup is several hours old. Yes, the fluorescent lights and dingy carpet aren't exactly setting the mood. I wish I felt more put-together, more prepared to be held and touched.

But Vincent doesn't seem to mind that I'm not perfect, and maybe that's all that matters.

Life is far too short to let my shot at feeling like I'm in a romance novel pass me by.

With a deep breath to bolster my bravery, I tilt my chin up again and offer my mouth to Vincent. He holds me with his thumb on my pulse point and his fingers in my hair as he brings his head down to kiss me once, gently, and then again. They're quick, featherlight brushes of his lips against mine—like he's teasing me. I make an impatient sound in the back of my throat, suspiciously like a whine, and Vincent laughs.

Then he kisses me properly.

I gasp as Vincent's mouth comes down over mine. My lips

part, and our tongues brush, tentatively at first and then with bolder, exploratory swipes and twirls. It's not like the clumsy, alcohol-soaked kisses I've had before—this is something entirely different. It's purposeful. Deliberate.

This is how it feels to kiss someone when the only thing clouding my head is a desperate need to know what he tastes like.

Vincent's tongue swipes over my bottom lip, followed by the gentle scrape of his teeth. I gasp. It's hard to hear anything over my heartbeat pounding in my ears. When he dips lower to brush kisses along my jawline, I shiver and reach up to thrust my fingers into his dark hair. It's thick and silky smooth.

I give his hair a soft, experimental tug.

Vincent groans against my neck. I feel it deep in my bones, reverberating like an echo and striking me right between my legs. I squirm against him and inhale sharply when I feel it— hardness beneath his soft black joggers. I don't know why I'm so shocked. I know, from my extensive literary research, how this all works. But the idea that Vincent is sporting an erection for me sends a flood of heat to my center. Instantly, I resent his pants and my own leggings for being in the way. I want them gone. I want only skin and for Vincent to press me open, warm and slick and vulnerable. I slide my hands to his biceps, clutching at the hard muscle under strained cotton, and use the leverage to roll my hips against his.

"Fuck," Vincent says against my cheek. "You're gonna kill me, Professor."

My center clenches at his words. And then a horrible thought occurs to me: *He doesn't even know my name.*

Four

I lean back and gulp in cool air, trying to get my bearings. Vincent takes the opportunity to duck his head and plant attentive kisses along my exposed collarbone.

He's good at this. Suspiciously good.

"Do you make a habit of seducing women in libraries, or is this a new thing for you?" I want it to sound like a joke, but I'm sure he can hear the anxiety seeping into my voice.

Vincent presses one last kiss to the base of my throat before straightening to look at me.

"No," he says, then amends: "I mean, I've seduced women, but never in a library. And that wasn't what I was trying to do. I really do have a paper due Monday, and this stupid fucking brace"—he lifts his injured arm and lets it drop back to his chest—"is real. I sprained my wrist during summer training. It's not just a bid for sympathy."

I watch him through narrowed eyes. "Just sprained?"

"Fell on it coming down from a contested layup."

"Hmm. The sling seems pretty serious."

"My coach," Vincent says tightly, "might've overreacted.

He doesn't want me to miss any more games than absolutely necessary."

I press my lips together, remembering all the footage I've seen of him getting rough with the opposing team on the basketball court. The words bubble up into my mouth before I can think them through. "You sure you didn't punch someone?"

Vincent sighs and tips his head back, eyes on the ceiling. "I take it you know who I am."

"Just because I don't go to parties doesn't mean I'm completely out of touch with what goes on at this school."

"Have you ever been to a basketball game?"

"No, but I saw the video of you breaking that guy's nose last year."

Vincent winces. "Not my brightest idea. That asshole had it coming, though."

"What'd he do?"

For a moment, he seems surprised—like he expected me to preach about violence never being the answer.

"He said something he shouldn't have."

"To you?"

"No. To my teammate. Jabari."

"Oh." I frown. "Well, then you fucked up, Knight."

"Really?"

"Yep. You should've gotten at *least* three more hits in before the refs pulled you off."

Vincent cracks a slightly sheepish smile that does terrible things to my insides. His good hand drops to my shoulder. I wonder if he knows that I feel electric sparks of pleasure every time the pad of his thumb traces my collarbone.

"Seems unfair that you know my name and I don't know yours," he murmurs.

I didn't realize until now that my anonymity was a comfort blanket. I could give Vincent a fake name, of course, but something about lying to him makes my stomach squirm with guilt.

"It's Kendall," I offer quietly.

"Well, Kendall," he whispers, my name soft in his mouth, "this sling isn't a pickup tool, if that's what you're worried about."

I bite back a smile. "I didn't think it was. It'd be kind of a lame pickup trick. I don't know how you could properly ravish a girl against a bookshelf with only one good—"

The only warning I get is the twinkle of mischief in Vincent's dark eyes.

And then he wraps his good arm around my waist, beneath my cardigan, and lifts me up off the ground. I let out a humiliating squeal of surprise and throw my arms around his neck, one hand clutching at his hair and the other tight around a handful of his shirt. I'm not a small person. I'm not built like the heroines who get tossed around in bedrooms and called *cute* or *feisty*. Despite the width of Vincent's shoulders and the impressive circumference of his biceps, I'm a little terrified shit could hit the fan very quickly.

"That was a *joke*. I was *joking*."

"And I'm not."

He shifts his hold on me. I feel fingers digging into my hip, just hard enough to hurt in the most glorious way. Maybe I'll bruise. I don't know why the thought of it thrills me.

"Do *not* drop me," I warn.

"You know I could squat lift you, right?"

The firm curve of his ass against my calves is proof enough of his claim.

"I'm just *saying*."

Vincent laughs, his hot breath feathering over my skin. "Just give me a minute. At least let me try to act smooth. I promise I've got you, Kendall."

My name in his mouth makes me needy all over again. Vincent must be able to tell, because he steps forward until I feel something hard behind me—a bookshelf. It's bolted to the wall, so I know we probably can't knock it over, but it still feels precarious to be pinned against it with nothing but open air under my feet.

This is all very dangerous.

"What were you saying," he murmurs, "about me ravishing you up against a bookshelf? Because I think it's clear I'm more than capable."

Giddiness floods my body. I duck my head so my lips brush his ear.

"Prove it," I whisper.

Vincent doesn't laugh, but there's a rumble in his chest— low and suspiciously like a growl—before he surges forward to kiss me again. This time, it's not so gentle. Our mouths meet with a hunger that makes my belly twist.

He can't be real. It's the thought on loop in my head as Vincent's hips roll against the cradle of mine. Where did this boy come from? Because it's so fucking *fun* to have a little verbal warfare with him and read my favorite poetry and then make out against the wall, and I can't believe I've made it almost twenty-one years of my life without feeling this way. My brain is going fuzzy at the edges. My world has collapsed to this: Vincent's solid and warm body, his hands cradling me, pressing me closer while his mouth—

Something hits the ground to my left with a heavy thud.

I jolt back from Vincent like I've been shocked.

It's a book.

I must've knocked it off the shelf. I'll have to figure out where it came from so Margie doesn't have to—

Oh, fuck.

Margie.

It's definitely been fifteen minutes by now, which means there's a very real chance she'll come up here to reshelve some books.

I tap Vincent's arm frantically. "Put me down, please."

He does so immediately.

The moment my feet are on the ground, I shuffle around him and put a few feet of space between us. His good arm falls back to his side. In the absence of the heat of Vincent's body, I'm reminded just how arctic it gets in this library, but I resist the urge to wrap my cardigan tight around myself and burrow into it. I will not hide. Not when Vincent's standing in front of me with pink cheeks, kiss-swollen lips, disheveled hair, and a dazed expression on his face.

I did that, I tell myself. *I made a mess of him.*

My roommates would *scream* if they could see me now. Harper and Nina have given me shit for years about being the homebody, the reasonable one, the mom friend of our group. Tonight? I'm unrecognizable. Out of my mind. Fully out of character.

"I told you," I say with a calmness I don't actually feel, "I'm *not* afraid."

Vincent's lips twitch. "Fair enough."

His voice is low and hoarse in a way that makes me feel wobbly. But I need to be more pragmatic. I'm on the clock. There's a supervisor who might come looking for me soon. And what next? Lose my virginity to a boy I've just met in a dark corner of Clement's only twenty-four-hour library?

Logic and reason are cruel bitches.

I smooth down the front of my shirt and clear my throat. "I should really get back to work. But if you want to follow me to the front desk, I can help you check that book out."

I take a step backward. Vincent smiles, but it looks a bit like a grimace.

"I'll meet you down there," he says. At my curious stare, he motions to the crotch of his pants. It's dimly lit, and his joggers are black, but I catch the outline of an impressive erection tenting the fabric. "I need a minute."

My face flushes. "Oh. *Oh*, right."

It feels like I should say something else—something to acknowledge the gravity of what just happened—but there's too much to cover. I don't even know where to start.

I don't look back as I leave the stacks, because if I do, there's a good chance I'll go running back to finish what we started.

At the top of the stairs, I hesitate before veering off down the hall to dart into the women's bathroom. The girl who looks back at me in the mirror over the row of sinks is a stranger—eyes wide, lips pink and puffy. A strangled laugh bubbles up in my throat. I have to be dreaming. I did *not* just make out with Vincent Knight. In the library. During my shift. After some (apparently very erotic) live reading of Elizabeth Barrett Browning.

What do we do now? Like, am I supposed to ask him out?

Does Vincent Knight even date? Or is this going to be a casual thing where he comes to the library during my night shifts and we come up with a million different ways to defile each section? Maybe that's too presumptuous of me. Maybe this was a weird, onetime thing. A moment of passion that we'll laugh off before we part ways.

I don't know what happens next. I've lost the fucking plot.

My hands shake when I reach out to turn the tap on and pat icy cold water on my overheated cheeks. Minutes pass—I don't know how many, since I don't have my phone on me—but my body doesn't seem to want to cool down.

I need to meet Vincent at the circulation desk.

So why aren't my feet moving?

"Shit," I say aloud. The word echoes down the line of empty toilet stalls. I meet my own eyes in the mirror again and realize, with startling clarity, that Vincent might've been right.

Maybe I *am* a coward.

• • •

After finally mustering up the strength to emerge from the girls' bathroom, I hurry down the stairs and head straight to the circulation desk, my shoulders hunched with shame. Margie is back, shuffling books around on one of the small rolling carts we use for reshelving.

There's no sign of Vincent.

"Did the printing go okay?" I ask.

Margie nods. "Poor kid has a career fair in the morning and couldn't figure out how to get the right margins on his résumé."

I hum sympathetically.

Margie heads off with a box of East Asian literature she wants to relocate to a display on the other side of the atrium. I scan the moonlit tables there for any sign of brown-eyed basketball players, then discreetly pull up the library's check-out database on my computer.

There's one new entry to the system: six minutes ago, Knight-comma-Vincent checked out *Engman's Anthology*.

I slump back in my chair, the air in my lungs leaving in a heavy whoosh. He's gone. He left while I hid in the bathroom like the coward he accused me of being.

If he wanted to, a voice in my head whispers, *he would've stayed*.

But he didn't.

It's probably for the best, actually. It would've been awkward to reconvene in the bright fluorescent lights here and try to pretend we didn't just maul each other. And it would've been painful to trudge through small talk as we discovered that, once the thrill of being alone with a member of the opposite sex in a dimly lit corner of the library was gone, the two of us have nothing in common. I still don't know anything about Vincent Knight—aside from the fact that he's an obscenely tall basketball player who hates English classes and has a mouth made for kissing.

He probably won't remember my name by next Friday. I'll be just another wild hookup story that he tells his teammates about over rounds of beer pong or in the locker room after practice. Because that's what nonfictional men do: disappoint you.

So, really, I should be thankful that he left without saying goodbye.

Wrapping my cardigan even tighter around myself, I reach for *The Mafia's Princess*, still face down where I stowed it on the desk. The naked torso on the cover feels like it's mocking me. With a heavy sigh, I lean down and stow it in my backpack.

I've had enough romance for one night.

Five

It's five thirty in the morning when I clock out of my shift, shoulder open the library doors, and emerge into the real world. The sky is still dark and star-speckled. In the orange glow of the lampposts stationed around the quad, there's a misty haze from the sprinklers in the grass. No one else is in sight. But that's typical—no one else has a good reason to be on campus before sunrise on a Saturday. I'm sure most of Clement's student body is still asleep.

An unwelcome image flickers into my head: Vincent Knight, curled up under a cloud of blankets and duvets, hair mussed and eyelashes like dark feathers in the hollows over his cheeks.

"Oh, fuck off," I grumble.

It's been a good seven hours now since he came into the library, and I'm stuck between wishing he never had and wishing I hadn't let him leave. Because what if that was it? My one chance to see what it feels like to live out my very own romance novel.

I don't need a man, I remind myself. *Nobody* needs *a man*.

I'm fine. I'll be fine.

I unchain my bike from the racks out front (with a bit more aggression than is strictly necessary) and pedal home, my teeth chattering in the cool California fall air.

Harper, Nina, and I lease an apartment a couple blocks north of campus. It's an old redbrick building nestled beneath wide oak trees that shed leaves onto the sidewalk below regardless of the season. They crunch under my sneakers as I tie up my bike and march up the front steps.

On most Saturday mornings, I'm as quiet as humanly possible when I get home so I don't wake up my roommates. But today, I don't have to bother—as soon as I step out of the stairwell on the second floor, I hear the unmistakable sound of Harper and Nina's laughter muffled through the wall.

I barely have the keys in the lock before the door flies open, and there's Harper, her corkscrew curls pulled back in a loose ponytail and fine glitter dusted across her dark cheekbones.

"Surprise!" she whisper-shouts. "We made you breakfast."

Over her shoulder, I can see Nina standing at the stovetop, spatula in hand.

"You guys are up?" I take in Harper's smeared makeup and Nina's deflated brown waves. They haven't roused themselves at the crack of dawn just to treat me to eggs and toast. "Oh my God, you haven't slept."

"Nope," Harper says with a giddy grin.

"We got home, like, half an hour ago," Nina tosses over her shoulder. "Do you want raspberry jam?"

"Yes, please." I toe off my sneakers and slide onto one of the stools at the kitchen island. "The party was good, then?"

"*So* good," Nina says as she pops a slice of bread into the toaster. "They hired a bartender, so the drinks were actually cold and not completely disgusting. I had a mai tai. A *mai tai*, Kendall. I never want to drink jungle juice again."

"God, I can't wait until we're all twenty-one," Harper says. "But until then, the basketball team knows how to throw a fucking party."

There's a soft, dreamy look on her face. Harper is a brilliant swimmer, a disciplined business major, and a complete and utter softy when it comes to stories of recovery, sacrifice, and generosity. Nina and I never go a week without her reading us some Humans of New York post or an inspirational news story. But this look? This one is new. I raise an eyebrow at Nina, who smiles knowingly as she slides my plate of eggs and toast across the counter.

"Jabari Henderson held her hand," Nina whispers.

I gasp with scandalized delight and turn to Harper, who throws herself onto the stool next to mine and hides her face behind her hands.

"Oh my *God*," she moans.

"What happened?" I demand. "Tell me *now*."

"After a few too many rum and Cokes, I got way too bold, and my dumb ass decided to ask him what he was drinking—"

"And then he took her to the bar to get her one!" Nina cries. "He held her hand—"

"Because it was crowded."

"That's still *flirting*, you moron. It's a *move*."

I nibble at my toast as I watch my giddy (and maybe still a little drunk) roommates make faces at each other. "I thought the team was on social probation before the season?"

"Oh, they are," Nina says. "But what a fucking joke. The

whole team was there, and I'm pretty sure I saw all the starters do a round of shots together."

"Except Knight," Harper amends.

My heart hiccups at the sound of his name.

Nina frowns. "Yeah, he was missing, which was weird. Usually, he's all over that shit."

Vincent left the library at about eleven o'clock last night. I figured he went home. But I'm fairly certain all the starters live in the off-campus house the basketball team leases, so that doesn't seem to line up. What, did he march through a sea of drunk kids and all his teammates—unnoticed—just to shut himself away in his room with *Engman's Anthology*?

"Maybe he went to a bar?" Nina suggests.

"I don't think he's twenty-one."

"But he's a senior, right?" I ask before I can shut myself up. "Maybe he decided to get serious and cut back on the drinking."

"Or," Nina says, "maybe he's got a girlfriend."

The toast in my mouth turns to dust.

Harper, savior of my sanity, shakes her head. "Knight's never had a girlfriend. He probably skipped the party because of his wrist. If he's on painkillers and he's not allowed to have any alcohol, I doubt he wanted to spend all night surrounded by drunk people."

Nina hums in agreement, then yawns. "God, I cannot wait to pass out."

"We're all sleeping in, right?" I ask.

"Oh, of course."

"Wait, Kendall," Nina says, "how was the library? Any new book recommendations for me?"

I smile down at my eggs. "I got through the first few chapters of *The Mafia's Princess*. I think you'd like it—the writing's solid, the love interest isn't obsessive or creepy, and I think it's going to get pretty spicy. I'll leave it on your desk when I finish it."

"You didn't finish it? It must not have been *that* good, then. You always finish books in one sitting."

I shrug. "I had a busy shift."

For a moment, I worry Nina is going to press me and I'll have to choose between lying to her (something I hate doing) and telling her what, exactly, made this shift so special. But then Harper finds glitter on her palm and asks if her eye shadow is smudged, and Nina cackles and informs her that her eye shadow has been all over her face for the better part of the night.

I decide not to tell them about my little rendezvous with Vincent.

If I don't talk about what happened, then it's *mine*. Mine to turn over in my head late at night and analyze. I don't want Harper and Nina's input to distort things, especially if one of them tells me something that'll completely rot the memory—like that Vincent Knight always wanders around campus looking for quiet corners to seduce naive girls, and that what happened between us was nothing more than a routine seduction for him.

It probably was.

But I don't want to know. I'd prefer not to ruin the story in my head.

● ● ●

All week long, I do my best to forget Vincent Knight—and all week long, I fail miserably.

I'm haunted by thoughts of dark eyes and love sonnets. There's no escape. Not when I'm brushing my teeth. Not when I'm sitting in the middle of a crowded lecture hall and frantically scribbling notes before the professor clicks to the next slide. Not when I'm scrolling through Instagram. Not when I'm snuggled under my covers at night, listening to podcasts about meditation or true crime. Not even when I'm at the grocery store with Harper and Nina, all three of us in our sweats and flip-flops as we congregate in the candy aisle to select our movie night snacks.

And definitely not when, instead of our agreed-upon movie, Harper turns on basketball.

"Hey!" I protest. "We agreed on a Tom Hanks movie."

"I just want to check the score, you big baby."

Clement's playing our first game of the season. It's only the end of the first quarter, but we're already up by twelve. I watch the players run up and down the court and tell myself that I'm not looking for floppy dark hair, devilishly intelligent brown eyes, and the mouth that kissed me senseless. But he's not out there. He must still be recovering.

I'm still recovering too. And that's a nice thought. That eventually I might be healed from this, and I won't have to try so hard not to think about being kissed by a boy who doesn't even know my last name.

Nina clears her throat. For a moment, I think she's on to me, but then she says, "Jabari looks good out there."

Harper chucks one of our decorative pillows at her. Nina cackles as it hits her square in the chest and knocks her backward in the armchair.

I laugh, too, but the camera angle shifts, and I almost choke on a peanut M&M—because there's Vincent Knight. On our television screen. In my apartment. Where I *live*. He's standing just behind Clement's bench in a suit jacket and a crisp white shirt with the top two buttons undone. The sling is gone, but he's still wearing the bulky black brace around his wrist.

He looks like a fucking prince. Beautiful, regal, and completely untouchable.

"Can we please change the channel now?" I snap, my heart hammering.

My roommates are too busy launching pillows back and forth—Nina has started making kissing noises; Harper is threatening to strangle her with her bare hands—so I'm the one who has to grab the remote.

I've never been so grumpy during a Tom Hanks movie.

Six

I blame stress for the fact that I wake up on Friday morning drenched in sweat and completely incapable of breathing through my nose.

I've had my flu shot. I'm up-to-date on all my vaccines. And I *never* get sick—not even freshman year when a nasty strain of strep swept through our dorm. So, I shower, even though there are black spots in my vision when I move my head too quickly, and I put on jeans, even though my bones ache and I want nothing more than to curl up in sweatpants, and I force myself to sit at my laptop reading an essay on feminist literature while my temples throb and my eyes burn.

Denial City, population one.

It isn't until my trash can is full of tissues and my head feels like it's splitting open that I finally admit to myself that there's no way I can make it to any of my afternoon classes, much less my night shift at the library. I text Harper and Nina, shoot Margie an apologetic email, and then turn to the student portal to find a replacement.

Within minutes, a girl offers to cover for me if I'll take her

Wednesday-morning shift. Nobody else is about to sacrifice their Friday night for a sick girl, so I have no choice but to agree to the switch.

I chuck off my jeans—horrible, uncomfortable, cursed denim—and pull on the sweatpants I've been dreaming of, then drag my traitorous corporeal form into bed.

My head feels like it's full of helium. My throat's so raw it's like I've gargled rocks.

"But you were fine last night," Harper says from the doorway as she tosses me bottles of Gatorade like a zookeeper lobbing fish to a sea lion. "You said you had a headache, but I didn't expect you'd be, like, on your fucking deathbed today."

"Neither did I," I croak. "Oh my God. Can you overdose on Advil? Is that a thing?"

"I'm making you chicken noodle soup!" Nina shouts from the kitchen.

Both insist on staying home with me for the night, even though I know the new going-out shirt Nina ordered two weeks ago finally arrived and she's dying to give it a test run. I prop myself up in bed and watch as they rearrange the furniture in the living room so I can see the TV through my open doorway.

"It's not too late for you to ditch me," I call.

"Shut up," Harper says. "What do you want to watch?"

"You guys should pick. I'm just going to fall asleep thirty minutes in."

Harper puts on *Pride & Prejudice*, which she knows is my all-time favorite and she can't stand. I'm about to thank her when she says, "I'm only watching this sappy shit for you, Kenny. As soon as you pass out, we're putting on something else."

"This movie is a masterpiece," Nina mutters.

"How the fuck am I friends with you guys?" Harper asks.

Because we love each other. The thought brings tears to my eyes. I didn't have this in middle school or high school. I got along well enough with people in my classes, but I was never anyone's first-choice friend—the one you invited to a movie and sleepover, the one you ran to with your secrets, the one you asked for advice. Which is fine. It was my own fault for being so reserved, and I probably saved myself a world of stress and heartbreak from all the messy politics of high school friendship.

But Nina and Harper are worth all the mess in the world.

I don't know how I got so lucky, to have found two people who still want to spend time with me when I'm at my absolute worst. As I watch Matthew Macfadyen's Darcy put his foot in his mouth and find I'm daydreaming of Vincent Knight's brown eyes, I realize that I've been keeping a secret from the two people whom I most want to confide in.

"I have to tell you guys something," I call out, "but you're not allowed to make fun of me."

"Oh, God, are you going to throw up?"

"No. No, it's just—it's sort of embarrassing."

Harper's head pokes around my door frame. "How embarrassing, on a scale of me sleeping through my sociology final to Nina getting kicked out of the art club's Bob Ross party?"

Nina gasps in outrage. "That was *one* time."

"Because they banned you for life."

"It's not my fault the only chaser they had was boxed wine—"

"I made out with Vincent Knight," I blurt.

For a moment, silence. And then both of my roommates appear in my doorway, scrambling over each other in their haste to see if I'm joking or if the fever has made me delirious.

"I'm sorry, you *what*?"

"Like, on-the-basketball-team Vincent?"

"When did you—and where did you—just, what?"

I wait until they've stopped blabbering to say, very calmly, "He came into the library during my shift last Friday needing help finding some poetry. We went up to the second floor, and one thing led to another, and we made out."

After my detailed recap, Harper and Nina obviously have some follow-up questions. *How big are his hands? Did he moan, because it's so hot when guys—wait, I'm sorry, he* lifted *you? I thought you said he only had one good arm! Did he get a boner? He did. Oh my God, Kendall, you* seduced *him!*

The two of them are giddy at the revelation that I've hooked up with one of Clement's star basketball players. They roll around on my floor and give commentary on my storytelling until I'm red-faced with mortification and laughing, even though my throat is killing me. Slowly but steadily, I feel the weight on my shoulders ease. It feels real now. Not like some weird fever dream. Vincent and I made out in a dark corner of the library, and it was insane and spontaneous and, in retrospect, a great story.

Maybe I'll be okay. Maybe having the story will be enough.

• • •

By Wednesday, my voice is practically gone and I'm still a bit shaky, but I feel human enough to crawl out of bed and climb onto my bike before dawn.

I take deep breaths of crisp morning air as I bike to campus. It feels weird to head to the library at the same hour I usually get off my shift—like the world has been flipped upside down, or like I've pulled a Harper and slept through my sociology final after accidentally switching the time zone on my phone. There's a knot in my stomach as I lock my bike up and head inside, but when I shoulder through the doors, the library feels perfectly unchanged.

I don't know why I was worried that coming back here would feel like returning to a crime scene. This is still my happy place.

The night shift kid—a tired-eyed boy with clunky headphones around his neck—looks at me like I'm his savior when I march up to the circulation desk and tell him I'm here to relieve him. While he's packing up his stuff, Margie comes out of the elevator with a book cart piled high with enormous science textbooks.

"Kendall!" she says when she spots me. "How are you feeling, kiddo?"

"I'm better," I croak, than laugh. "Obviously, I don't sound like it, but the student health center says I'm not contagious."

The doctor I saw there agreed with me—stress, not a viral infection, was the most likely cause of my weekend malaise. She's seen hundreds of Clement students with similar symptoms that happened to line up with final exams, group projects, and other major deadlines.

Margie nods sympathetically. "There's a fresh box of herbal tea and an electric kettle in the back office. Help yourself."

"Thank you," I say, exhaling heavily.

I stow my backpack under the desk, pull out my plastic baggie of cough drops, and start toward the office door.

"Oh—before I forget," Margie says, stopping me. "A boy came in on Friday and asked for you."

Everything goes still. I think there's a ringing in my ears.

"What boy?" I ask, even though I think I already know the answer.

"I don't remember his name. Tall son of a bitch. Very handsome. He checked out two different books of Elizabeth Barrett Browning poems and an autobiography on some famous college basketball coach."

Vincent. He came back.

"I explained you were out sick," Margie adds.

I die a little inside, even though Vincent couldn't possibly have known how snotty and sweaty and miserable I was this weekend. Fuck. I can't believe I missed him.

He asked for you.

I'm not sure how to interpret that. Maybe he wanted to check in and figure out why I'd disappeared after we made out. Maybe he wanted a repeat of the last Friday night. Or maybe he just wanted to make it clear that what happened between us was a onetime thing and that he'd prefer it if I didn't run my mouth about it.

"Did he say why he was looking for me?" It's a loaded question, but I have to know.

"He said he needed an English tutor, but he left a note for you. Hold on—I put it on my desk in the back—"

Margie ducks into the office and reappears a moment later with a little scrap of torn paper in her hand. My first thought when she passes it to me is that Vincent's handwriting is surprisingly neat—two little lines of perfectly even block letters. He does his As the same way I do mine.

STILL SUCK AT POETRY. PLEASE HAVE MERCY.
VKNIGHT@CLEMENT.EDU.

I turn it over, hoping for some more insight, but the other side is blank.

"Should I have told him to screw off?" Margie asks.

I croak out a laugh. "No, I can handle him. Thanks, Margie."

After tucking Vincent's note into the back pocket of my jeans, I get to work. There's much to be done before the morning crowd arrives to print homework and essays before classes. As the sun rises, light streams into the atrium like liquid gold and casts the whole library in a warm glow. I stock shelves and process returns and help a group of chemistry students game our e-book checkout system so they don't have to pay two hundred bucks for a textbook.

And the whole time, the scrap of paper burns in my pocket.

Because it can only mean one thing: the story isn't over.

Seven

Harper and Nina ask me to put Vincent's note in the center of our coffee table so they can huddle over it like two historians examining a precious artifact.

"It sounds like he wants her to tutor him," Harper says, like it's obvious.

"But *tutoring* might be code for sex," Nina argues.

"Why would a fucking college basketball player not just tell a girl if he's interested? Straight men are, like, notoriously unsubtle when they're trying to fuck."

"It's not like he could just give a *librarian* a note that says, *Had fun kissing you up against a bookshelf last week, I'd really like to put my penis in you now.* What if she read it before it got to Kendall? This"—she taps the note—"is definitely code."

Harper is unconvinced. "If he wanted to keep the note clean, he could've asked her out or told her to come to a party at the basketball team's house. He didn't. He definitely just wants her to help him pass his class. And you know what? He's banking on the fact that she'll be all soft for him now and won't charge him."

"He wouldn't—" Nina begins, then sighs. "No, I take that back. Men are garbage."

I slump down on our couch, which is hard and creaky and banged up in the way furniture in student housing tends to be. Nina appeals to the hopeless romantic in me, but Harper's pragmatism is more in line with my gut feeling. Vincent Knight could've written anything in this note. He chose to ask for help with poetry.

I shouldn't add context that isn't there. I shouldn't allow myself to project the traits of all my favorite romance novel love interests on a real-life man. It's a recipe for disappointment.

Still, I can't help but think that if this *were* a romance novel, tutoring would be the plot device that throws Vincent and me back into each other's orbit. I am the reluctant heroine turning down the quest. But act two is inevitable. When I think about it that way, it's not so intimidating.

Still, it takes me a few days to work up the courage to email him.

I decide to play it straight, to avoid the horrible scenario in which I think Vincent is propositioning me and assume he genuinely needs help passing English lit.

To: vknight@clement.edu
From: kholiday@clement.edu
Subject: Tutoring

Hi Vincent,
The librarian gave me your note. I am available Mondays
and Wednesdays between 10:00 a.m. and 3:00 p.m, and
Friday evenings before my shift at the library (10:00 p.m.).
My usual tutoring rate is $25/hour, but I can be flexible.
Best,
Kendall

As soon as it leaves my inbox with a little whoosh, I doubt every word.

I can't tell if it's too professional or not professional enough, and *fuck*, what if Nina was right and his note was code and I've just somehow offered to prostitute myself? *I can be flexible* suddenly feels like the most overtly sexual thing I have ever ended an email with.

Not even five minutes later, there's the telltale ping of a new message. The little red dot next to the mail icon sends my blood pressure through the roof. I breathe out through my mouth, reminding myself that it could very well be spam from a clothing store or an updated homework assignment from a professor, and click open my inbox.

To: kholiday@clement.edu
From: vknight@clement.edu
Subject: RE: Tutoring

Kendall,
Monday works. 10 a.m. at main Starbucks. I'll bring the book. Venmo or cash?
V

My palms are clammy, because fuck, that's tomorrow, and *fuck*, he's giving me nothing to work with here. Half of me wants to call Harper and Nina in to get their thoughts, but the more I read over his message, the more I know that I'm grasping at straws.

There's nothing romantic in his response. Nothing even remotely flirty. Which means it's time for me to get my head out of the clouds and plant my feet firmly on the ground.

● ● ●

I wake up the next morning soaked in sweat. At first, I think I'm getting sick again, but then I check the weather app on my phone and realize it's going to be absurdly hot today for fall in Northern California. Perfect. Because on top of my anxiety about seeing Vincent again, I really need to worry about sweat stains and sunburns.

I'd normally turn to Harper to talk me down from my catastrophizing, but she's at the gym for her morning swim.

Nina's the one who helps me get ready.

"Wear my green dress," she tells me. "The one with the spaghetti straps. You look so hot in that dress. Think about it. You can wear one of your grandma cardigans over it, so he suspects nothing. You get inside, and oh, what's that? *It's so warm in here*. You take off the cardigan, and *boom*. He's overcome with lust. You fuck on the floor of the Starbucks."

"You're hereby fired as my life coach."

I appreciate Nina's enthusiasm and flair for the dramatic, but this isn't a date. I pull on a simple T-shirt and some jean shorts. Nina glares at me with disappointment and disgust as I reach for my battered white sneakers and lace them up.

"I'm so disappointed," she grumbles as she walks me to the door.

"I know."

"At least give him a handie under the table or something."

I shut the apartment door in her face.

Outside, I shove on my sunglasses and try to keep to the shade, like the gremlin I am, as I march onto campus. There are three different Starbucks on or near Clement's campus. The main one is at the corner, right between the engineering and the journalism schools. It's always packed, but the crowd today is sparse for a Monday. Looks like most of Clement's student body is taking advantage of the sunshine and lounging around in the rolling green grass of the quad.

I order a tall cold brew and hunt for a good table.

There's an open one tucked in the back corner. Shrugging off my backpack, I slump down into a leather armchair with a clear view of the front door. When I check my phone and realize I'm a solid twelve minutes early, I feel a tiny twist of embarrassment. But it's fine. I'm fine. Nobody in this coffee shop knows what's happening in my head. I'm just a girl having some coffee and scrolling through social media. Besides, there's no sign of Vincent yet. I can always tell him I got here two minutes before he did.

So, I settle in, and I wait. And wait. And *wait*.

He's late.

Five minutes late. Then ten. Then fifteen.

I pull up his email again, just to check that I haven't accidentally fucked up the time, date, or location for this meetup. But I'm right.

I think I'm being stood up.

It's a good thing this isn't a date, because being stood up for my first would probably hurt.

Still, the caffeine in my stomach churns like battery acid.

You know what? No. I'm not about to let my day be ruined. I've made the effort to haul myself onto campus, I'm at a coffee shop with soft ambient music playing, and I have a cup of delicious cold brew in my hand. Everything is in place for me to have a lovely fucking morning. Without another second of hesitation, I reach for my backpack and pull out *The Duke's Design*, a vaguely Regency-era romance novel about a headstrong woman and a duke who, in a rather convoluted chain of events, needs her to pose as his fiancé to prevent all his inheritance from going to his irredeemable rake of a younger brother.

The pretty pastel illustrated cover is far more suitable for public reading than the brazenly naked chest on *The Mafia's Princess*. I haven't touched that book since the night at the library—I just left it on Nina's desk. I couldn't even look at it without remembering the way Vincent tastes.

Which is absolutely *not* what I should be thinking about right now.

I take a long gulp of my coffee, so cold it makes the roof of my mouth ache, and start reading.

The Duke's Design is clever and witty in a way that makes me want to read the author's grocery lists. The main character, Clara, is probably a bit too progressive to be a believable upper-class white woman of early nineteenth-century England, but I've always preferred modern sensibilities to historical accuracy when it comes to romance novels. The duke is everything I expected—tall, broody, a little too concerned with propriety—but every now and again he has a line of dialogue that leads me to believe he's going to say wicked things in bed, and I am very much into it.

I'm so into it, in fact, that I'm beginning to have a bit of a problem.

Jean shorts were a horrible idea. My thighs are sticking to the leather under me, and each time I squirm in the armchair—crossing and then uncrossing my legs—the seam shifts and presses against my crotch. It's delicious and wonderful and absolutely *not* what I need while I'm in public.

I don't register that someone is approaching my little table in the corner until it's too late. But before I even lift my chin, I know it's *him*. I recognize the sound of him clearing his throat. I recognize the feeling of being loomed over by someone who's taller than anyone has any business being. So, when I tear my eyes away from the sex scene in front of me and look up, I'm hardly surprised to find I'm no longer alone.

Vincent Knight smiles down at me.

"How's the book, Holiday?"

Eight

I'm absolutely fucked, because Vincent is even more beautiful than I remember.

It's not fair. None of it is. Not the dark, disheveled hair. Not the warm brown eyes. Not the bright-white Clement Athletics T-shirt that's doing *wonderful* things for his sun-kissed skin and sculpted arms. He's still wearing that black brace around his left wrist. I wonder if he has tan lines from it. That thought triggers an avalanche of very inappropriate musings about where else Vincent might have tan lines, and if he'll show me them if I ask nicely.

Oh, I am in so much trouble.

"You're late," I blurt, frustrated with myself and him and also the universe for throwing me into Vincent's orbit with a romance novel in my hands for the second time in as many weeks.

"My lab ran longer than it was supposed to."

That's all he says. No apology, no further explanation. This is the same proud motherfucker who came into the library two weeks ago with a stick up his ass, so I don't know why I expected him to be any better behaved now.

I arch an eyebrow. "Your lab?"

"I can show you my schedule, if you don't believe me."

There's a teasing lilt to his voice, and it makes me unspeakably furious. I've been sitting here for almost an hour because he needs an English tutor—and because I'm an idiot who thought today could go one of two ways: either Vincent would show up and disappoint me, allowing me to write off whatever magic happened at the library as a result of my own loneliness and one very smutty novel, or Vincent would show up and realize he wanted me to be more than his tutor. But instead, it seems the most realistic—and disappointing—order of events will happen. He's going to pay me for my completely nonsexual services, and then we're going to call it a day and go our separate ways because he's a Division I basketball player and I am a girl who spends an alarming percentage of her waking life buried in books.

I sit straighter in my seat, suddenly very aware of my warm face and how far my denim shorts have ridden up my thighs.

"It's fine," I say, even though it isn't. "Can we get started?"

I motion toward the empty chair opposite mine, but Vincent doesn't budge. There's a little wrinkle between his eyebrows as he watches me stuff *The Duke's Design* into my backpack and tug at the hem of my shorts with an indignant sigh. He looks unsettled.

"What are you drinking?" he asks.

I lift my cup and shake it so he can hear the ice rattle. "It *was* a cold brew."

"You want another one?"

I've probably had enough caffeine, since I'm already on edge and cranky, but I'm feeling petty. "If you're offering, then sure."

Vincent nods his head once, like a soldier saluting his captain, before he drops his backpack to the floor next to the chair opposite mine and marches up to the counter. There's no line. It's quiet enough in here that I can hear him tell the barista his order. *Our* order.

Stop it, I tell myself. *We are not a unit.*

I tear my eyes off Vincent. As it turns out, I'm not the only one in Starbucks who's watching him: there are two girls at a table across the coffee shop, a group of boys lounging on a bench against the window, a lone older woman—probably a professor—hunched over her laptop. They're all looking. Even the other baristas are leaning forward attentively, just in case Clement's star basketball player needs a chocolate croissant, pronto. And I can't blame any of them. Vincent is devastatingly handsome and carries himself with a magnetic kind of confidence. It's hard *not* to stare.

I wish he asked me here just to see me again. Not because he wanted me for my English literature expertise but because he genuinely wanted to spend time with me and get to know me. And that realization hurts, so I cram it down and cling to my pettiness like a life raft.

Several pairs of eyes stay locked on Vincent as he heads back to my corner of the coffee shop, an enormous plastic cup in each hand. He sets one of them down in front of me. It's definitely a venti. I think this is his attempt at an apology. I gape at him as he settles into the armchair across from me, his too-long legs crowding mine under the table between us.

He sighs. "What's wrong with it?"

"This is—this is way too much coffee."

"You don't have to drink it all."

"I don't think I *could*. I'd be a mess if I drank this much coffee."

"I like you when you're a mess," Vincent replies without blinking.

The blunt reminder of what we did two weeks ago hits me like a bolt of lightning to the chest.

My face goes bright red. The flicker of satisfaction in Vincent's eyes tells me he was banking on it. And maybe he just wants to toy with me for his own enjoyment, but there's an endearing twinkle in his eyes that makes me feel like he wants me to be in on the joke with him.

I've spent two weeks trying to convince myself that what happened between us was nothing, and that Vincent isn't to be trusted or daydreamed about. But when he's here, in front of me, I have to admit that he's not exactly the stranger or the villain I've made him out to be in my head. He's the same boy I met in the library—quick-witted, too proud to apologize or ask for help without being a smart-ass, and far too much fun to flirt with.

Except he didn't bring me here for that. He brought me here to tutor him.

So how fucking dare he flirt with me?

I take a gulp of my (free) ice-cold coffee and clear my throat. "What do you need help with? That's why we're here, isn't it? Because you're bad with your words."

Vincent's bravado falters. I refuse to feel guilty about it.

Thankfully, the insult seems to flick a switch in him.

Vincent clears his throat and reaches for his backpack, suddenly all business. "I have to write an in-class essay next week on this tiger poem"—his biceps flex against his sleeves, but I absolutely do *not* stare—"and honest to God, I'm lost. I told you I suck at poetry. And I figured, you know, you're brilliant."

"Obviously," I murmur into my cold brew.

His lips twitch. "And humble about it. Which is why you're going to help me figure out what the fuck this Blake guy was trying to say."

Vincent pulls out a book, flips it open to a dog-eared page, and passes it to me. I put down my coffee and wipe my damp palms on my shorts, eager for something to do and something to distract me from the boy across the table. It appears our subject matter for the day is a William Blake poem—arguably his most famous.

"Oh," I say, "I know this one. I've gone over this in, like, four different classes."

"Of course you have."

"It's a classic. I had to memorize it my sophomore year of high school. *Tyger Tyger, burning bright—*"

Vincent shifts in his chair. The leather creaks under him. I'm suddenly and violently reminded of the fact that the last time I read poetry aloud to him, we mauled each other.

"—and, you know, the rest of it."

"Right," he says. "Give me your translation, Holiday."

There it is again—my last name. He's used it twice now, and I can't decide if I like it or if I want to grab him by the front of his shirt and demand he stop with the nicknames. I tuck my hair behind my ears and scoot forward in my seat.

When my knee bumps Vincent's, I immediately angle my legs to one side and pretend nothing happened.

"So," I begin, clearing my throat, "Blake published two companion collections: *Songs of Innocence* and then, a few years later, *Songs of Experience*. Have you covered any of his other work in your class?"

"We read the child labor one, I think."

I snort. "It's called 'The Chimney Sweeper.' That poem has two parts: one in *Songs of Innocence* and another in *Songs of Experience*. Blake was really interested in dichotomies—good and evil, heaven and hell—so he did a lot of companion pieces across the two collections. This one"—I tap the page—"has a sister poem in *Songs of Innocence* called 'The Lamb.'"

Vincent nods. "This one's about violence, and the other one is about peace?"

"In essence, yes. But Blake's not just contrasting two animals. If you look at the way he's framing it and how he's using repetitive questions, it's more than just setting up a dichotomy." I open my mouth to start reading, then stop and press my lips together. I'm suddenly self-conscious about my own voice—and not entirely sure if I'll make it through the poem without combusting. So, I shove the book at Vincent and say, "Read the first stanza for me."

It comes out more brusque and demanding than I meant it to, but he doesn't even flinch. Vincent dutifully takes the book from my hand, flips it around, and starts to read the poem aloud.

I immediately regret asking.

Nine

The sound of Vincent's voice makes my entire body clench.

We're tucked in a somewhat secluded corner of the coffee shop, and the gentle indie music playing over the speakers is quiet, so Vincent doesn't have to project all that much. He reads softly and deliberately. His voice is a low, rumbling, intimate thing. It reminds me that on the Friday night we met, when I was still thinking about a sex scene in *The Mafia's Princess* and was struck dumb by the tall and brooding stranger who needed a reading recommendation, I briefly imagined Vincent reciting poetry to me. It seemed like a nice fantasy. Now I realize I was Icarus: an absolute fucking fool hauling ass toward the sun, completely unaware that the heights I sought would wreck me.

And oh, it's wrecking me—the way his mouth forms the words. The way his wide palms and long fingers cradle the book. The way a stray piece of his dark hair drapes romantically over his forehead.

"Tyger Tyger, burning bright, In the forests of the night; What immortal hand or eye, Could frame thy fearful symmetry?"

Vincent lifts his eyes expectantly. I try to reconcile myself to the fact that my insides have melted and my underwear is a little bit damp.

"Keep reading. I mean, in your head, if you—if you want, just to speed things up."

Vincent, a man of no mercy, shrugs. "I don't mind reading it out loud."

I sit there, a trembling mess of caffeine and desire, as Vincent Knight reads the poem in its entirety. He trips over a few words and awkward, old-fashioned turns of phrase, but there's something charming about it. Everyone else in this Starbucks probably thinks he's as close to a deity as a college student can get, but I get to watch him smile in that slightly self-deprecating way when he slips up—and I get to listen to the confident cadence of his voice when he nails an entire stanza in two steady breaths.

I let my eyelids flutter closed, embracing my newest kink: being read to.

When Vincent reaches the last line, a part of me wants to tell him to read it again. He probably wouldn't fight me on it—I'm the expert here, after all. Reluctantly, I peel open my eyes and meet Vincent's. A moment passes in perfect silence. Then he looks back down at the page.

"Did he who made the Lamb make thee?" he repeats from the second-to-last stanza. "So, he's talking about God. He's asking how God could make both of these animals."

I clear my throat. "Exactly. You have to think about what Blake believed in, and what was going on around him with the industrial revolution. It was a lot to process. He's asking himself how God could make something so innocent, so agricultural and romantic as the lamb, and also make a tiger—this beast from a faraway land that needs to kill the lamb to feed itself."

Vincent stares at the page for a long moment, his dark eyes tracing laps over the lines.

"This is actually kind of fucking cool," he says.

I hope he's not being sarcastic. "You think?"

"Yeah. I finally get why you picked your major."

"For all the high-paying job prospects, *obviously*."

Vincent snorts. "You could definitely teach at the college level if you wanted to. You might be better at this than my tenured professor. I went to his office hours last week. Complete waste of time."

"Let me guess," I say. "Old white guy?"

"His name is Richard Wilson. Think he's in his late sixties."

"Knew it." I lean back in my chair and fold one leg over the other. "I almost took a class with him my freshman year, but his Rate My Professor score was abysmal. Honestly, though, you could get the same interpretation I just gave you from a few Google searches. Like I said in the library . . ." My eyes skitter away from his. The next few words come out slightly choked. "The trick to most poetry is context. It's like talking to a person. The more you know about where they're coming from, the easier it is to understand them."

Vincent leans back in his chair too and studies me for a moment.

"Have you always been a big reader?"

"Oh, yeah. I had sort of a rough start—I was diagnosed with dyslexia when I was in first grade—so it took me a little longer to learn than most of the kids in my class. But then

I was insatiable. My parents used to take me to our public library twice a week because I kept blowing through the checkout limit every few days."

"Damn."

I feel my cheeks heat. Then, because I'm prone to over-sharing, I say, "It's easy to read that much when you're a shy kid. I didn't really have friends until the end of high school. And even then, it was mostly the people I sat next to in class. Books have always been a major part of my personal and social life."

Vincent tilts his head. "Do you write at all?"

"I try to. I'm not as good at it as I'd like to be. But I'm taking a creative writing workshop this semester, so fingers crossed it helps. My professor is great. He's written like twenty-five sci-fi novels, so he's not super stuck-up about genre fiction, which I appreciate."

It's sometimes difficult to be a romance novel enthusiast in a sea of academia and internalized misogyny that suggests the genre is somehow less important and less worthy of praise than literary fiction.

Vincent nods. "Are most of the English professors at this school stuffy white guys like good old Richard, or do you have a good mix of women and nonwhite faculty? I don't know much about Clement outside of my major."

"There are a lot of younger women in the department, actually. And at least a third of the professors I've had are openly LGBTQ+." Then, against my better judgment, I ask, "What is your major, anyway?"

"Human biology."

I scrunch my nose. "Oh, yuck."

"Told you. English was never my thing. I'm a STEM guy."

"Wait a minute. I thought you hated memorization. Isn't bio all about memorization?"

He shrugs. "It sticks better than poetry ever did. The material makes more sense to me—maybe because I've been playing basketball since I was seven or eight, so I've always thought a lot about our anatomy and the way our bodies work."

I'm also thinking a lot about how our bodies work.

I shake my head. "You insufferable nerd."

Vincent tosses his head back and lets out a surprised bark of laughter. The sound of it is glorious. "What? You don't care about mitosis?"

"I'd rather take a class with Richard fucking Wilson."

Vincent laughs again, and I'm so proud of myself for pulling the sound out of him that I have to press my lips together to hold back a self-satisfied smile. I shift in my seat, uncrossing and then angling my legs. Vincent's gaze drops and lands on my bare thighs—the right one now sporting a big pink oval where it was sandwiched under the left—and his laughter dries up in his throat.

When his eyes meet mine again, there's a curiosity burning in them that makes me feel like he can clear the distance I've tried to put between us.

"Maybe I can tutor *you* sometime," he offers. "You know, in exchange."

The heat in his eyes tells me that both our heads are in the gutter.

It's both a thrilling realization—that maybe I'm not entirely alone in my thirst—and a terrifying one. Because I bet a more experienced girl would know what all the teasing smiles and innuendos meant. What if this is how Vincent is? What if he flirts with everyone (baristas, professors, classmates in his labs) and I'm just a girl who overthinks everything and has a bad case of main character syndrome?

The smile falls off my face. I tug at the hem of my shorts again and tuck my hair behind my ears. Vincent notices I'm pulling back. That little furrow between his eyebrows reappears.

"Are there any other poems you need to go over?" I ask. "I have a lot of reading to do before my class this afternoon, so if we're done . . ."

Vincent's eyes are heavy on me. The heat of his assessing stare makes me squirm, but then the seam of my denim shorts rubs the exact right spot and I'm reminded that I liked his little poetry reading a little bit too much.

"What?" I demand.

"Nothing." Then, like it's an afterthought: "You look good, Kendall."

A startled laugh escapes me. "Oh, fuck off."

"No, I mean it," he says. "It's nice to see you in broad daylight."

I wish we weren't in public. I wish I had the nerve to tell him, point-blank, that something about reading poetry with him makes me wet and wanting like a pent-up Regency woman.

Instead, I say, "Yeah."

Yeah, it's good to see you too. Yeah, I still think about you too. Yeah, I'll let you bend me over this armchair and—

"You never answered my question, by the way," Vincent says.

I frown. "Which one?"

He nods toward my backpack. "How's the book?"

Ten

Right. I guess he's not letting that slide.

I fight the urge to angle my knees and block Vincent's view of my backpack. The boy may be perceptive as fuck, but it's not like he can see through canvas and three layers of notebooks. Still, I feel weirdly exposed. I catalogue the faces of the scattered students and professors and baristas around the Starbucks, but they're all fully absorbed in their conversations and laptops and caffeinated beverages. The only eyes on me are Vincent Knight's.

"It's a good book," I say. Then, more honestly, I amend: "Actually, it's a little silly."

Vincent waits. He wants me to elaborate.

"Okay, so," I say, taking a giant breath and hooking one foot up underneath my butt, "this duke asks this woman who can't stand him to pose as his fiancé because there was a clause in his father's will that says the title will get passed on to his shitty brother if he doesn't marry in a year. And the brother's addicted to gambling and knocked up a married woman back in London, so it's all very high stakes and—well, messy. There are lots of balls and scandals and plot twists. It's not at all historically accurate, but it's fun. And silly. But in the right way. If that makes sense?"

If Vincent thinks my book sounds like a waste of time, he doesn't show it. He doesn't laugh at me. He doesn't shame me.

But he does say, "So, college boys are trash, but a duke with family baggage is fine?"

A laugh bubbles up in my throat, partly because I'm relieved he's not being completely judgmental about my genre of choice and partly because he actually remembers what we talked about in the library. I wonder if he's replayed our conversation in his head the way I have.

"In my defense, dukedom is the highest possible rank of the peerage."

"So, he's rich," Vincent says flatly. "That's the appeal."

"It definitely helps." I lift my straw to my mouth. "But he's also responsible and educated and apparently very talented at horse riding and other . . . physical things." I'm proud of myself for not stumbling over the words. I feel very cool. Very casual.

Vincent arches an eyebrow. "Yeah?"

I nod and take a sip.

He smiles wickedly. "And how do I measure up?"

I choke on my cold brew, which is neither cool nor casual. But in my defense, I'm a little caught off guard. If I'd known we were going to do this—this flirty, bantering thing—I would've coordinated my underwear. I would've taken Nina up on the devious dress idea and asked her to be out of the apartment for the rest of the day in case Vincent and I needed somewhere private.

I glance around Starbucks again and lock eyes with a barista. Nope. No privacy here.

"Measure up how?" I ask. It feels like a dangerous question, so I pad it with: "Last time I checked, you don't own any land in England."

"But I'm a good kisser."

My heart hiccups. "Well, that's presumptuous of you—"

"I've also been playing basketball since elementary school, so I'm disciplined and I understand the value of hard work. I've been a team captain before too, so I can handle responsibility. Leadership. All that good shit. And I have a 3.7 GPA, so I probably won't graduate summa cum laude, but I'll definitely get magna—"

"Is there a reason you're giving me your résumé?" I interrupt.

"I'm trying to prove a point, Holiday." Vincent shrugs. "Seems like you have pretty high expectations for your love interests. You don't seem interested in being courted by anyone who isn't a billionaire or a royal or some kind of supernatural creature."

That one hits a little too close to home, so I resort to my usual defense mechanism: snark.

"*Courted?* I'm sorry, is this Victorian England?"

"No, this is Starbucks."

I could kick him. I really could. "You're incorrigible."

"And *you* have unrealistic standards."

His knee bumps against the inside of my thigh—the one that isn't tucked up on the chair. I startle at the contact, but he doesn't move to break it. He lets the weight of his leg and the heat of his skin press into mine.

I think of Nina's parting words to me this morning: *At least give him a handie under the table.*

In one unrestrained burst of imagination, I see the appeal. I have long arms. All it would take is some clever but discreet maneuvering, and I could have my hand tucked under his shirt and pressed to the soft skin just above his waistband. At least, I imagine that it's soft. My brain is pretty good at summoning the rest of the scene: the little trail of hair below his belly button tickling the pads of my fingers. The tug of elastic as I slip my hand into his shorts. Hot skin hardening in my palm while Vincent's dark eyes pin me to my seat and say, wordlessly, all the things I want to hear.

I want you. I feel this too.

A little harder, Holiday, you won't break it.

The trouble, of course, is that I don't have a fucking clue what I'm doing. I've read enough romance novels to appreciate the mechanics of it all (the positions, the movements, the dialogue), but reading about sex feels different from staring into a boy's eyes and knowing you want him inside you.

Vincent isn't an empty shell I can project onto. Not anymore.

Right now, I don't feel the same electric confidence I felt in our dark corner of the library. In fact, it's hard to feel any confidence at all when I consider how Vincent left me that night. He didn't stick around to say goodbye or let me help him check out *Engman's Anthology* or talk me down from my panic attack in the girls' bathroom. He's given me no indication that he wants me in his life as anything other than a tutor. So, what does he want? A one-night stand? A girlfriend? A little fool he strings along for months just to see how far she'll run after him?

"Talk to me, Holiday." Vincent nudges his knee against mine. "You look like you're spiraling."

Because I am.

I huff and slam my iced coffee onto the table between us. "What do you want from me?" It comes out much harsher than I mean it to. "Because your note—I just—I thought this was a tutoring session, and then I get here, and you're—" I gesture vaguely at the way he's lounging in the chair across from me, arms wide and legs sprawled so they cage mine.

Vincent's expression shifts. He sits upright, hunching his shoulders. It's a move that, as a tall girl, I recognize well. He's shrinking himself. Making himself smaller.

"I really did need help with the poem," he says. Then, more softly, he admits, "But I wanted to see you again. *Obviously.*"

My heart is hammering. I really shouldn't have had so much of the coffee he bought me.

"Obviously?"

Vincent sighs, exasperated. "You know why I'm here, Kendall."

But I don't. He watches me blink at him, open-mouthed and too stunned to speak, and leans over the table, close enough that I catch the scent of laundry detergent and warm, spiced cologne (a scent I didn't realize I missed until right now).

"The real question," he says, eyes narrowed, "is why are *you* here?"

Because I wanted to know. Because I *had* to know if what happened two weeks ago during my night shift was a fluke, or if I could feel that way again. And now I think I regret that curiosity, because seeing Vincent again has confirmed that something about him in particular makes me feel giddy and grounded all at the same time.

I've never felt this vulnerable before.

So, I say the safe thing: "Because you needed a tutor."

The words come easily, even if they're patently false, and they land like a belly flop in a swimming pool. Vincent leans back in his chair, his face suddenly blank. His dark eyes—so hauntingly pretty under those thick, feathery eyelashes—give nothing away. I watch him rub his palms on the front of his athletic shorts, my eyes catching on the muscular slope of his thighs, and realize I've fucked up harder than I previously believed possible.

"Great," he says with a smile I don't believe. "Glad we've cleared that up."

No, wait.

My stomach twists. I feel like I've lost my grip on the English language. I don't know which words to pluck out of the file cabinet inside my head to fix this. I wish I knew how to drop a scene break here and get us somewhere new and secluded and full of all the right narration and dialogue that will lead to Vincent's mouth being on mine again.

"I mean—" I blurt, then wince. "I *didn't* mean—"

Vincent shakes his head, and it's very kind, but in a detached sort of way that stings. "Don't worry about it. You said Venmo was good, right?"

I deflate like a popped balloon. I don't want this to be just a transaction. But my heart is lodged in my throat, and Vincent is reaching for his pocket and pulling out his phone, and if he pays me for this, so help me, I'll *lose it*. My hand flies out before I'm entirely aware of what I'm doing. It lands on Vincent's wrist. The one without the brace. The feel of his bare skin against my fingertips sends a jolt up my arm. When he stills and looks me in the eyes, I feel it in two places: between my legs and in the hollow of my aching chest.

"Don't," I say with far too much emotion. I clear my throat and reel it in a little. "Don't pay me. Please."

Vincent stares at me like I'm speaking Latin.

I wish, in this moment, that I was more of a writer than a reader. I wish I knew how to steer a plot and how to make things happen the way I want them to. Reading is so much fun, but I'm tired of feeling like all the best parts of my life have been lived inside my own head.

I meet Vincent's eyes and hope that he sees written on my face all the words I'm incapable of summoning.

I want you. I feel this too.

Please don't listen to the shit I say when I'm scared.

And then, over his shoulder, I catch a blur of movement.

There's a group of six extraordinarily tall boys—a few of them in matching white Clement Athletics T-shirts—filing through the door and into Starbucks. I recognize Jabari Henderson first. After that, it's easy enough to identify the other basketball players with him. Most of them are starters. A couple of them are second string. All of them are incredibly large humans.

Jabari and I lock eyes. He turns away immediately, and it's almost believable that we're just two strangers in a Starbucks who accidentally looked at each other. But a moment later, he turns to say something to the guy beside him before tipping his head very discreetly in our direction. Whatever he said is then relayed to the rest of the group, and the six of them quickly shuffle over to a table on the other side of Starbucks, directly across from where Vincent and I are seated.

And as clueless as I feel right now, I'm quick enough to catch on to what's happening.

We're being watched.

Eleven

I don't know how this could get any more mortifying, but the addition of a small crowd of basketball players to witness it all definitely doesn't help.

My hand is still wrapped around Vincent's wrist, which is too big for me to touch my thumb to my middle finger. Belatedly, I realize how this must look, so I try to play it off like I'm brushing away an imaginary piece of lint that's caught in the fine, downy-soft hair on his arm. This, unfortunately, means I end up stroking the back of his forearm in a way that is a hundred times more incriminating.

Vincent arches an eyebrow.

I press my hands together and sandwich them between my thighs. "You had some—never mind. Sorry. Continue."

"I'm definitely paying you," he insists, still watching me warily. "You earned your money, Holiday. You're good at what you do. And I made you wait half an hour for me to come, so I'm paying you for an extra hour. Don't fight me."

I really hope his friends are out of earshot, because paired with my semierotic arm touching, everything that just came out of his mouth could be *dramatically* misinterpreted.

"I don't care about the money. This was good practice for me." *Yes, that'll definitely clear up what we're talking about.* "I love teaching poetry," I add a little too loudly. "And free coffee. And this was—this was fun."

Vincent laughs, more in disbelief than anything else.

"You know," he says, "sometimes you're harder to interpret than Shakespeare."

"I fucking hate Shakespeare," I admit.

Vincent smiles. "I knew there was a reason I liked you."

The words wrap me up tight like a weighted blanket. For one pristine moment, there's no professor three tables over shuffling through papers. There's no girl at the counter asking the barista to please make sure they're giving her oat milk, because her lactose intolerance will not forgive her for a transgression. There's no group of basketball players cataloguing my every move so they can break it down later like postgame ESPN broadcasters. It's just me, my pounding heart, and Vincent's soft, easy smile.

A distant laugh shatters the illusion.

It's Jabari. We lock eyes again. Not for the first time in my life, I feel like an animal in a zoo—or maybe the punch line of a joke that I haven't even heard the setup to. It seems like Vincent's teammates knew exactly where to find us, which leads me to wonder if Vincent told them to come here and watch . . . whatever *this* is.

To come watch him play with the girl who kissed him in the library, during her shift, while there were people in the building. To come see if she'll do it again.

Jabari, biting back a grin, nudges the boy next to him with

his elbow. That boy lifts his phone and not-so-surreptitiously angles it in our direction—and this is my breaking point, because now I know I'm not just overthinking things.

I'm definitely being laughed at.

Vincent's eyes go wide as I lurch up out of my chair, bumping the table between us so that the legs make a high-pitched scraping noise on the tile floor. I yank down the rolled hems of my jean shorts, wipe my palms on the front of my shirt, and then bend down to collect all my things—books, backpack, first empty coffee cup, second (larger, mostly empty) coffee cup. Maybe if I hadn't chugged so much cold brew, I wouldn't be this shivery and anxious.

There's a telltale stinging in my eyes. I fight it. I will *not* start crying in a Starbucks. That is a rock bottom I will not let myself hit.

"I should get going," I say, the words coming out in a rush as I loop the straps of my backpack over my shoulders. "Seriously, though. We're even. Thanks for the coffee."

I make it two steps before Vincent catches my hand. He doesn't have to pull on me. Just the feel of his skin—his fingertips against the back of my hand, his thumb pressing into my palm—is enough to make me stop. I'm anchored by his side, torn between my desperation to get the fuck out of here and the desire to stay and bask in the warmth of his attention. Because he's looking up at me through those thick lashes, and the curve of his mouth is so pink and plush and—

"My birthday's on Thursday," Vincent says.

I blink, unsure what to do with this revelation. "Happy birthday?"

"We're having a party at the house. You should come. You can bring your roommates."

"I—we—Thursdays are—"

"Movie night," Vincent finishes for me. "I know. But you're invited, if you want to come."

I hate that he remembers the things I mentioned in passing three Fridays ago. I hate that it sparks a silly, stubborn hope in me. Hope that he's just as sentimental as I am. That maybe he can't stop thinking about how I tasted and how I laughed and how it felt when we were pressed up against the bookshelves.

"I'm not going to make out with you in public again," I blurt, fear overwhelming my better judgment.

Vincent rears back. There's genuine hurt in the startled look he gives me.

"I wasn't asking you to," he says.

"Sorry," I add, my voice breathless and watery. "I know that's not what—*obviously*, you didn't—I don't know why I said that. It's not your fault. I'm just—I'm out of my element. Not with the tutoring stuff but with the rest of it. The flirting. The innuendos. I'm not good at this game, and I don't know the rules, and I don't think I want to play."

He lets my hand drop. I miss his touch immediately.

"There's no game," Vincent insists, twisting in his chair so he's facing me straight on. "Look, I'm not great at this either. You don't have to come to the party if I've made you uncomfortable, but I—I'd like to have you there, and your roommates might have fun, and there's gonna be a ton of free alcohol, and I'm sure we could get a poetry reading going once everyone's played a few rounds of beer pong."

I want to laugh. I do.

Instead, I say, "I'll think about it."

Vincent opens his mouth like he's going to argue. "Okay."

"I really do have to go."

"Thank you. For helping me with the poetry. I mean it, Kendall."

I nod, turn on my heel, and start toward the door.

But I can't help myself from adding one last comment over my shoulder.

"I think your friends are here for you."

My tone is *just* bitter enough that I'm sure Vincent will connect the dots between my departure and the arrival of his teammates. But I don't stick around to hear him try to explain why half of the basketball team is posted up at a table across the coffee shop.

Outside, it's hot and bright. I'm immediately miserable. The whole walk home, birds chirp and sunlight winks through the trees and students laugh as they breeze past me toward campus, and it's all so cheerful and picturesque that it makes me want to throw my head back and scream into the cloudless sky. Because honestly? How dare everyone have such a delightful day while I'm trying not to think about what's being said about me in the team group chat.

I get the Venmo notification when I'm crossing the street in front of my building.

Vincent Knight paid you $100.

The subject line is a lone tiger emoji.

And somehow, this is the final slap in the face. The cherry on top of the shit sundae. I'm grateful I'm already bounding up the front steps of my building. I don't need any of the students walking by to see me fighting back tears.

• • •

Harper is sprawled across a yoga mat on the living room floor, her bare feet in the air and her legs all twisted together like a soft pretzel. She always stretches after her swims. When I shoulder through the front door of the apartment, her head pops up, corkscrew curls tumbling everywhere as they slip loose from her topknot.

"She's back!" Harper hollers.

There's a distant sound of scrambling, and then Nina's bedroom door flies open. "Already?" She marches out into the living room with her reading glasses on. This just goes to show how concerned she is about the events of my morning—she *never* lets us see her with her reading glasses on. "How did it go? Did you guys hook up in the bathroom?"

"That's so fucking unsanitary," Harper says.

"I'm gonna second that," I grumble.

Nina, in true empath fashion, frowns. "What's wrong?"

"He paid me a hundred bucks," I announce with a laugh that is not at all funny. "For the tutoring. I got the notification on my way back here."

"Why are you saying that like it's a bad thing?" Harper asks.

Nina sighs. "Because that's not what she wanted."

I drop my backpack, collapse onto the couch, and recount it all—the late arrival of Vincent, the gifted cold brew I absolutely should not have chugged, the poetry analysis that somehow turned into what I can only describe as foreplay . . . and, finally, the way it all came crashing down.

"Are you sure they weren't just grabbing coffee?" Nina asks.

"They didn't even go up to the counter. And I saw one of them take out his phone and point it at us like he was taking a picture. Vincent definitely tipped them off."

She sighs and scrubs her hands over her face. "What did he say when you left?"

"He"—I scoff because it seems so absurd now—"*invited me to his birthday party.*"

"He *what?*"

"I shit you not. Just when I thought I understood men."

"He invited you to his birthday party?" Nina repeats, stunned.

"It's on Thursday, apparently. So, unfortunately, we won't be attending, since we've already got plans. Harper, I'm pretty sure it's your turn to pick the movie."

But Nina isn't ready to have our bimonthly argument about the objective ranking of Sandra Bullock's filmography. "Kenny, *please* tell me you didn't tell him you're not coming."

"I said I'd think about it."

"You—" Nina has to stop and collect herself. "Kendall, what the *fuck?*"

"The whole thing had bad vibes once the team arrived. I panicked and booked it out of there."

I sprawl backward across the length of the couch. It creaks unflatteringly under my weight. I try not to take it personally. Nina walks over, her hands balled in fists on her hips, and looms above me in a menacingly maternal way.

"What's our most hated trope?"

I frown. "Our what?"

85

"Answer the question. What do we always bitch about in books?"

"Slut-shaming?"

"No—I mean, yes, obviously, but I'm talking about a *trope*."

"Surprise pregnancy?"

"Oh, *God*—" There's fire in Nina's eyes like she's prepared to rant. "Yes, all right, we hate a lot of tropes. But I was talking about *miscommunication*, Kendall. We both hate when two stupid characters could solve all their problems by saying one honest thing. So, instead of assuming you know why a bunch of basketball players came into Starbucks—when you know for a *fact* that you and Harper once put on hoodies and fake moustaches to spy on me when I had that date with that girl from improv—why didn't you ask Vincent what was up with them?"

Admittedly, Nina has a very good point.

So, yes. I fucked up. I fumbled. I goofed my first ever not-a-date Starbucks trip with a boy.

But if I trace out all that's happened between Vincent and me, this feels like it could be the midpoint: that spot in the story where it all goes wrong and some sort of twist or plot device is needed to push the main characters back together again so they can fall in love properly. Maybe Vincent's birthday party is our plot device. Maybe there's still hope for me.

If nothing else, I know I want to kiss him again. Even if it all ends badly. I'm young—like he said. I can do casual. I can have fun. I can be okay with the idea of not getting a *happy ever after* if it means I get another shot at kissing Vincent.

Because more than anything, I want one last chance to feel that way again.

So, my choice is clear.

"All right," I say with a nod. "What do we do?"

"We're going to go to his birthday party," Nina tells me, "and you're going to get him alone, and you're going to *talk to him*. You need to tell him, to his face, that you refuse to tutor him ever again and that you want to fuck him six ways to Sunday. Okay? Because he deserves to know where you really stand."

I keep nodding. "Cool, cool, cool."

"You look pale as fuck," Harper says.

"Yeah, I think I'm gonna throw up," I croak. "We'll pregame the party, though, right?"

Nina claps me on the shoulder. "That's the spirit, champ. Keep up that nervous wreck energy. All my best going-out stories start with some anxiety and too many tequila shots. I have a good feeling about this."

Weirdly enough—despite the knot in my stomach—I do too.

Twelve

Over the next two days, I read eight different contemporary romances with a pen in one hand so I can underline particularly good lines of dialogue and take notes in the margins.

"You know," Nina says while we're curled up on opposite ends of the couch, "this whole birthday party thing doesn't have required reading. You can just get drunk and show up."

"Like you did with your Spanish final?"

"I'm a *native speaker*, and the foreign language requirement at this school is bullshit."

To be fair, I do feel a bit like I'm studying for an exam—except it's somehow more stressful than any final I've taken, because it feels like I missed the lecture where I was supposed to learn how to have a crush without letting it consume me body and soul.

I want to have fun. I want to stop overthinking it. Plenty of people have flings in college. Surely, I'm not so much of an outlier that I can't do the same. I'm determined to try. Even if all goes terribly—even if the magic I felt that night in the library is gone, even if I do something embarrassing, even if

Vincent flat-out turns me down in front of my friends—failure will be a hell of a lot better than spending the rest of my life wishing I hadn't been too proud and too scared to try.

I'd rather have one night with Vincent than nothing at all.

"I need to prepare," I admit. "I want to know what to *say*."

"Well, that's easy."

"Please don't—"

"Ask him to take off his pants and—"

"*Nina.*"

I blame her for planting the seed of depravity in my head. Because in the late hours of Wednesday night, in what I can only describe as a moment of weakness, I look up highlights from the basketball team's last season on YouTube. And fine. Maybe I pause the videos more than a few times to get a clear shot of Vincent, his face glimmering with sweat under the bright lights of the court. Maybe I smile to myself like a dork when he sinks a game-winning buzzer beater from beyond the three-point line. And maybe I'm four minutes deep in one of Vincent's postgame interviews when I notice something in the column of recommendations below.

The video of Vincent getting ejected from last year's big game.

It's only three minutes long. With my heart in my throat, I click on it.

Jabari has the ball. He's dribbling, dribbling, and passes—lightning quick—to another Clement player, who sinks a three. The camera briefly tracks the celebration. But then, in the corner of the screen, I catch the other team's point guard ram Jabari with his shoulder. The guy's face is twisted into a horrible snarl. His lips move, but I can't make out what he says.

Jabari's expression tells me all I need to know, though.

And then, a few feet away from them, Vincent Knight turns on his heel, takes two long strides toward our rival point guard, and delivers one swift right-handed uppercut before the guy even realizes it's coming.

The trash-talker crumples immediately, clutching his already dripping nose.

Admittedly, I read a lot of romance novels with strong, violent, *touch her and you die* love interests. But that's fiction. In my real life, I've never been attracted to aggressive men with short tempers; it's impossible for me to reconcile the fantasy with the reality of a man who might turn that anger and strength against the people he claims to love. But Vincent doesn't look out of control or unhinged or bloodthirsty. It's deliberate. It's quick. And if the shock on Jabari's face is any indication, it isn't something Vincent makes a habit of.

I'm on my fourth or fifth rewatch of the video when I realize I only have one hand on the phone. The other, which seems to have developed a mind of its own, is straying dangerously close to the waistband of my underwear.

"Oh my God," I whisper-hiss, slipping my arm back out from under the covers and smacking myself in the cheek. "What is *wrong* with you?"

Even as I ask the question, the answer comes with striking clarity.

I'm always skeptical about nonfictional men. They are, as Nina puts it, *garbage*. And I know that's a generalization, but it's scary to be a straight woman when you never know if your new crush might actually be a closeted racist, a serial killer, or a cryptocurrency enthusiast. So, yeah. Seeing Vincent Knight deck a guy really does it for me—not because I have a thing for violence and aggression or the white knight trope, but because I know now that Vincent and I share some of the same values: we stand up for our friends.

He's one of the good ones.

I think. It might be a bit of a jump to make the conclusion based on a three-minute YouTube clip, but maybe I'm blinded by the pretty brown eyes and the memory of his mouth on mine.

Someone needs to put me out of my suffering.

Tomorrow can't come quickly enough.

• • •

When I get home from my women's literature seminar the following evening, there are clothes draped over the couch and an open bottle of pink lemonade on the kitchen counter. Rap music drifts from Nina's open door. It sounds like she's doing that phone-in-a-cup thing, which means her portable speaker must be out of charge again. The whole apartment smells of perfume, extra-strength deodorant, alcohol, and hair that's been pulled through a straightener.

This can mean only one thing: my roommates are already pregaming for Vincent Knight's birthday party.

"It's not even seven!" I holler into the apartment. "You guys have zero chill!"

Nina pops out of her bedroom in her fluffy pink dressing gown (pausing to strike a pose in the doorway) and comes padding into the living room. She has a child's paper party hat on her head. It's way too small, and the elastic band looks like it's strangling her, but there's a delighted smile on her face and a flush to her cheeks that tells me she's already too drunk to care about something as trivial as breathing.

"Zero chill, yes," she says, "but *mucho* tequila. How was class?"

"Violently feminist, as usual. Where'd you get the hat?"

"They had them at the liquor store!" Harper calls a split second before she pops out of her own room in jeans and a bralette.

Harper is also wearing a party hat, although hers has had the string cut off and is held in place with an aggressive number of bobby pins. Her corkscrew curls have been painstakingly straightened into one long, silky, jet-black curtain. I'm so distracted by how gorgeous she looks that I don't notice the enormous handle of tequila cradled in her arm like a newborn baby until she hoists it up onto the kitchen island. I'm not exactly a connoisseur of wines and spirits, but I recognize this particular brand as one that's usually kept high up on a locked shelf at our local grocery store.

"Holy shit," I say. "Why did you guys buy the good stuff?"

"Because it's your boy's birthday," Harper says.

"He's not my—"

"And because your virginity deserves a proper send-off," Nina adds.

Rather than argue the second point, I steer the conversation elsewhere. "I've never been to the basketball team's house. What should I be expecting there? Is it more of a wine and weed sort of kickback vibe, or a little tailgate party, or should I expect, like, fifty people?"

"Fifty?" Harper repeats with a laugh. "That's cute, Kenny.

You should expect half the fucking school to show up. Knight's turning twenty-one. People go fucking feral when starters turn twenty-one. The basketball team dropped two grand on alcohol for tonight, and I know for a *fact* that every student athlete at this school is gonna be there. Also, I heard someone invited the slam poetry club, and you know how those artsy kids go wild."

Nina nods. "True. We're heathens."

"The slam poetry club?" I repeat, my fingertips tracing the hollow of my collarbone.

That can't be a coincidence, can it?

"Wait, who'd you hear all this from?" Nina asks.

Harper shrugs and picks at the label on the tequila bottle. "I may or may not have matched with Jabari Henderson on Bumble."

Nina and I both gasp.

"What?" Harper demands, instantly on the defensive.

"Don't girls have to message first on Bumble?" I ask.

Nina gasps again, louder. "What was your opening line?"

"I'm not talking to you right now."

"Ooh, I like it. Keep him on the hook. Show him who's boss."

"I meant *you*, bitch."

Harper storms back into her room with a shouted declaration that she's taking off the hat and it better not have left kinks in her hair, because she doesn't want to go to the trouble of heating up her flat iron again. I slide up onto one of the stools at the kitchen island. Nina shuffles to the other side and grabs a hand towel off the oven handle, draping it over one shoulder before she reaches for the plastic bag of red cups by the sink.

"What do you want, Kenny?" she asks. "I'm playing bartender."

"I might as well just have a shot. We've got the good stuff, right?"

We turn on a pregame playlist that has Harper's favorite dance music (and Nina's favorite Spanish rap that she knows all the words to) and we each have a shot (and then another) before we move the party to Nina's room. She lets me borrow her lucky going-out shirt—a long-sleeved black bodysuit with a plunging V-neck that dips right down to my sternum—and Harper gives me free rein over her extensive collection of makeup (except the foundations and concealers, since those are nowhere near my shade). I swipe on winged eyeliner and red lipstick like it's battle armor, because I meant what I said to Vincent Knight the night we met.

I'm *not* a coward.

Thirteen

The basketball team leases an old Victorian house on a sleepy, tree-lined street that connects Clement's campus to the downtown area.

I've walked down this street at least a hundred times. Whenever I head into town (which is really only when I need to buy clothes that seem too risky to order online or when I want to spend the afternoon in the romance section at the rambling old bookstore), this is my route. I know it like the back of my hand—all the university flags and decals in the windows, all the folding chairs on the front porches, all the neighborhood cats who technically shouldn't be kept in student housing.

I know this street. But I've never felt the pavement under my feet tremble in time with the bassline of a Post Malone song playing ominously in the distance.

Nina and Harper pass a water bottle filled with lemonade and tequila back and forth while they talk strategy.

"Bar first, beer pong, then—"

"No, no. Bar first, *then* we find your boys, *then* beer pong—"

I'm only half listening because I'm more interested in watching students spill out from houses and side streets and double-parked Ubers to join our pilgrimage, the flow of people building and building until, at last, we reach our shared destination.

The house explodes with light and sound and collegiate chaos that spills out onto the dark street below. There are balloons (in Clement's school colors, naturally) tethered to the railing on the front porch, and all the downstairs windows have been blacked out with what looks suspiciously like black trash bags taped together. Most of the second- and third-floor windows are lit up, and there are people leaning out of them to shout down to friends below on the packed front lawn.

As soon as I see how many people are here, I instinctively hug my arms over my chest.

This bodysuit was a terrible idea. What possessed me to come to a party with my tits halfway out? And who let me wear ankle boots with a three-inch heel? I'm towering over almost all the girls here, and a decent number of the boys. There's no hiding. There's no blending in.

I'm one big beacon of red lipstick and cleavage.

It's only once I push past this initial panic that I realize it's not just a crowd—it's a *line*, winding across the lawn and wrapping up onto the porch. There are two lanky kids (both freshmen; I recognize their faces from the basketball team roster) manning the front door with clipboards under their arms.

"Holy shit," I croak as we come to a stop on the sidewalk. "There's a *list*?"

"It's fine," Nina says, looping her arm through one of mine and squeezing tight. "We're fine. Don't panic. It'll move fast, and it's barely past nine o'clock, so we have plenty of time to do everything—and everyone—we came to do."

"I am *not* waiting," Harper announces.

"But we're already here!" Nina protests. "And we pre-gamed, and we look *hot*—"

"Calm down. I'm not leaving either."

And then Harper executes what I can only describe as a magic trick.

She whips her phone out of the back pocket of her jeans, pulls open her texts, and taps out a one-word-long message before hitting Send.

Not even fifteen seconds later, *poof*.

Jabari Henderson appears on the porch, his own phone in one hand. The other hand is rubbing over the side of his fade and adjusting the buttons of his (very trendy) short-sleeved shirt like he's frantically trying to make sure he's presentable. I watch him preen nervously and realize that Jabari is, without a shadow of a doubt, smitten.

"What the *fuck* was your opening line on Bumble?" Nina whisper-hisses.

Harper studiously ignores the question and lifts one hand high into the air, gold bracelets glinting in the soft glow of the porch lights. Jabari spots her in the crowd. I catch the split second of childlike joy on his face before he manages to pull it back and play it cool. He tips his chin up, motioning for her to come up to the front of the line.

With a flip of her dark hair over her shoulder, Harper marches across the grass. Nina trots along after her, head held high as she basks in the jealous stares of all the kids who've been waiting out here longer than we have to prove that their name is on the list. I follow, biting back the urge to apologize to each and every one of them.

Jabari lets out a low whistle as Harper climbs the porch steps. I scrunch my nose warily, but Harper laughs.

"Behave, boy. Behave."

Jabari presses his lips together, biting back a smile. "You made it."

"Me and half the school," Harper snaps. "You're just asking for your neighbors to report y'all to DPS at this point. I thought this thing was supposed to be invitation-only since you're on social probation?"

Jabari shrugs. "We sent out a lot of invites."

Harper arches an eyebrow.

"Don't give me that look, girl. You're my only plus-one."

Harper . . . giggles.

This is a new development. I've never seen Harper smile at a boy like this. Actually, I've never seen Harper look at a boy with any emotion other than distrust or outright hostility. So, this? This is a big fucking deal.

I'm still not one hundred percent sold on the guy. Not after Starbucks. But if the way Jabari is staring at Harper like she hung the moon is any indication, he understands what a big deal it is that she's allowing him the honor of speaking to her.

So—reluctantly—I'll give him a point.

"Hey, Henderson," Nina says.

Jabari startles like he's just noticed that Harper isn't the only woman in the world. "Nina," he says with a cordial nod. "Welcome back. I'll let everybody know that the reigning beer pong champ is in the building."

Nina blooms at the compliment. "Don't warn them. I like when they underestimate me."

Fine. That's two points for Jabari.

But then he's turning to me, and I'm suddenly and violently reminded that 1. I'm a real human being who can be perceived by other human beings and 2. three days ago, he and his teammates sat on the other side of a Starbucks and laughed at me. There's no time to hide. All I can do is stand there like future roadkill in the headlights of a semitruck. Jabari's whole face lights up with recognition and then—to my horror—a look of utter delight that I've only ever seen on Nina's face when she's about to do something I absolutely do not want her to do.

"I don't think we've met," he says, offering me his hand like we're at a career fair. "I'm Jabari."

You know damn well who I am, I want to say. Instead, I take his outstretched hand in what I hope is a bone-crushing grip and settle for a monotone: "Kendall."

"Kendall," Jabari repeats like he's never heard the name before in his life. "It is *so* great to meet you, Kendall."

I feel the corner of my mouth tug.

But I won't smile. Not yet.

Not until I know I can trust this guy.

"The three of us live together," Harper says.

Jabari's jaw drops. "You're *kidding*."

"Where's the birthday boy?" Nina asks.

I cut her a glare that could melt plastic. Nina doesn't so much as wince. She and Jabari are looking at each other like two people in a crowded lecture hall who've wordlessly agreed to partner up on a semester-long project.

I don't care for this development. Not even a little.

"He should be somewhere around here," Jabari says, brow knitting thoughtfully. "You guys want something to drink? I'll take you to the bar, if you're thirsty."

"Oh, we're *parched*," Nina replies.

Jabari takes Harper's hand, Harper takes Nina's hand, and Nina catches my wrist before I can wriggle out of her reach and sprint off into the night, never to be seen again.

Outside, the house is chaos.

Inside? It's somehow worse.

Darkness. Neon lights. Bodies packed tight, almost shoulder to shoulder, swaying in time with pounding music or streaming up and down hallways and in between rooms. Red cups in hands. The pungent scent of alcohol.

It's a cacophonous overload to my senses.

And yet everyone else looks like they're having the time of their fucking lives. Packs of girls dance in tight circles together, hips swinging as they shout song lyrics into one another's faces with the uninhibited passion of high school theater kids. Guys erupt in laughter and cheers as they stumble into some other guy that they loudly proclaim to be *my guy* to everyone within earshot. It seems everyone knows one another—from class, from sports teams, from prior hookups, from friends of friends of friends.

I've never wanted to be the center of the room or the girl who has a million acquaintances. I keep a small, tight inner circle. But clearly, Vincent has a much different concept of *social life*, because these beautiful, rowdy people are Vincent's friends. This is his tiny universe in which he is the sun and everyone revolves around him.

I feel like a passing asteroid.

We're not compatible.

I shake off the thought. It doesn't matter if Vincent and I aren't endgame. I'm not looking to marry the guy—that's ridiculous. I just want to climb him like a tree.

I can do this.

I'm going to fucking do this.

Jabari takes us on a quick lap around the dining room, where crowds have gathered around two different beer pong tables, and then doubles back across the hall and into the living room.

"I thought we were getting drinks," I shout to Nina.

Jabari definitely hears me.

"Bar's this way," he calls over his shoulder. "How do y'all feel about jungle juice?"

I don't think he's really listening for an answer.

Jabari cranes his neck and scans the living room, huffing a little in frustration. I get the sense that he's used to being able to see straight over everyone's heads, but this party is full of student athletes who play basketball and volleyball and football and other sports typically played by large humans. And maybe I'm a *little* thankful for the abnormally tall crowd, because I don't feel *entirely* out of place, but it's still a clusterfuck of drunk strangers bopping around in the dark while music thumps so loudly I feel the beat rattling around in my bones, and I'm suddenly terrified of having to pretend I'm not on the brink of an anxiety attack when I finally find—

"Knight!"

Jabari's voice rings out over the pounding music and strikes me square in the chest. Before I have time to mentally or emotionally prepare myself, he slips through an opening in the crowd, dragging the rest of us along after him to the far corner of the living room.

And there's Vincent.

Fourteen

Vincent doesn't see me at first—the crowd is too thick, and I'm half-hidden behind my friends. But I see him.

His dark hair shines under the neon glow of the cyan and magenta lights, and his face is something carved out of Greek antiquity—all hard angles and romantic curves cast in chiaroscuro. Even surrounded by assorted student athletes, Vincent is impressively tall and broad. He looks more dignified than a prince of the underworld. More dangerous than a Mafia hit man on the job. More dominant than a billionaire in a tailored suit. Which is an utterly silly thing for my brain to decide, since he's just wearing a black T-shirt, dark-wash jeans, and scuffed white sneakers—basic college boy party attire.

The brace that's been on his left arm for weeks is gone. The sight of his bare wrist, lightly freckled and covered with fine hair, shouldn't be this erotic, but *fuck*, I'm gawking like a Victorian who's spotted a stray ankle.

My gaze trails up a few inches and lands on the two black marker lines drawn on his forearm. Tally marks. I'm not so totally out of touch with campus culture that I don't know about the old Clement birthday tradition of having a drink for each year of life you've survived, but it's a little hard to believe that our star basketball player is only two drinks deep at nearly ten o'clock on his twenty-first birthday.

And then I see Vincent's face, and I know for a fact that he's sober.

The boy looks *exhausted*.

Jabari claps him on the back—a move that seems half comforting and half mocking—and Vincent startles, then sighs wearily when he recognizes whose arm is slung over his shoulder.

"Vinny, I've got some good news—"

"Oh, God. What did you do?"

"What do you mean, what did I do?"

"You look like you did something. I don't trust you."

"*Damn*, you're in a mood. Do you need another drink? Because I'll get you a drink. Vodka Sprite? Rum and Coke? I don't know what the fuck goes in an old-fashioned, but I'll do my best."

Vincent cracks a smile—reluctantly—and scrubs a hand over his face. "I don't need a drink. I *need* about two hundred fewer people in this house. We're going to get shut down before everyone who was actually invited gets here. Seriously. Who are half these people?"

"All right, all right," Jabari concedes. "I'll tell Griffin to turn down the music, and I'll personally keep an eye on the freshmen and make sure none of 'em end up with alcohol poisoning. But before I go do that—"

"I told you, I'm not doing body shots."

"—I got you a birthday present."

Vincent winces like he's expecting the worst, but then Jabari steps aside, presenting me with a sweep of his arm like he's one of the showgirls on *The Price Is Right* and I'm a brand-new Jet Ski that some poor bastard is going to have to pay exorbitant taxes on.

Vincent, the poor bastard in question, goes slack-jawed.

"Holy shit," he says. "Kendall."

Jabari throws back his head and hollers, "Suh-*prise*, shawty!"

It's not exactly how I pictured our reunion (it definitely doesn't have the sublime romantic impact of Mr. Darcy marching across the misty moors to tell Elizabeth he loves her), but I try to push through the disappointment. It's fine that it's almost too loud to hear each other and too dark to see each other. It's fine that there are sweaty drunk people on all sides of us. It's fine that Jabari, Nina, and Harper are watching Vincent and me stare at each other like we're exams that the other hasn't studied for.

I'm suddenly hyperaware of the fact that my shoulders are hunched and I've got my arms wrapped around myself. I let them drop to my sides and try to hold my chin high. Vincent's eyes immediately dip to my collarbone, and then down—all the way to the base of my bare sternum. I feel the heat of his gaze like a physical touch. He tugs his eyes back up to mine and swallows hard.

"You came," he rasps.

It's too easy of a double entendre. A cheap shot, really.

"I was promised a poetry reading."

"Right." The corner of Vincent's mouth twitches. "Prepare

to be blown away, Holiday. I memorized some Shel Silverstein just for you."

I laugh, too relieved to do much else. Because this? The bantering thing? This is comfortable and familiar and so fun it makes me dizzy.

I could do this shit all night.

"Is this really how y'all flirt?" Jabari asks.

The question is delivered with a surprising amount of fondness, but Vincent still startles like he's only just remembered that his friend is standing next to us. His expression smooths over into a hard mask. I'm reminded of the boy who came in during my shift three weeks ago: cold, confident, stuck somewhere halfway between *aloof* and *asshole*. He was embarrassed that night. Out of his element, out of sorts, and frustrated that he needed my help.

This brooding thing he does is his defense mechanism.

"Hey, Henderson," Vincent says, "can you fuck off?"

Jabari doesn't seem the least bit offended. He salutes his teammate, turns to Harper, and says something to her that I can't catch over the music. She nods and gestures to Nina, then grabs me by my sleeve and hauls me close so she can shout into my ear.

"I'm gonna go upstairs and meet some of Jabari's teammates. I'm leaving Nina to wing-woman for you, because you're hopeless and I don't trust you, so do what she says, okay?"

"But—"

"Nope. The boy wants you, Kenny. Don't fuck it up for yourself."

Harper gives me a soft—yet slightly condescending—pinch on my cheek, and then she and Jabari are lost to the crush of the crowd. I look to Nina, who folds her arms over her chest and widens her stance, like a bouncer outside a bar, before nodding at me.

"He didn't give you any trouble, did he?" Vincent asks like it's supposed to be a joke, but there's a worried edge to his voice, and his eyebrows are pinched.

"Is he always like that? So . . ." I search for the right word. ". . . forward?"

"He's a shooting guard, actually."

I blink.

"It's a basketball joke."

"Oh. See, I don't know all of the positions."

Vincent bites back a laugh. It takes me a second to catch up, but when I do, I fold my arms across my chest and sigh witheringly.

"So immature," I grumble.

"I can teach you, Holiday. Just ask."

I'm glad for the neon glow to hide my blush. "All right, fair enough. I walked into that one."

It's Vincent's turn to laugh. It melts something in me.

Harper's words echo in my head: *The boy wants you.* And I want him. But how in the hell does a girl tell a boy, in the middle of a very crowded and very public birthday party, that she wants to do very private things?

Nina leans in to my ear and says, "Ask him where the bar is. Jabari promised me a drink."

It's like she's sneaking me answers during an exam.

"Hey, Vincent, where's the—"

The song playing over the speakers switches, and suddenly all I can hear is the familiar opening bars of a 2016 throwback and the scattered gasps and cheers of people hurrying to find some open space to dance in.

Vincent's eyebrows furrow. I don't think he heard me.

I roll up onto my tiptoes at the same moment that he ducks down, turning his head to offer me his ear. I'm so surprised by his closeness that I wobble and have to hold an arm out to regain my balance. Vincent's hand comes up to cup my elbow. It's barely a touch, but it's somehow enough to make my whole body rock forward, seeking the solid heat of his.

"Can we get drinks?" I ask, my voice suddenly hoarse.

Vincent straightens and nods. The hand on my elbow drops down, ghosting over my forearm. I turn my hand over instinctively to catch his. And then our palms are pressed together, our fingers lacing in a way that feels far too practiced and familiar for a first time, and I'm fairly certain that I'm fucked.

Behind me, Nina laughs. I'm reminded of what she said about Jabari Henderson holding Harper's hand to lead her to the bar at a party.

That's flirting, you moron. It's a move.

Vincent's hand in mine is an anchor in the storm as we push through the living room and into the kitchen. At least ten different people call out birthday well-wishes. A few guys reach out to Vincent for a high five or a clap on the back. One is so intent on engaging him in a conversation that he throws an arm over Vincent's shoulder and walks along with us while the crowd splits for Vincent and his commandingly broad shoulders.

This is a whole new side of him that I've never seen.

I knew, of course, that he was one of the big fish in the

campus pond. But it's another thing entirely to witness him in his element, surrounded by people who know him and love him and want a piece of him. I already feel like he's mine—and that's not right, because I can't own him. I don't want to. Nobody should feel ownership over another person. I've critiqued way too many overpossessive alpha love interests to become one myself. But as I watch Vincent mingle with the crowd, I feel the worst sting of longing.

I squeeze his hand tighter on impulse.

He casts a glance over his shoulder, eyebrows knit with worry. I give him what has to be the weakest smile anyone's ever flashed at a party.

Pull it together, Holiday.

Do it for the plot.

Fifteen

The music is only marginally quieter in the kitchen.

Everyone congregates around the bar, which isn't really a bar so much as a long table constructed out of plywood that's being staffed by two very tall boys and a dark-haired girl with a gold hoop in her nose. Half the room is carrying a red cup. The other half is shouldering their way forward in the hopes of getting one. I brace myself against the swaying crowd and tighten my grip on Nina's hand (so I won't lose her) and Vincent's (because I don't want him to lose me either).

"It's the birthday boy!" the girl with the nose ring shouts when we reach the bar.

Vincent laughs. "Hey, Priya. Any chance we get VIP access?"

Priya shifts some cases of beer and bags of red cups out of the way, revealing an opening under part of the bar. Vincent presses a hand to the small of my back, guiding me forward, and then I'm ducking to get under the plywood. Nina's next.

"Oh, I like this," she says when she pops up with me on the other side. "I like this a lot."

There's actually breathing room back here, in the open space behind the makeshift bar. My shoulders sag with relief. Then Vincent ducks under the bar to join us, and suddenly there's less space, but I'm not mad about it. Not at all.

"What do you want?" he asks.

You. "I don't know. What are the options?"

"Beer, wine, vodka, tequila, whiskey. Anything you want. Just . . ." Vincent winces, then reaches out to pat the side of an enormous plastic Gatorade barrel perched up on the bar. "Don't touch the jungle juice. It's got like six different types of hard alcohol in it. You'll be blacked out before you finish your first cup."

Nina wordlessly slips around us, plucks a cup off the stack, and dispenses herself a glass.

"Are you serious?" I ask.

She takes a sip and smacks her lips. "I'm never serious. Oh, wow. This is poison. Yep. Okay. You stay and do your thing, and I'm going to challenge someone to beer pong before this stuff hits. I'll be making friends and enemies, if you need me." She adds, in a mock-whisper she hides from Vincent with one hand, "Don't need me."

Then Nina slips out from under the bar and disappears, leaving me with Vincent.

Alone—and also very much *not* alone.

"I'll take some red wine," I blurt. "If that's okay?"

I want to kick myself. Who asks for red wine at a house party? My drink of choice for cozy nights in with my roommates is a disaster waiting to happen with so many elbows flying around.

But Vincent doesn't even blink. He flags down Priya,

who's busy distributing cans of beer to half the lacrosse team, and relays my order to her. She reaches for the boxed wine. Vincent redirects her to an unopened bottle hidden in a cabinet on the other side of the bar. Priya cocks an eyebrow and gives me a look that's a little impressed and a lot intrigued.

"What's the special occasion?" she teases.

"My birthday," Vincent says. His tone is bored, but there's a pink flush to his cheeks.

I watch as the cork is popped and my own personal wine is poured into a red cup.

"Here you go, babe," Priya says.

"Thanks so much." I put my nose over the rim and sniff. "Shit. Is this real wine?"

Vincent cracks a smile. "Of course it's real wine."

"I know! I just meant—it smells good. Not like the boxed stuff."

For a solid three seconds, I'm convinced there are honest-to-God stars twinkling in Vincent's eyes before I realize it's just the reflection of the string lights pinned up around the crown molding over the kitchen cabinets. He looks so beautiful. And he's so tall that, even in my heeled boots, I have to tip my chin up to look at him. The last time we saw each other, he was sitting down. Now that we're both upright, I'm reminded how well our bodies slot together when he lifts me and I can wrap my legs around the middle of him. He was able to pick me up with only one good arm. I wonder what he could do with *two*.

Oh, God. Maybe red wine is a bad idea.

"How's your wrist?" I blurt.

A bolder girl might stroke the back of his hand or trace

little patterns on his skin with her fingertip. Instead, I clutch my plastic cup of wine in both hands, white-knuckled, absolutely *killing* this whole seduction thing.

"It's better," Vincent says. "The physical therapist cleared me to play again. I actually got to handle the ball in practice yesterday, which was a relief."

I'd like you to handle me—

"Were you going to get anything?" I ask, suddenly not keen to be drinking alone.

Vincent shakes his head. "I'm good. Trying to keep a clear head."

"For the poetry reading?"

"Obviously. I already butchered Blake sober. Can't make a fool of myself again."

"You did fine. Don't be so hard on yourself."

The corner of Vincent's mouth curls up into a half smile, and it's like the best shot of hard alcohol I've ever had—none of the burn, just a slow shot of heat that lands deep in my belly. It's almost too much. I look down at my cup of wine.

Vincent bumps his hip against mine.

"I'm really glad you're here, Holiday," he says. "Especially after Monday. I know it was. . ." He trails off and grimaces, which just about sums up the catastrophe that was the end of our little tutoring session.

"I wanted to talk to you about that, actually—"

The words are out before I can stop them. *Shit.* This isn't going to plan. I'm supposed to keep it light and fun. I'm not supposed to make a big speech—not when I'm pretty sure I'll say the wrong thing again and ruin this. But Vincent stands straighter, like he's physically bracing for whatever verbal hellfire I can rain on him, and suddenly it feels imperative that I clear the air. Even if I have to scream the words over a Doja Cat song.

"Vincent, I—"

"Knight!"

All my courage evaporates.

There's a basketball player standing on the other side of the bar. He's an absolute unit of a human (seven feet tall, give or take an inch) but his cheeks are round and his face is decidedly boyish. I think he's a freshman. I'm not entirely sure, though, because most of my roster stalking has been focused on Vincent and the boys I saw in Starbucks.

A muscle in Vincent's jaw ticks—the only indication he gives that he's annoyed by the interruption.

"What's up?" he demands.

Vincent's teammate isn't dissuaded by his sharp tone. "Do you have a copy of the key to the basement? Jabari said there are some kegs down there we can bring up." His eyes shift past Vincent and land on me. "Hey, I'm Griffin—"

He attempts to reach a hand across the bar for me to shake, but Vincent steps forward and creates a human wall between me and his teammate. I'm quietly glad for it. Maybe he's learned his lesson about keeping his teammates out of our business.

"The key's in my room."

"Cool. Do you want to give me your room key? Or do you want to go get it?"

"I don't remember where I put it. But I don't want you turning the place inside out. Why do we even need kegs? There's plenty of alcohol."

"But we wanted to have a keg stand competition," Griffin says forlornly.

Vincent sighs and turns to me. I get the odd sense that he's about to ask for my permission, and I'm again reminded that I can't own him.

"Go take care of business," I say, giving him what I intend to be an encouraging pat on the shoulder but turns out to be just an excuse to run my palm over the curve of his muscle. I can't remember the name of it right now. Maybe I should ask him later for an anatomy lesson.

God, I *really* need to put down this wine.

Luckily, it's dark enough in here that Vincent can't see how badly I'm blushing.

"You're staying, right?" he asks, still looking uneasy.

"No, I did my hair and makeup and walked all the way over here for the free wine." I give him a pointed look. "Of course I'm staying. Someone has to make sure Nina's not breaking international beer pong ethics."

"I'll find you later," he tells me. It sounds like a promise.

As soon as Vincent disappears into the crowd, though, I'm suddenly and painfully aware of the fact that I'm standing completely on my own in a house full of strangers. With a deep breath, I duck back out from behind the bar and dive into the crowd, joining the stream of people heading into the dining room.

I'm relieved when I find Nina posted up on one side of a beer pong table.

She's not as happy to see me as I am to see her, though.

"Where's Vincent?" she demands.

"He had to go take care of some official party business."

Maybe tonight wasn't the ideal night to try to talk to him privately. People are drunk and loud and desperate for a piece of him. His teammates, the other athletes, the kids from his classes, the girls who are watching from all corners of the room and waiting for their chance—all of them are playing a strategic game to win Vincent's attention, if only for a few minutes before someone else swoops in to steal the birthday boy.

It hits me, then, that I'm playing too.

"Go after him," Nina orders, reading my mind. "Assert yourself."

"He said he'd find me again . . ." As soon as I say it, I know Nina is right. Waiting around is only going to give me time to overthink and convince myself that this won't end well. Or, worse, result in me going all night without being able to actually *talk* to Vincent.

"You can't say you hate passive main characters and then be passive, Kendall."

"I know," I huff. "Give me a minute, okay?"

What I need is a moment in relative silence to compose myself, fuss with my hair, blot my lipstick, and remind myself that I am a bad bitch who is totally capable of seducing Vincent Knight and then not freaking out if it all ends in anything less than us riding off into the sunset.

Nina whoops out a cheer as she lands another Ping-Pong ball into a cup across the table. The two boys at the other end look at each other like they've realized they're in over their heads. I would stay and delight in her triumph, but I have an agenda tonight.

"I need to find the bathroom," I announce.

"It's upstairs at the end of the hall. You want me to come with you?"

I shake my head. This is a solo mission.

"I can find it," I say. "Stay right here, okay? I'll be back in five."

Sixteen

There's no way this is taking five minutes.

The line for the bathroom is about a mile long and takes up half of the upstairs hallway. I fall into place behind a pair of girls who immediately notice that I'm out of sorts and take it upon themselves to compliment every inch of my outfit, then my makeup, then my bone structure.

Now I remember the only thing I've ever liked about college parties: the warm sense of community and camaraderie formed between drunk girls waiting for their turn to pee.

Someone down the line shouts for lip balm.

Immediately, there are four offers.

It's more fun than the actual party, and it's exactly the environment I need to take a deep breath and *think*. It shouldn't be this hard for me to go after what I want. And that's Vincent. Judging by the way he looks at me and the near-constant stream of flirtatious jokes and double entendres, he wants me too. So why is my anxious little brain complicating things? Why am I so worried about our friends? Speaking of—I should make sure they're holding up without me.

I'm checking my phone for any texts from Nina or Harper when I feel it: the familiar invisible tug that urges me to lift my head.

Vincent is coming down the crowded hallway in the opposite direction. He looks thoroughly annoyed. It doesn't take a genius to figure out why: he's a few steps behind Griffin, who's swinging a lanyard with what must be the key to the basement and whistling along with the pounding music that's drifting up through the floor. Griffin breezes right past me. For a moment, I think Vincent will too.

But our eyes meet like magnets snapping together, and he comes to a stop at my side.

"Hey. You good?"

"I'm fine," I tell him. "Just waiting for the bathroom."

Vincent looks up and down the row of girls like he's just noticed that we're all lined up for something. A trio of lacrosse boys try to slide past Vincent in the crowded hall, and he shuffles forward, toward me. There's enough room between me and the wall that I could probably take a step back, but I don't. I let Vincent get so close I can feel the heat of his chest radiating against me. He smells divine. Laundry detergent and something subtle and spiced that's achingly familiar now. I have to tip my head back to meet his eyes.

"Do you want to use mine?" Vincent offers.

I scrunch my nose. I'm not quite drunk enough to tolerate the sight of a urinal.

"I'm in a single," he adds. "I have my own bathroom. I promise it's clean."

Out of the corner of my eye, I register that the girls ahead of me in line are watching us with open mouths. The taller of the two gives me a pointed look that says, *Go with him, obviously.*

"Fine," I relent. "But I reserve the right to roast you if all you have in your shower is that shampoo–body wash combo shit."

"I wouldn't expect anything less from you, Holiday."

For a split second, I think he's going to take my hand again, but the hall isn't quite crowded enough to justify the need to form a human chain. I shoot the two drunk girls I've been bonding with a sheepish smile (*Can you believe this is happening?*) and they return the gesture with a thumbs-up (and some obscene gestures that I take to mean *Get it, girl*) before I turn and follow Vincent back down the hall the way he came.

He pulls his keys out of the back pocket of his jeans and unlocks a door at the end of the hall.

His room is nicer than I was expecting.

Admittedly, I've come to believe that most college-aged boys who don't live in the on-campus dorms sleep on air mattresses or futons they found on the side of the road and have decor made exclusively from empty vodka bottles and beer cans. But Vincent's room is more like an IKEA staging room than a dilapidated frat house. His bed is made. His desk is stacked tall with textbooks and stray papers, like he's been doing homework, but none of those papers are crumpled or scattered on the floor. The only true mess in the room is the mountain of athletic gear on the floor beside his wardrobe—a few duffel bags, some practice jerseys, and some basketball sneakers that are so enormous I briefly do a double take at Vincent's feet.

He clears his throat and gestures toward the door to my left.

"Bathroom's through there."

"Right! Right. Thanks."

I pull the door shut behind me. How on Earth have I just finessed this? I'm in his *bathroom*. I didn't even really need to pee (I just wanted a quiet moment to myself) and now Vincent and I are in what has to be the quietest corner of the house. His sink is clean, the mirror above it clear of any water splatter or toothpaste stains. The towels on the wall-mounted rack are navy blue and unwrinkled. I slowly pull back the shower curtain, hoping the rustling fabric and the sliding of metal rings on the curtain rod isn't too loud. Shampoo. Face wash. Body wash. Three separate bottles. Well done, Knight.

With my inspection complete, I flush the toilet (to keep up the illusion) and then lean over the sink, palms braced on the rim, to stare hard at my reflection.

"You're a strong, independent woman in control of your own life," I whisper. Then, as an afterthought: "And your tits look phenomenal."

When I slip out of the bathroom, Vincent is perched on the side of his mattress, his phone in his hand. He slips it back into the pocket of his jeans and stands as soon as he sees me.

We're alone together, finally.

In his bedroom.

The floor underneath my feet trembles in time with the bassline of a Spanish song I know Nina and Harper must be screaming the lyrics to, wherever they are. I could head back downstairs and join them. I could smile, thank Vincent, and walk to the door. It's propped open a few inches. I can hear the distant chatter and footsteps of people down the hall. Vincent could reach for the door too, and hold it open. He could sigh and say something about getting back to his party.

But he doesn't move. And neither do I.

We stand, rooted, our eyes on each other.

He steps forward, and the black tally marks on his forearm catch the light.

"What are those for?" I blurt, pointing at them.

Vincent looks down and blinks, like he's forgotten the lines were there. "Drinks. I'm supposed to make it to twenty-one by midnight."

"You're running a little behind."

He shrugs. "It's only ten. I've got time."

"Unless your very reasonably sized and superchill party gets broken up by DPS, you mean."

Vincent exhales a laugh. "It's not really *my* party."

"It's your birthday, isn't it?"

"I just meant that this party isn't for me. It's for the team. They've had to pull all the weight this season, so yeah, I would've done things a little differently—maybe invited about two hundred fewer people—but the team's worked hard. They deserve some good old-fashioned chaos."

"Spoken like a true captain."

Vincent shrugs. "What can I say? They're my boys."

"So, you're the team daddy," I say, then immediately realize my mistake. "Team *dad*, I mean."

He doesn't let me off that easy. "I'm sorry, could you repeat that first part?"

"No."

"Did you say—"

"You know what I meant."

"You're a *mess*, Holiday. A mess. I've never seen you so off your game."

I huff and perch on the corner of his desk. "Big parties overwhelm me. I like the dancing, sometimes, but mostly I just feel claustrophobic and self-conscious."

"About your dancing?" Vincent asks. "I took a ballroom dancing elective freshman year. I could teach you some moves."

He sounds way too excited about the prospect of embarrassing me.

"My dancing is *fine*, thank you very much."

My eyes land on the stack of books on his desk—one of which is familiar.

I hold up *Engman's Anthology* and arch an eyebrow.

"You know you have to return this, right?"

Vincent shrugs. "Not for another week."

I do the math myself to confirm. I hate that so much time has passed. It feels like I'm losing bits and pieces of the memory, even though I've been replaying it in my head religiously. The details are smoothing over—the specifics of the conversation and the little touches during our kisses are becoming one big, amorphous feeling. A vibe, if you will.

I zone back in and realize I've been staring at Vincent's mouth.

He's noticed this, of course, and watches me with eyes so dark and smoldering that I feel like he's struck a match along my spine.

"Read me something," he murmurs. "Out loud."

He must know what he's asking of me. He has to. My heart hiccups as I push off the desk, take a few steps into the middle of the room, and let the book in my hands fall open, pages sliding over each other until I spot a yellow Post-It peeking out from the top. I flip forward to it and find an Elizabeth Barrett Browning poem. My face splits into a grin.

"Did you bookmark this?" I ask, holding it up so he can see.

Vincent hums noncommittally.

"Say over again, and yet once over again, That thou dost love me," I read.

Outside, somewhere down the hall, someone screams, "Sarah! Where's Sarah? Bitch, you took my phone—"

Vincent huffs and marches to the door.

"Can I close this?" he asks me, suddenly a little shy.

My entire body heats. "Sure. Totally. Of course."

Vincent presses the door shut and, after a moment's hesitation, twists the lock. He shoots me another glance, to check if I have any objections. I suppress the urge to shoot him a very dorky thumbs-up. Instead, I look down at *Engman's Anthology* and clear my throat. Before I can begin reading aloud again, Vincent crosses the room in three long strides and stands behind me, so close I can feel the heat of his body in the inch of air between us.

He's reading over my shoulder—just like the night we met.

I have to swallow hard to prevent a shiver of heat from rolling down my spine.

"Say thou dost love me, love me, love me—toll The silver iterance!—only minding, Dear, To love me also in silence with thy soul."

I read slowly. Meticulously. Selfishly, because I want to stand right here until I've memorized every detail of this moment. The warmth. The smell. The gentle thump of distant music, the muffled chaos down the hall. The indescribable feeling of relief, that somehow we've made it back here. Back to each other.

"Well, Professor Holiday," Vincent murmurs when I reach the end of the sonnet, "what do you think?"

"This one's too easy," I croak, voice as weak as my knees.

"Tell me your interpretation anyway."

I consider the page again. "She wants to be told she's loved, but it has to be true. He has to mean it. It has to be more than just empty words."

"Actions speak louder than words," Vincent murmurs, more to himself than to me.

"Exactly."

"I'm pretty sure I'm going to ace this poetry class because of you."

"You know, technically," I say, pointing a fingertip at his floor, "this is tutoring. Like, right now. So, I should probably charge you."

He nods solemnly. "I'll Venmo you."

I press my lips together and cover the bottom half of my face with the open book to stop myself from giggling. Vincent's eyes drop. I briefly imagine him ripping the anthology from my hands, tossing it across the room, and kissing me full on the mouth.

But he doesn't. He's still. Patient. Waiting.

"You know how you offered to pay me back?" I ask.

He nods.

I reach up and trace a fingertip over the curve of his shoulder. "What's this muscle?"

Vincent exhales hard.

"Deltoid," he answers.

I nod and let my arm drop to my side.

"Is that all you wanted to ask?"

"Yep. Curiosity satisfied."

I turn to set *Engman's Anthology* back on his desk. But Vincent follows—and this time, he presses his body flush against my back. I stop breathing entirely.

"You sure you don't want to know what this muscle is?" he asks, tracing a fingertip up the outside of my forearm. I shiver when his knuckle passes over the tender skin in the crook of my elbow and continues up and over my—

"Bicep," I croak. "Everyone knows that one."

My hair tickles the back of my neck as he pushes it to the side. The only warning I get is his hot breath on my skin, and then his lips are pressed against the curve of my shoulder—so gently that at first I wonder if I'm imagining it.

"And this one?"

I can't think straight.

"Um." My voice is a soft croak. "Don't say it. I know it."

His lips press against my shoulder again, and this time there's no mistake. My mouth falls open and heat pools low in my stomach as Vincent nips at the skin.

"Trapezius," he whispers.

I spin to face him, immediately going weak in the knees when I realize we're so close that I can feel the length of him against the front of me now. His mouth is inches from mine. I press a hand to his chest, trying to keep that precious sliver of space between us. I feel like I'm about to launch myself at him, but I can't stumble into this blindly—not when miscommunication is the worst trope. If we kiss now, that'll be it. I'll forget everything that's been bothering me and every question I need answered. And I know I told myself I was coming here for a onetime thing, but this feels like something worth the effort. Worth the risk.

I want to do this right or not at all.

"Kendall," Vincent murmurs. It sounds like a plea.

"Wait," I say, swallowing hard. "I have something I want to say."

Seventeen

Vincent doesn't get frustrated. He doesn't get angry or distant or weird. Even if he finds my request to *talk* a total mood killer, the measured step he takes back from me isn't passive-aggressive or cruel. It's patient. It gives me the space I need to march into the middle of his room and pace a few laps, sucking in deep breaths of cool air and trying to clear my head before I turn to face him again.

He leans against his desk and nods, giving me the floor.

"So." I clear my throat. "I ran. On Monday."

"I know. I was there."

I huff and shoot him a warning look.

"I have stage fright, I guess. Not that I was handling everything great before that—"

"I was about to say," he quips with a smile that's more kind than it is teasing. "Look, I don't blame you for leaving. I didn't know the guys were going to come spy on me. My friends are idiots. I apologize on their behalf."

"Don't apologize yet," I snap. "Can I at least make my points first?"

Vincent holds his arms wide open. "Apology rescinded. Give me your worst."

I take a deep breath and fold my arms over my chest to steady myself.

"I don't like that your friends knew where to find us. And I know I can't ask you not to talk to them about this kind of stuff, because obviously I've told Harper and Nina everything—of course I did. And I'd be a hypocrite to be mad at you, but the fact that they came into Starbucks and sat there and *watched us* and probably took pictures to send to some sort of team group chat made me feel so—so—" I let out a strangled groan. "So *attacked*. Like, when girls talk about toxic masculinity and guys being gross with each other? It's *that*. That feeling of being made fun of, being watched and harassed."

The whole time I'm speaking, Vincent's smile falls.

When I'm done, he swallows hard and says, "I'm sorry, Kendall. It wasn't my intention—it wasn't *our* intention. I promise. But intention doesn't matter. I hurt you. And I'm sorry."

I can tell this one's not on behalf of his team. This apology is his. I bite back the impulse to say it's okay, because it's not. But I do nod—just so he knows that his apology is acknowledged.

"I also ran because I was . . . confused."

"About what? Let's talk it out."

I arch an eyebrow. "Really?"

"Of course. I don't want you to be confused about anything."

It's so not what I expected—and it's so *validating* to be

treated like my overactive emotions aren't irrational or an annoyance.

"I told you already that I'm not good at this game," I begin.

Vincent opens his mouth.

"I know." I cut him off. "I know you said it's not a game. But that's the only way I can describe what it feels like. And it feels like I missed something, or nobody gave me the rule book, and maybe I'm just not very smart, but—"

"You're smart," Vincent interrupts sharply. "Ask me something. Anything."

I chew on my lip and search his face for any hint of humor. There's none. He's dead serious.

"When you left the note at the library," I begin, my voice wobbling just a little, "was that code for, like, wanting to go on a coffee date? Or hook up? Or was it really just for tutoring? Or—I don't know. I didn't want to read too much into it."

I wring my hands, willing my heartbeat to calm the fuck down and stop acting like I'm standing on the edge of a roof twenty stories up from a busy street. *So overdramatic.*

Vincent frowns. "Which note are we talking about?"

"*The* note."

"No, I mean—the first one or the second one?"

It's my turn to frown. "Wait. What?"

Vincent stares at me for a moment like he can't tell if I'm joking or not, and then he does the last thing I expect. He laughs. I watch him, dumbstruck, as he sits down on the edge of his bed and scrubs his hands over his face. "Oh my God," he moans, then he drops his hands into his lap. "I knew it."

I feel like my brain is lagging.

"Knew what?" I ask.

Vincent shakes his head. "It's my fault—it was a dumb idea. It was that first night, when I came in during your shift and we—" He tilts his head in silent acknowledgment of our make-out session. "The librarian was helping me check out the anthology you gave me, and I—" Vincent laughs again, like he's embarrassed, and hides his face behind one hand. "I wrote you a little note and my phone number on a piece of paper. I put it in your book."

"What book?" I ask, and then abruptly I remember *The Mafia's Princess*. The book he caught me reading. The book I left on the circulation desk when we went upstairs. The book I never finished reading because I couldn't look at the cover without thinking about how badly I'd fucked up with Vincent. "Stop. You're kidding me."

Vincent bites down on his lower lip and nods.

"Fuck!" I cry.

All this time—three *miserable* weeks—and I had his phone number in the book I couldn't bring myself to finish. I had solid, tangible proof that Vincent Knight wanted me, and I passed it off to Nina and told her she could either read it or toss it in a donation bin.

I bury my face in my hands.

"I didn't finish the book," I groan into my palms. "Oh my God, I—I told Nina she could have it. Shit. She probably donated it." Because if she'd found a note from Vincent Knight tucked in my romance novel, she never would've shut up about it.

"No wonder you were so pissed off at Starbucks."

"Oh my God, I was furious. I thought you were

purposefully sending mixed signals. You kiss me, and then you disappear, and then I don't hear from you again until you need a tutor—like, what was I supposed to do with *that*?"

"I thought *you* ghosted *me* after the night we met. I never got a text from you, and I thought maybe you weren't interested, but I had to know for sure. Asking for help with poetry was, like, my Hail Mary to see you again. And then you emailed me, and it was so stiff and formal, and I thought—"

"That I didn't want to see you again," I finish.

He nods. "And *you* thought I just wanted a tutor."

It's both satisfying and infuriating to finally clear this up.

One thing I'm definitely sure of: miscommunication truly is the worst trope.

"Well, we're *brilliant*," I announce.

Vincent laughs. It's loud and loose and makes the knot in my chest come undone.

"I'm not very good at asking for what I want," he admits, his cheeks and the tips of his ears tinged with pink as he picks at invisible lint on his duvet. I've never seen him so bashful. "If I'm advocating for someone else, it's easy. I'm just being team captain. But if it's just for me, I—I don't know. I feel greedy."

The idea that Vincent—confident, quick-witted, flirty, dirty-minded Vincent—doesn't like advocating for himself doesn't seem to fit. But the puzzle piece slots into place.

He's never been good at asking for help, has he?

I think of the way he kissed me in the library, and his offer to let me practice on him. How sheepish he was when he asked me to be patient and let him try to lift me with one arm, for my own enjoyment. The way he teased me at Starbucks, the whole time thinking I'd just come for the money but hoping, quietly, that I wanted him the way he wanted me. He's always left the door open for me. Even when I slam it shut in his face, he opens it up again.

But all this time, he's been too afraid to ask me to come inside.

It's enough to break my heart. It's enough to make me want to clutch him tight and pepper kisses over every inch of his face, to apologize for being a coward—and to reprimand him for being a coward too.

"Well," I say. "We're just going to have to communicate better, aren't we? Be honest with each other. Clear. Direct."

Vincent swallows and sits up straighter.

"Then for the sake of being direct," he says, "I can't stop thinking about you, Kendall. And I've read every goddamned poem Elizabeth Barrett Browning ever wrote. In three weeks. For *fun*."

I bark out a surprised laugh and press my hands to my overheated cheeks.

"What have you done to me?"

It feels like a small sacrifice of pride for the sake of honesty, so I return the favor.

"I watched your highlight reel on YouTube," I whisper.

His eyes twinkle. "And?"

"I still don't know how shot clock violations work, and at this point, I'm too embarrassed to ask."

Vincent throws his head back and laughs again. But it's not exactly at my expense, because I'm laughing too, at the utter absurdity that *this whole fucking time*, we've been on the same page without realizing it.

This is it. This is where I could borrow any number of

lines I've memorized from my novels about declared feelings and deepest desires. But both Vincent and Elizabeth Barrett Browning made a great fucking point: actions speak louder than words. And right now, I want to be *loud*. So, I cross the room to where Vincent is sitting on the side of his bed, clamp my hands down on his shoulders for balance, and then—in one solid burst of bravery and determination—press one knee to the mattress and swing my other leg over his lap.

Eighteen

This was, perhaps, a bit impulsive.

I'm straddling Vincent's lap, hands clutching fistfuls of his shirt so I won't fall backward and land ass-first on his bedroom floor, perched high on my knees because I'm not totally ready to put my full weight on his thighs.

Vincent's eyes are level with my collarbone. If he looks down, he'll see straight into the plunging neckline of my borrowed bodysuit. If he looks up, he'll see a double chin. Nothing about this is flattering or seductive, but it's too late to back out without awkwardly climbing off his lap. So, we're just going to roll with it.

Because I am definitely still not good at this, I lean back—just enough to look him in the eyes—and ask, "Is this too direct?"

Vincent snorts and ducks forward to hide his smile in the crook of my neck. His hands briefly bracket my hips, then drop to my thighs, like he can't decide where to put them.

"Please try to help me maintain *some* semblance of my dignity," I scold.

"Sorry. I'm sorry. I'm not laughing at you, I promise." Vincent's breath is hot against my pulse point. I try not to shiver. "I'm laughing because if I don't laugh, I'm going to explode. I've never gotten this hard this fast."

Heat blooms in my cheeks and rushes between my legs.

I lower myself down onto his lap—because surely he's just joking—and the laugh in my throat immediately turns to dust. He's actually hard. Vincent is *erect*, pressed right where he'd slip inside me, and the heat of him seeps straight through both of our jeans and makes me immediately and humiliatingly wet.

Vincent groans. I startle and sit back, so my weight is on his thighs. He groans again.

"I'm not hurting you, am I?" I ask. "I'm not very small. But I guess neither are you."

"You're the perfect size for me," Vincent says. His eyes dip down, following the neckline of my bodysuit, and then meet mine again. He bites back a smile. "And your tits look phenomenal."

For a moment, the compliment is jarring. And then I recognize the words as my own.

I go very still. "You did *not* hear that."

"It's okay. We've all hyped ourselves up in a bathroom mirror."

The long, strangled groan of mortification that leaves my body sounds like the dying wail of an animal. I let go of his shoulders and hide my face in my palms.

If the floor could go ahead and swallow me up, that'd be great.

Vincent gently takes my wrists and pulls my hands down between us.

"Can you please put me out of my misery and kiss me?" I grumble.

Vincent exhales a laugh, his smile heartbreakingly soft.

His lips land on my cheek first. He kisses it once, softly, before shifting to the other side of my face to do the same. I sit very still, my eyes shut and my heart lodged in my throat, as he marks a slow trail up to my forehead, then down the bridge of my nose—pausing to press butterfly-soft kisses on my eyelids—before resuming his path toward my mouth. At the last moment, when I'm sure he'll end this torture and kiss me properly, he dips past my jaw and presses a hard, wet kiss to my pulse point.

I let out a ragged and rather humiliating whine.

"Vincent." I'm *begging*. Feminism is dead. I killed her, and I don't care.

"Oh, all right," he sighs.

He tips his chin up in offering, and at last, I kiss him—open-mouthed and greedy.

It's divine. It's music, and poetry, and every other over-blown metaphor I've ever heard about kissing. Vincent's lips are familiar in a way that makes my heart ache. The nudge of tongue against mine before it strokes over my bottom lip is so soft, so *gentle*, and simultaneously hungry in a way that makes my stomach coil with heat.

"Happy?" he murmurs against my lips.

"Don't patronize me," I whisper. But my answering kiss says, *Yes—incandescently*.

Tentatively, I rake my fingernails up his chest, dragging at the soft cotton of his shirt. Vincent shudders under my hands and tightens his grip on my hips, tugging them forward until my pelvis is pressed to his stomach.

I like the way he handles me. The way he positions me just how he likes. There's something thrilling about his strength and the unpredictability of his desire. It's not like having a dirty daydream before bed and having to come up with the whole plot yourself. I'm not alone. He's here. He's real. He's participating.

It's so nice to want and be wanted. I could drown in this feeling.

Unfortunately, my body hasn't caught up to the metaphors racing through my head—I have to come up for air at some point. When I do pull back to catch my breath, I'm startled by the sight that greets me: Vincent has my red lipstick smudged all over his face, from nose to chin. It's so startling—and so *filthy*, so *obscene*—that I choke out a strangled laugh.

"What?" Vincent demands.

"You've got lipstick—" I gesture around my own mouth.

He arches an eyebrow. "So do you."

I gasp, pull my sleeve over my hand, and rub furiously. Vincent laughs.

"Shut up," I beg. "Twelve hours of smudge-proof coverage, my ass."

"You should write a one-star review."

I wipe hard at the corners of my mouth. "There. Am I better?"

"Much."

"Here. Let me clean you up."

Vincent props his weight back on his arms and lets me tend to him. I brace one hand on the back of his head, holding him in place while I wipe his mouth with my sleeve.

"Your hair is so soft," I grumble. "Do you really not use conditioner?"

"You looked through my shower?"

"Of course I did. I warned you I would."

If Vincent notices that I run my bare thumb back over the curve of his lower lip a few times more than is strictly necessary, he doesn't mention it. But he does let out a soft, content breath and close his eyes when my other hand—the one braced against his stupidly soft hair—starts moving, fingers flexing so my nails trace a slow rhythm against his scalp.

It takes his eyelids a moment to flutter open again when I release him.

"All better?" he rasps.

"All better," I confirm. "Sorry I made a mess."

Vincent groans low in his chest. "Say that again."

"What? Sorry?" Realization hits me. "Or *I made a mess*?"

He runs his tongue over the ridge of his teeth. It makes me dizzy.

"You"—I press an accusatory finger to his chest—"are a dirty boy."

"This is new for me," he says, palms held out in defense. "Dirty talk has never done it for me, but you and your damned poetry . . ."

"Maybe we should keep talking, then," I say, trying to sound sultry.

Vincent snorts. "Given our track record with communication? Yeah, I think so."

A laugh bubbles up in my throat. Vincent catches it with a hard kiss. And then I'm not laughing anymore, because the only thing that exists in the world is the heat of his mouth on mine. My fingers thread into his hair again. Vincent returns the gesture by stroking one hand down the length of my spine, from my shoulder (trapezius) to the curve of my ass. A split second after I think that I'd pay good money to have him squeeze me there, he spreads his hand and grips me so hard I let out an involuntary grunt.

I go rogue and grind down on his lap.

He's *harder*. I didn't think it was possible.

And suddenly there's no doubt. No fear. No hesitation. It's like some intimidatingly complex algebra equation has suddenly been simplified, and now the answer is clear as day.

I lean back again and cup his jaw in my hands. "I want to do more than kiss."

Vincent nods. "You know how I ravished you up against that bookcase?"

"Rings a bell."

"Well . . ." One corner of his mouth hitches. "If you thought that was impressive, imagine what I can do with *two* hands."

"Show me," I demand.

"Show you what?"

"Do you really need me to say it?"

He blinks, a picture of feigned innocence. It's a battle of wills. Me, glaring at the enormous, dark-eyed basketball player whose hands are on my hips and whose muscular thighs are braced under me. Vincent, smiling back at me benignly, eyelashes fluttering.

"Come on, Holiday," he murmurs. "Use your words."

This . . . does something to me.

"Stop teasing," I say breathlessly, "and fucking *touch me*."

I reach for the wrist of the hand that's still cradling my ass and try to redirect it toward the front of me. I can't believe I wore jeans. I can't believe he's wearing jeans too. I hate them. I want them gone, immediately, and I never want to see them again.

"One or two?" Vincent asks, voice rough.

"What?"

He blinks slowly. His eyelashes really should be illegal. "Hold your hand up."

I have no clue where he's going with this, but I follow the order. Vincent lifts his hand and presses his palm against mine, lining our fingers up. His hand is enormous, of course. The man can palm a basketball. But it's not until he wiggles his index finger, drawing attention to the fact that his is an inch longer and nearly twice as wide as mine, that I realize what he's on about.

Oh. *Oh.*

I'm shaking, just a little, as I reach out and catch Vincent's hand in both of mine. He lets me hold it and turn it over, examining his broad palm and long fingers before I smooth my thumb over the joint of his wrist. Vincent shivers, just a little. I think I might have imagined that, though.

"I'm asking what you can handle, Holiday," he says. "One finger, or two."

"Two," I blurt. "I can do two."

I hope. At this rate, I'm not sure I'll survive the night.

"Good. So, I'm going to put two fingers inside you," Vincent says as he flips over his hand gently, so I'm still holding it in mine, "and then I'm going to curl them up, like this, and you're going to come on my hand."

The words alone make me feel like I'm on fire. But then Vincent crooks his fingers the way he's saying he'll crook them inside me, and the brush of skin—the *strength* he has in one stupidly enormous hand—makes a muscle deep in my stomach clench.

"All right," I say with a shaky laugh. "Let's not be *too* confident in our abilities."

Vincent blinks innocently. "I'm just trying to communicate clearly."

He knows exactly what he's doing. And he'd better not stop.

I sprawl back on the bed, a soft gust of air escaping his pillow when my head hits it. His duvet is smooth and crumb-free under my hands. It's not the kind of unmade, bedbug-infested mess that Nina, Harper, and I always joke about college boys having in their rooms. Vincent keeps his space clean and bright. (I don't know what it says about me that this is a huge turn-on.)

Vincent follows, one knee braced between mine and hands on either side of my head. He looks so beautiful above me. Dark hair falling in dark eyes. Biceps straining against the sleeves of his T-shirt, which has ridden up just enough to reveal a sliver of skin above the waist of his jeans.

This is happening.

I've spent so many hours of my life reading about characters getting naked. I've lived vicariously through a thousand different rituals of kissing, undressing, and exchanging heated words and tender confessions. And now that I'm here, actually living it, all I can think is that I really, really hope Vincent thinks I'm pretty. It's such a silly thought. I swore to myself, back during freshman year, that I'd stop letting the male gaze influence any of my decisions. But this one male's gaze has single-handedly fucked me up.

Vincent must know me well enough by now to recognize the agonized look on my face, because he nudges the side of my calf with his knee.

"Talk to me, Holiday."

My eyes refocus on Vincent, who's watching me with a little concern.

"Go easy on me, okay?" I try to make it a joke, but my voice wobbles.

Vincent catches it. His hand—the one that's finally free of the brace—finds mine and weaves our fingers together. It's so soft. I hate him for it, a little, because it makes something in my chest clench so tight that it's almost too much.

"Hey," he says.

"Hey," I parrot.

"I'll do whatever you tell me to do. You're in charge here."

I can't tell if the room has inexplicably grown smaller or if the low and rumbling cadence of his voice is like a weighted blanket draped over my shoulders, but I'm suddenly ten degrees warmer. The weird shivering thing my body has started doing fades. I go still. Calm.

You're in charge.

"I trust you," I blurt, even though he didn't ask.

Vincent stares at me for a moment, his dark eyes sparkling in the soft light, before rolling forward on his knees to place a gentle kiss to my forehead. It's a moment that's far too serious and sentimental to match the muffled sounds of college debauchery seeping through the floorboards.

"I won't let you down, Holiday," Vincent says. Then, with the same seriousness: "Now let's get your pants off."

Nineteen

Vincent—a true gentleman—pops open the button and un-zips my jeans for me. He tugs them down my thighs and calves and then over my sock-clad feet, which look utterly silly now that my legs are bare. But Vincent doesn't laugh at my dorky mismatched socks (one dotted with flowers, the other with a cartoonish black cat by my toes). His eyes are locked onto the place where my borrowed bodysuit snaps together between my legs.

"This," he says, hooking a finger under the fabric at my hip and letting it snap back to my skin. "I love this thing. Whatever the hell it is."

I snort. "It's called a bodysuit."

Vincent sucks his lips in like he's trying to stop himself from saying something.

"What?" I demand.

"Okay, you're going to hate me for this, but have you ever seen those warm-up pants that basketball players wear before their games? The ones with the snaps up the sides? And then they just, like, fucking rip 'em off?"

A laugh rips out of my mouth. "Vincent! Why would you say that—"

"Is this one of those situations?" he asks through his own laugh.

"Oh, absolutely not," I say, trying to look stern despite the fact that I'm still grinning. "This bodysuit belongs to my roommate. It's her favorite, and I'm just borrowing it, so I'm going to need you to please refrain from dramatically tearing it off me."

Vincent puts his hands up in surrender. "Well, now I don't trust myself. Could you do the honors?"

I make a show of sighing, like this is a huge inconvenience, and reach down between my legs. Vincent's eyes track my every move as I gently pop open the snaps of my bodysuit. It takes me a few tries, because I'm trembling, but eventually I get them undone. Now I'm glad I wore nice underwear tonight—plain, inoffensive, forgiving black cotton.

It's fitting that I've worn black for, as Nina would probably put it, the funeral of my virginity.

"There," I say, stacking my hands one over the other on my stomach. "Please proceed."

Vincent's eyes rake up and down my body, leaving trails of heat wherever they've been. Down my neck; the valley of my breasts; between my hip bones.

"God, I'm in trouble," he whispers, so softly that I'm not entirely sure he means for me to hear him. He reaches out and strokes his fingers against the cotton of my underwear where it's stretched taut over my cunt—and it's the first time in my life I've thought of it as that. *My cunt.* I've only ever encountered that terminology in erotic novels, and it's never seemed to fit into my everyday vocabulary. It's too blunt a word. Too harsh. But the gentle press of Vincent's fingertips and knuckles has me thinking all kind of blunt, harsh words.

I let out a heavy breath.

"Let's get these off of you too," Vincent murmurs.

I don't wait for him to help. I hook my fingers under the waistband at my hips, press my heels into the bed, and arch up off the mattress. With a few tugs and a bit of pulling my knees up to my chest, I've got my underwear off and in one hand. I chuck it indiscriminately across the room. I don't even watch to see where it lands.

And then it's done. I'm half naked in front of someone else for the first time.

Vincent won't stop *staring*.

"What?" I snap.

"Nothing," he says. Then, softly: "You look good in my bed."

My heart clenches. I try to deflect the feeling, because it's too much. "I'd better look good. It took me half an hour to do my makeup. You have no idea how hard it is to get your eyeliner even."

Vincent's lips twitch. "You're right. I have no idea."

He leans down to kiss me. I'm glad for the momentary break from being viewed. This all feels a lot easier when my eyes are closed and Vincent's mouth is on mine—or sliding along my jaw, down my neck, into the valley between my breasts.

His eyes land on the place where Nina's bodysuit stretches over the curve of my right tit. The flicker of heat in his expression leaves me winded. Vincent looks like he's suddenly thinking of a hundred ways to ruin me. And I'd let him. I want him to slide a hand under the fabric and do whatever the hell he wants with my phenomenal tits. I don't care if he brushes a thumb over my nipple, featherlight and tender, while I squirm and giggle. I don't care if he takes an entire tit in his hand and squeezes it, like he's rock climbing and needs to find purchase. I don't care if he twists and sucks at my nipple until I'm screaming and sobbing and begging him to do terrible things to me.

I just want to see what he wants to do. I want the surprise of his desire.

But then Vincent inhales hard, like he's pulling himself together, and settles back on his knees between my legs.

"I think I should warm you up," he says.

"Warm me up?" I croak.

And my liquefied little brain is too slow to catch on—because even when Vincent crouches low and wraps his arms around my thighs, I don't understand what he means. Not until he ducks his head and licks one long, slow stripe right up the seam of me, from opening to clit. His mouth is so hot and wet, and the sight of his dark hair between my legs and his eyelashes against his cheeks is so utterly erotic, that I gasp in shock.

When Vincent lifts his head, there's a proud gleam in his eyes.

"Like that."

I don't have it in me to make a witty comment—or to rocket launch myself into self-consciousness about how I must look at this angle or what I taste like. The world has narrowed into one small point of light. My whole face is hot. Even my neck and chest are on fire.

"It's your birthday," I say, a weak attempt at a joke. "Shouldn't *I* be giving *you* a gift?"

"Believe me, Holiday. You are."

And then he ducks his head and seals his mouth over me. I let out a shuddering breath and grab one fistful of the duvet beneath me. My other hand knots into Vincent's hair while he works his jaw like he's kissing me. Or like he's trying to devour me. It's hard to tell. His tongue traces laps up and down, swiping inside and then flicking at the bundle of nerves that makes my right hamstring tremble.

Vincent moves his tongue and slips one finger inside me. It goes in so fucking easily. If I weren't halfway out of my mind right now, I might blush at the soft, slick *pop* of him sliding in right to the second knuckle. But it's not enough—not even close—so I rock my hips up, seeking more friction, more pressure, more *anything*.

Vincent grunts and pulls back to say, "Greedy."

"Stop teasing," I demand, giving his hair a sharp tug.

Vincent's answering groan tickles against the inside of my thigh. "I just want to make sure I'm not hurting you."

"Shut the fuck up."

That does the trick.

Vincent slips a second finger inside me. The stretch is glorious—just enough to pinch a little, just enough that I really feel it when he spreads his fingers inside me, pressing on opposite walls and stretching the muscle, testing it. I groan and let my head fall back, eyelids fluttering shut.

"Okay?" Vincent asks.

"Mmh."

"Good girl."

A strangled laugh rips out of my throat.

"What?" Vincent says. "I thought you wanted me to keep talking."

I press my lips together. I'm not going to admit that those two words do . . . *things* to me. Vincent knows. He can feel it. And I can hear in his voice that he's teasing me.

"I said *talking* was good. Not *dirty talk*. Dirty talk is—"

He withdraws his fingers almost all the way, then thrusts them back in at a new, better angle.

"—cheap," I croak.

"So, you *don't* want me to tell you how hot and wet you are?" Vincent asks, feigning innocence. "You don't want me to say that you're dripping? That I can't wait for you to ruin my sheets? And I *definitely* shouldn't tell you how tight you're gripping my knuckles and how fucking sweet you taste, right?"

I open my mouth, fully determined to tell him to fuck off.

What comes out instead is a low and throaty moan.

"'Attagirl, Holiday."

Vincent pumps his finger in slow, terrible strokes and presses his face to the inside of my thigh, kissing my skin and mumbling words of praise that I barely catch over the sound of my own pounding heartbeat and the wet little squelches coming from where we're connected. I press my heels into the mattress and clench down. Vincent groans, his movements stilling before he shifts his weight and starts pressing harder, faster, and razes his teeth over the tender skin on the inside of my thigh.

I let out something like a strangled laugh, because this just isn't fair. On the few occasions that I've tried fingering myself, it's been a waste of effort—I just end up sweaty and underwhelmed, my hand cramped and back aching from contorting myself in a sad attempt to reach *something*. To make it feel the way romance novels have told me it should feel. I just figured I was one of the many women who prefer clitoral stimulation to penetration.

I thought I knew myself.

But I guess I was wrong, because when Vincent's fingers curl and bump against a tender spot inside of me along my front wall again, I nearly come on the spot.

"That," I gasp. "Do that again—"

The words are barely out of my mouth before Vincent's fingers are back against that front wall again. But this time, his other arm loops around my thigh, anchoring me to him, and the heel of his palm lands on the tender skin between my pubic bone and my belly button. He presses down.

My muscles flutter, my abs contract, and my hips buck up against Vincent's hands. But he holds steady, an immovable wall of muscle and bone. I'm pinned. I have nowhere to go. And there's a tide rising in me, threatening to wash me right over the edge of something enormous and a little bit terrifying. I grab at Vincent's wrist, not sure if I'm trying to pull his hand away (to tell him that something is building and that the magnitude of it scares me) or if I'm trying to hold him closer (because I think I might actually kill him if he stops what he's doing).

"Don't fight it," he murmurs. "You're okay."

"Vincent," I say, and it's a warning—or maybe a plea. I can't tell.

"I've got you, Kendall," he says. "Come."

He presses his mouth to my center again and sucks hard.

The knot inside me pulls tight and, in one burst, comes

undone. My eyelids flutter. My mouth falls open. I dig my fingernails into Vincent's skin and hair, tensing involuntarily as I gasp for air. And then the pressure moves through me, like a wave in a storm, leaving behind slack muscles and over-sensitive nerves. I shiver and sob beneath him, but Vincent doesn't let up. He keeps pressing, pumping, sucking at me until I'm pressing at his head and begging, in a mess of words I can't even untangle, to have mercy.

The mattress dips and bounces, and then Vincent's up above me again and pressing a kiss to my mouth. I'm too dazed to do anything but mimic him, my tongue clumsy and my breathing still quick. When he pulls back to look at me, his eyes—the warmest shade of brown—are sparkling with something like triumph and wonder.

I feel more than pretty.

I feel like the fucking main character.

And now there's a new hunger growing in me, sparked by that flush of confidence.

"My turn," I demand.

Vincent barks out a laugh. "You just had your turn."

"Not what I meant." I shake my head. "I get to touch you now."

Vincent props himself up on one hand and uses the other to push the hair back from my sweat-dampened forehead. "This isn't a favor-for-a-favor kind of thing, Holiday."

"I don't think you're listening, Knight." I reach one hand between us and grab the waistband of his jeans. "I. Want. To. Touch. You."

He swallows hard. "Well, since you're *begging*—"

I let the heel of my palm brush his erection through his

pants. Vincent's smug smile disappears and his chin tips back, a low groan rumbling in his throat. It's deeply satisfying to know I'm capable of wiping that smirk off his face. I want to make him come undone too.

"Who did you say was begging?" I ask.

And I'm a little bit giddy with power now, because *I can do this*. I can be the girl from the romance novel—except it's real, and I'm me, and it's not all in my own head.

"Pants off," I command.

Vincent nods and reaches for the front of his jeans. I'm glad the boy can take directions, because if I don't see his dick (cock? penis? I'm undecided) in the next six seconds, I think I'll combust.

But I barely hear the soft metallic hiss of his zipper when he tugs it down, because outside, in the hall, there's the thundering echo of footsteps—like a herd of cattle stampeding—and loud laughter. It grows closer and closer, and then there's the jarring sound of someone pounding on a door.

On Vincent's door.

"Knight!" a voice I recognize as Jabari's shouts from the other side. "It's bar time! Get your ID and let's roll."

The doorknob rattles—still locked, thank God—and I am suddenly and painfully aware of the fact that I'm halfway naked in Vincent Knight's bed, *underneath him*, face flushed, chest heaving, in the afterglow of what might very well be the best orgasm of my life, with my hands reaching out for his still-hidden dick.

So honestly? Fuck the basketball team.

Twenty

What sounds like half of Clement's basketball team is outside, and I'm in Vincent's bed with my bare legs tangled between his. I'm not a party person to begin with, but this? This is a nightmare. Vincent must see the panic painted across my face, because the annoyed twist of his lips immediately falls into something far more solemn.

"You're fine," he whispers. "The door's locked. It's fine."

But it's not fine. His teammates are outside his door, and I'm naked from the waist down, save for my mismatched cat socks. I've never been so afraid—or so frustrated, because I almost had everything I've ever fantasized about. I think there are actual tears welling up in my eyes.

"Are you *kidding* me?" I whine.

Vincent pushes himself up to his knees, eyebrows pinched with determination.

"I'll get rid of them," he whispers.

"I'm hiding in your bathroom," I whisper back, rolling away from him.

"You don't have to—"

I'm already scrambling off the side of the bed, ducking down to pick up my jeans.

"Knight!" Jabari calls again, and he's parroted by a few other voices before someone bangs on the door again. It makes me suddenly and inexplicably furious.

"Where the fuck is my underwear?" I hiss. "I don't want your friends to see me like this!"

Vincent makes a face, then gives a pointed look down at his own crotch, where his unbuttoned jeans are stretched taut over a rapidly softening yet still impressive erection. Right. I'm sure he doesn't exactly want to be seen by his friends right now either.

It seems like a bad time to point out that they've ruined our happy ending in more than one sense of the phrase.

While I duck into the bathroom, Vincent presses his cheek to his bedroom door. He clears his throat twice, but his voice is still incriminatingly low and rumbling when he speaks.

"Hey, Jabari?"

"What's up?" Jabari's response comes muffled through the wood.

Vincent's mouth opens, and I'm about a hundred percent certain he wants to say *fuck off*, but what comes out is: "Can you give me, like, twenty minutes? I'll meet you downstairs."

"Don't give me that shit. You're ready. No more procrastinating."

"Henderson," Vincent croaks. "I swear to God. Ten minutes. Fuck, I'll take *five*."

"Nah, man. C'mon. We're on a mission to—"

"Fuck. Off."

Vincent turns to me, his expression one straight out of a Shakespearean tragedy. Without a single word exchanged, I know we both understand that his teammates aren't going anywhere until they get what they want.

Vincent crosses the room in a few angry strides and snatches his wallet off his bedside table, hesitates, then comes toward me instead of heading right for his door. He presses a hand to the wall just outside the bathroom and leans in to look at me.

"I'll take them down the hall and get them to do another round of shots or something," he whispers. "You can sneak out when the coast is clear, and I'll meet you downstairs. Or—or you can stay here, and I can come back?"

Even as he suggests this with a spark of hope in his eyes, I can tell he knows it's going to be impossible to slip away from his friends again.

It's not fair. I'm not ready for tonight to be over.

"I should go downstairs," I say, moving to shut the door.

"Kendall."

I freeze and meet his eyes.

"I'm sorry," he says.

"I might hate your friends," I reply.

"That makes two of us."

Vincent turns to go.

"Wait," I say. He does. I wrap one hand around the back of his neck, my fingers tangling in his thoroughly rumpled hair, and pull myself up onto my toes to kiss him. Vincent returns the gesture with equal fervor, rocking against me so eagerly that I have to arch my back and shift my feet to accommodate him. Our lips separate with a wet smack.

"One for the road," I whisper.

Vincent shakes his head. "This isn't helping with the boner."

He kisses me again—this time on the forehead—and then takes a step back and exhales hard. For a long moment, we stare at each other. I try to memorize this moment—to soak it all in—just in case it's all I ever get.

It doesn't feel like an ending, a hopeful part of me whispers.

And oh. Oh no.

I told myself I could be a grown-up about this. I told myself I could have *one* night to stop being such a coward and have some fun. But here I am, getting immediately and inordinately attached to the first boy I've ever felt this way about. I want Vincent to do something completely disproportionate to the situation, like storm downstairs, cut the speakers, and send everyone else home. I wish he'd be a romance hero, even if that's ridiculous.

Jabari Henderson pounds on the door again.

"Go," I tell Vincent, giving him a little push—one last excuse to touch his chest.

The look he shoots me over his shoulder as he crosses his room is both agonized and apologetic. I hide next to the shower, out of sight, and listen to a long moment of silence before he unlocks his bedroom door and tugs it open.

"Took you long enough," someone in the hall shouts.

"Sorry, sorry," Vincent says apologetically. He's a surprisingly good actor. "Couldn't find my wallet. Jabari, you still have any tequila in your room?"

The answer is: "Oh, *hell* yeah."

Vincent slips through the door, pulling it tight behind

him. I listen for the telltale sound of fading footsteps and merriment as he shepherds his teammates down the hall.

I stand in Vincent's bathroom, my back pressed to the wall, and stare at my reflection in the mirror. My hair is wrecked. My lipstick is gone. My face is flushed, and there are pink spots on my neck—not quite hickeys, but maybe they will be tomorrow. I hope they will be. I want concrete reminders of what we did. I want *souvenirs*, dammit.

Because otherwise, I might not believe this happened.

He brought me to orgasm. In the middle of his own birthday party.

For a moment, the giddiness cuts through my anxiety. I grin at my own reflection. But the longer I stare, the more my dazed smile falls and the more my stomach knots.

It was perfect. *He* was perfect. It was like something straight out of the best kind of romance novel, where the boy worships the girl and actually pays attention to what makes her feel good. There wasn't a single moment when I didn't like what Vincent was doing—and I don't mind if he's had tons of practice, because I'm not about to slut-shame anyone, but it's hitting me that the whole encounter was fairly lopsided.

For fuck's sake, he didn't even *come*.

He gave, and he gave, and even when I pawed at his pants and demanded to see his dick, he seemed hesitant. And I know he wanted me. He said so. I saw the desire in his eyes, and I can't think of another reason why a boy would look at a girl like that. But now that I'm alone in his bathroom, my hands shaking as I smooth down the front of my wrinkled bodysuit, I wonder how much of that was in my own head.

A knot forms in my throat.

I can't explain it. I can't put my finger on it.

I just feel like I've done something wrong.

•   •   •

Despite my best efforts, I can't locate my underwear. I know I took it off, and I know I chucked it somewhere vaguely in the direction of the desk, but it's nowhere to be found. Apparently, I've launched it into another dimension. I give up after a few minutes of searching and tug my jeans back on over my snapped-up bodysuit, blushing hard at the memory of Vincent's face when I undressed.

This. I love this thing.

I huff and scrub my hands over my face. I just had the best orgasm of my life. I just did everything I've been wanting to do. I don't know why I feel so off-kilter.

Legs still shaky from my orgasm, I pull open Vincent's door and check both ways before I slip out into the hall, undetected, and stumble downstairs into the dining room. The crush of the crowd doesn't help my anxiety. There's no sign of Nina around the beer pong tables. I do a lap around the kitchen. I'm about to brave the living room when I hear the unmistakable sound of Nina calling out my name.

She's in a little hallway off the kitchen, between a sliding glass door that leads to a back porch and a small door that must be a closet or a pantry. From here, I can see straight into the entry hall, where people are pouring up and down the stairs and in and out of the front door.

"Harper really wasn't kidding about half the school coming," I mutter.

"Where have you been?" Nina demands. Then she registers the sight of me, with my mussed hair and missing lipstick, and her eyes blow wide. "Oh my *God*. You didn't."

I try to smile. "I did."

The grin that splits Nina's face dissolves when the small door behind her clicks and swings open. It's a laundry room. I catch sight of a double stack of washers and dryers before my eyes land on Harper, whose mascara is gone and whose eyes are pink and watery.

She's been crying.

She never cries.

"What happened?" I demand.

"It's nothing," Harper snaps, sniffling hard. "I'm getting some jungle juice."

"Harper, wait—"

She's already shouldering her way into the kitchen.

As soon as she's out of earshot, Nina grabs my arm and leans in.

"We saw Jabari with another girl," she whispers as well as one can whisper in the middle of a crowded house party. "He was upstairs with Harper and a bunch of the team, and he got a text, and he said he'd be right back, but then Harper followed him down here a few minutes later and we saw them. He was holding her hand. He was taking her to the bar. And Harper played it cool, but then we overheard one of his teammates talking about some sort of big team mission to get someone laid and—"

Nina stops talking abruptly, her face crumpling as she takes in my rumpled hair and missing lipstick. She thought they were talking about Jabari. But now that she's said it out loud—and now that she's seen me—I think she realizes they were probably talking about someone else.

The birthday boy.

Twenty-one

I've always hated the *it was only a bet* trope.

Right now, I have the same sinking feeling of nausea I get when I'm reading a book and the pieces start to fall into place. Because maybe this is why Jabari was so excited to see me. I really was Vincent's birthday present—wrapped up in a neat bow and hand-delivered. And what about Griffin, the kid who came and asked Vincent for the key to the basement? Was that an attempt to get me upstairs to Vincent's room? Was this whole night one big, coordinated team effort to get my pants off?

My underwear. Maybe it's still up in Vincent's room, wherever it landed. But maybe—just maybe—it's in his pocket, a trophy to be shown off to his friends.

My brain has no brakes. I'm just a passenger, my grip on my seat white-knuckled as I go barreling toward the worst-case scenario. I can't stop myself from replaying the events of the night, wondering if I somehow misread it all. If I somehow got the story wrong.

"I'm ready to go home," I say, my voice high and tight.

"Hey, hey, hey," Nina says, gripping me by my biceps. "What happened upstairs? Did you guys make out?"

I laugh weakly. "A little more than that."

"Oh, God. Did you . . ." She trails off.

Maybe the basketball team will be able to tell you all the dirty details tomorrow.

And *fuck*, now I wish we hadn't come at all, because this *hurts*. The same part of my imagination that's so good at painting everything in romance tropes is turning the whole night into a horror movie. I press my fingertips into my chest, prodding at the tight lump where my heart should be. I think I'm going to throw up. Can stress kill you this quickly?

"Did he do something you didn't want him to?" Nina demands.

"No. No, I—it was all consensual, and it was—"

My throat is too tight. I can't finish the sentence.

Perfect. It was perfect.

"Kenny," Nina says gently.

Her eyes are focused somewhere over my shoulder.

I turn just in time to see Vincent coming down the stairs. He's not alone—a small crowd of his teammates surrounds him. Jabari Henderson is right behind him, a hand on either one of Vincent's shoulders as he speaks into his ear like some kind of hype man. Their little cluster quickly grows as other partygoers are swept up into orbit around the birthday boy. I watch Priya, the girl from behind the kitchen bar, who's pretty and sweet and exactly the kind of girl I'd want to be friends with, ruffle Vincent's hair, and I have to look away.

Because I want him.

Despite every warning siren blaring in my head, there's

still a part of me that trusts him. That sees him in the crowd and thinks, *mine*.

All night, I've been falling.

And for him, it was all just a plot to get laid on his birthday.

"Kenny, listen to me," Nina presses on. "Everything is going to be—"

"Holiday!"

I have to take a deep, steadying breath before I turn and meet the footsteps coming our way. When I do, Vincent stands above me, all broad shoulders and broad smile. He looks confident. Of course he's confident—his friends are watching from the other end of the hall, by the front door. I feel frozen with something suspiciously like stage fright.

He told them. He told them about me, about what we were doing in his room, and now he's come to—what? Claim his prize? Reveal the whole deceit like some kind of archetypal villain?

He wouldn't do that, I want to scream.

But what if he did? What if he hurts me, and I walked right into it?

And even as a knot of cold dread forms in my stomach, the sight of him melts something in me. Magenta and cyan lights from the living room dance floor spill into the hall, catching in Vincent's hair and twinkling in his eyes. The sight of his face shouldn't be able to set off this many fireworks in my chest.

You could be my worst mistake, I think.

"What do you want?" I ask, voice barely audible over the pounding music.

"Come to the bar with us," Vincent says, still smiling, and holds out a hand.

There's a third tally mark on his forearm now. The logical part of my brain knows it's probably just because he did another shot. The paranoid part of my brain wonders if that wobbly permanent marker line is *me*.

Does he actually want me to come, or is he just trying to parade me around as his conquest?

If I were brave, I'd ask. I'd tell him I'm scared, and that I don't know how to do this. I don't come to parties. I don't straddle boys and ask them to touch me. I'm in way over my head. He was so patient with me upstairs. He listened. I felt like I could say anything. But now? With all his friends in earshot? I won't embarrass myself like that.

So, I just inch backward and say, "I'm not twenty-one."

Vincent's confidence cracks, just a little. I see it in the downward tilt of his mouth before he catches himself.

"Are you free tomorrow, then?" he asks. "Before your shift? Or sometime this weekend?"

"I'm actually not free ever."

Nina nudges me with a sharp elbow to my ribs. I grunt but don't stand down. Her rose-tinted romanticism isn't going to thaw my ice-cold panic. My walls are up. The drawbridge is shut, the turrets barricaded, the moat crocodile-infested.

Vincent Knight isn't getting anywhere close to me. Not now. Not like this.

His mouth parts, then closes. He glances at Nina, then back at me, looking lost.

"Are you okay?" he asks, shuffling a step closer. I feel the heat of his body and have to take a bolstering breath. "We can go somewhere quiet, right now. If the bar sounds too overwhelming, or if you just want to talk—"

Vaguely, I'm aware that he's offering to pick me over his team and their birthday celebration plans. I feel myself trying to latch on to that.

"No," I blurt, folding my arms tight over my chest. "I don't want to go anywhere."

I feel too exposed, too out in the open, but I know that if Vincent gets me alone again, I'll just fall back into that strange sense of security that leads me to do impulsive and ridiculous things, like kiss him and ask him to touch me and demand that he take his pants off. But I don't say all that. I just stare at him with every ounce of distrust roiling in my body.

I don't like how he's looking at me. It feels like he can see straight through me—and like somehow, I've hurt him and not the other way around. It's not fair. And then whatever emotion is written across Vincent's face falls away and is replaced with that cold, confident, brooding thing he does. His mask. His defense mechanism.

Or maybe it's not that at all—maybe that's who he really is.

How many villains start out looking like the good guys?

"So that's it," he says. "You got your story, and now you're done?"

I flinch. "What's that supposed to mean?"

Vincent shakes his head. "Nothing. Just . . ." He scans my face, and I catch another flash of hurt before he pulls his eyes off mine and lets out a shaky breath. "I hope you find what you're looking for. Really. There's gotta be a billionaire with a big dick out there who needs an English tutor to rip him to shreds."

I think it'd sting less if he slapped me.

Vincent's made fun of me for reading romance novels before. More than once, in fact, he's pointed out that maybe my standards are unrealistically high. I have the sudden and horrible feeling that he'll make fun of me if I tell him how scared I am. How much I want from him. How quickly I've gotten attached. He'll think I'm silly. Immature. Inexperienced.

And he'd be right.

I don't know what I'm doing. I don't know how to be in love. Not for real.

"I think you should go to the bar," I say, voice shaking.

For a moment, Vincent looks like he's going to argue, but then his lips press into a flat line and he offers one sharp nod—deciding I'm not worth the trouble.

"You're in charge, Holiday," he says.

You're in charge. Words uttered half an hour ago in much different circumstances, in a much different tone. I feel like I'm standing outside my own body, watching us careen toward each other like cars on an icy freeway, incapable of stepping in to stop the catastrophic collision.

My anger explodes like an airbag.

"Have fun with your boys, then," I snap. Despite my best efforts not to say anything else, I add a very soft and slightly sarcastic: "Happy birthday."

I turn on my heel and march into the kitchen, determined to have the last word. The second I'm swallowed up by the crowd and the booming bassline of a dark, moody song, I feel my heartbeat pounding in my temples and against my ribs. People are laughing and dancing all around me, drinks sloshing out of red cups in their hands and hips swiveling in time with the music. Everyone's having the night of their lives.

And I've just imploded mine.

It all happened so fast. It feels like a fever dream.

Oh, God. What did I do?

What had to be done. I refuse to be the girl who gets blindsided. I'm smarter than that. And I'm certainly smart enough to clock a trope when I see one, so really, I'm disappointed in myself for letting this go so far. *I let him see me naked.* I flinch. *I let him eat me out. I came on his hand.* I lunge for the now-unmanned makeshift bar and surge up on my tiptoes, suddenly glad for my height and my long arms as I lean over the counter and rifle through empty red cups and glass bottles.

I need alcohol. Immediately.

I need to be so drunk that tonight becomes the kind of night that Nina and Harper always talk about having. The kind of night that ends with your head in the toilet but makes for a good story once you've left the embarrassment (and the hangover) far behind.

My mind gives a sharp tug. The specifics of my conversation with Vincent are already becoming a blur of anger and fear and disbelief, but I distinctly remember him saying something along the same lines. *You got your story, and now you're done.* My skin prickles with unease.

What the hell did he mean by that?

I feel a hand on my back, and for one split second, I think Vincent has followed me—but when I turn to look over my shoulder, it's Nina.

I'm furious to find that I'm disappointed.

"Did he leave?" I snap.

Nina bites down on her bottom lip, and I have my answer.

Well. Good. I don't want to spoil his birthday. I hope he has a fantastic time at the bar with all his buddies. I hope he gets his twenty-one tallies—by whatever means necessary—and that he has tons of fun telling all his friends about how I begged him to make me come.

"Kendall," Nina says, and her sympathy stings like a knife.

"Don't," I rasp. I snatch up the first red cup I see on the kitchen counter, drain it, and let out a spluttering cough. It's straight vodka. It's like liquid fire—but I'd rather burn down the rest of tonight than think about Vincent. "If you need me, I'll be chugging jungle juice with Harper."

I'd rather be the supporting cast in her tragedy than the main character in mine.

Twenty-two

I've never been so hungover.

My Friday-night shift at the library is brutal. Almost not survivable, really. It has to be some kind of human rights violation to force a student worker to stare into the glare of a computer screen, drag around a cart of books (with a broken wheel that squeaks so loudly it's like an ice pick to their frontal lobe), and argue with other students about their overdue books all while battling what is categorically the worst hangover of their life.

"Are you getting sick again?" Margie asks me when she catches me slumped over the front desk with my head buried in my arms. "Because if you are, just go home. Don't even clock out. I'll say you were here, and they'll pay you for the full shift."

I almost take her up on the offer. But I'm stubborn, so I stay. That's why. No other reason. Not because I keep watching the front doors. Not because I keep imagining that I hear them creak open, see a glint of light off the glass, catch the movement of a tall, dark-haired boy coming inside. Every time, my chest seizes up with panic.

Because if Vincent walks into the library, then I'll have to face what happened last night. Which means I'll have to confront all the evidence indicating Vincent hooked up with me more for his friends' sake than for his own—the audience at Starbucks, Jabari presenting me as a *birthday gift*, the kid at the bar trying to get us upstairs to Vincent's room, our unbalanced alone time (Kendall, 1; Vincent, 0), my missing underwear—and, perhaps even worse, all the evidence I'm still clinging to that it all meant as much to him as it did to me.

But luckily for me, I don't have to unpack all that tonight.

There's no sign of Vincent.

Of course there isn't, that pessimistic voice in my head whispers. *He's already gotten what he wanted.*

• • •

On Saturday, Clement has an away game. I only know this because I make the mistake of opening Twitter while I'm supposed to be reading Chaucer, and the first thing that pops up on my feed is a clip of Vincent triumphantly sinking a three-pointer.

I slam my phone face down on the kitchen counter. It doesn't help. When I squeeze my eyes shut, I still see him—his bare arms flexing, his hair dark against his sweat-dampened forehead, his mouth curled up into a cocky smile as the blurred crowd in the background jumps to their feet to cheer and applaud him.

Good for him. Glad he's doing well.

I snatch up my highlighter and recommit myself to wading through Chaucer and his archaic English, which is suddenly less painful in comparison. Nina, who's washing her weekly collection of water glasses and mugs in the sink across from me, arches an eyebrow.

"You good?"

"Fantastic," I mumble.

"I've been thinking about it," she says, "and you should reach out to Vincent."

I flip the page of my book a little too hard. It tears a little at the bottom, right along the spine.

"And why would I do that?"

Nina slaps the faucet off and sets another glass on the drying rack. "Because your pity party has turned into a forty-eight-hour rager, and it must be getting exhausting. You did it. You were appropriately miserable. Now can you please talk it out with him so you can either make up or, like, vandalize his car Carrie Underwood style? Anything but this sad girl hour shit."

"I am not *sad*."

"Right. Sorry. My bad—you're a *coward*."

The word lands like a brick.

"I beg your pardon?"

Nina smiles, just a little, like my reaction confirms it. "I'm not trying to insult you, so I'll make this nice and simple. Do you still want to be with Vincent or not?"

I swallow hard. "Not anymore."

"Because his teammates will know? And you can't bear the thought of people knowing that you—a grown woman—want to fuck another consenting adult?"

"Because I felt *objectified*," I correct. "You were there,

Nina. I saw your face. You got the same sketch vibes that I did. Jabari left Harper upstairs and went to hold another girl's hand. The rest of the team was trying to get me alone with Vincent. There was a *team mission*. What if it was a game to them? What if they were keeping score? Boys do that. I've read articles about sports teams that have *spreadsheets*."

Nina narrows her eyes at me. "You think Vincent's teammates tried to hook you guys up?"

"I'm sure of it."

"So, they did exactly what Harper and I were doing?"

I open my mouth, then shut it, then try again. "It's different. You know it's different."

"How is it different?"

Why does it feel like Nina's not taking my side on this?

"They're *boys*, Nina. And if you list out every little shred of evidence I have from that night, it's the classic setup for the *it was all a bet* trope."

Nina smacks a palm to the counter.

"There it is! I knew it! You make a narrative out of *everything*. Look—yes. Sometimes art imitates life. But you always oversimplify things so you can tuck them into neat and tidy boxes. It's like you're doing a literary analysis of your own fucking life to avoid actually living it."

"I don't do that," I argue. *Oh, God, I do.*

"You do," Nina says. "It's self-sabotage. Because if you can convince yourself you already know how it ends, then you get to walk away without having to actually be a real person and live your life. Sometimes it feels like you don't want to do *anything*. I get that you're not a big fan of parties and crowds, but sometimes it feels very *I'm not like other girls*."

It's like she's struck me across the face.

"I *am* like other girls," I argue. "I make a point not to think I'm better than other women, and you *know* that."

"So why were you able to full-on maul Vincent when it was just the two of you, but Harper and I had to physically drag you into the basketball house to get you to fucking talk to him? Huh? What's all that about?"

"Because I was nervous," I splutter. "I'm not good at this stuff, Nina. I'm not like—"

"Other girls?"

"That is *not* where I was going with that!"

Nina huffs, turns to shove her favorite mug onto the shelf, and then presses the cupboard door shut. When she spins to face me again, her expression is maternal in a way that makes me feel like I'm in elementary school again and my mom is asking me why I can't just go over and say hello to the other kids instead of clinging to her leg.

"I love you, Kenny," Nina says. "And that means I have to tell you when I think you're in the wrong before you make a complete mess of everything."

I think of Vincent's face, bathed in magenta and cyan party lights. The ragged sigh he played off with a shrug. I've already made a mess.

"Can you please stop treating me like a child," I beg Nina. I feel nauseous. My skin is tight. "Just because you like parties doesn't mean I have to. And just because you go on tons of dates and hook up with people all the time—"

"So, I'm the whore best friend?"

I frown. "The what?"

"I'm just saying." Nina shrugs. "It sounds like you're the

poor virginal main character, and I'm the whore best friend who's only around to cheer you on while you go after the guy. I'm a supporting character. A plot device. I lent you my hottest bodysuit, dragged you to a party—because *God forbid* the bookworm go to a party of your own free will—and then I strategically slipped out of the picture so you could get the golden boy alone." She folds a damp tea towel on the counter and gives it a proud pat. "I'm the whore best friend."

"No, you aren't," I protest. "You're not a whore, Nina."

"And you're not a child. So, stop acting like one and have some fucking agency."

I'm so stunned, and my body is so shivery and overheated, that all I can think to do is slide off the kitchen stool and storm off to my room.

Like a child.

• • •

The next few days are miserable.

Chaucer kicks my ass. Then I learn we're doing some Shakespeare next. Someone in our building takes my laundry out of the dryer and puts theirs in instead, stealing a dollar and wasting an hour of my life. I trip over a curb while crossing the street onto campus and make eye contact with a girl from my women's literature class.

I don't see Vincent at all, except in a very vivid nightmare.

(We're in the basketball team's house, except the floor plan is all scrambled and wonky, the way they tend to be in dreams. I'm chasing Vincent. I try to scream his name, but nothing comes out, and he keeps getting swallowed up in the crowd of faceless strangers.)

It's a rotten week.

It doesn't help that Nina and I are in some kind of horrible Wild West–style standoff, and Harper, who's made it clear she won't pick a side, has gotten mad at us for fighting and decided to ice us both out too. The three of us don't fight often. We've never shuffled around the apartment in silence, coming and going without a word and waiting until the coast is clear to use our shared bathroom. I know I'll have a break from the tension this weekend—Nina's improv class is taking an overnight road trip to do a festival, and Harper's headed home for the weekend to celebrate her grandmother's hundredth birthday.

I can't tell if I'm thankful that we'll all have time away from one another or if I'm dreading the possibility that our standoff could trickle over into next week.

I feel sick. I can't eat.

Because now, I'm able to admit to myself in the quietest of internal monologues, *I know I have three people I have to apologize to*.

Thursday evening, I curl up on the living room couch with my (horrible, boring, overrated) anthology of Shakespeare's sonnets. Nina's at the kitchen counter with a history textbook. Harper is in her room, the door wide open as she packs her bag for her trip. We're still not talking, and it's tense, but we've all made the decision to be in one another's space. It's a little passive-aggressive. It's also a clear sign that we're all desperate to make a point, to be seen and heard, and to settle things.

I know I should be the one to apologize first.

But Harper, of all people, is the one who cracks.

"You guys," she announces from her bedroom doorway, her voice small and tired and a little bit furious, "I'm really tired of this."

And then her face scrunches up, and the tears come.

Nina and I freeze, then lurch into action. I pop up off the couch, my Shakespeare tumbling to the floor (where it belongs), and hurry across the living room as Nina leaps up from her stool and throws her arms around Harper's shaking shoulders.

"I'm tired of this strong Black woman shit," she croaks into Nina's armpit.

My stomach sinks like a rock. Maybe I've made Nina into my whore best friend, playing right into the stereotype of the sexually liberated bisexual Latina, but I've done worse with Harper. I've made her the cynical, strong, hardworking friend, and I've ignored that she too had everything blow up in her face at the party.

"Fuck," I say, surprised to find myself crying too. "I'm sorry—oh, God, these are *white woman tears*—"

Harper laughs. I know it's not for my sake, because it's her worst laugh. The one that's half cackle and half scream. It's a little waterlogged and sadder than usual, but the sound of it is still a comfort. Nina releases Harper, and I dart forward to help wipe her tears with the sleeve of my oversized cardigan.

"Listen, I *am* a bad bitch," Harper says, sniffling. "I *like* being a bad bitch. But just once, I'd like everyone to go soft on me." She sits down on the stool Nina has vacated and slumps over the counter a little. When she speaks again, it's quiet.

"That's why I liked Jabari. He was so over-the-top, and so goofy, and I make fun of simps, but fuck. It was so nice to be treated like that."

Nina winces. "I'm sorry I was selfish this week. You deserved some support." She glances at me and winces again. "Both of you. You needed a friend, and I let you guys down. I'm sorry about what I said to you, Kendall. I mean, I stand by some of it—"

"Stop," I interrupt, wincing hard. "Please, Nina. You should stand by all of it, okay? You were right. I'm sorry I got so defensive. And I'm sorry I made you feel like the slutty best friend—"

"The *whore* best friend. Please, Kendall. Respect my title."

It's my turn to ugly laugh. "I'm sorry I made you feel like a supporting character. And you too, Harper—I'm sorry if I've ever made you feel like you're an archetype."

"I don't actually know what that is," Harper says, "but apology accepted."

Nina cups my face in her hands. "I love that you think in stories, Kendall. I do. It's beautiful, and romantic, and deeply entertaining. But sometimes, when I crack a dirty joke, I wish you wouldn't sigh and act like you're not thinking the same thing. Because I've read some of the books you read, girl. They're *filthy*."

I laugh, but my cheeks get hot.

Nina takes my face and forces me to meet her eyes. "You're allowed to be horny, and you're allowed to be sensitive and nervous and all the other things you are. You don't have to be an archetype either. You can change. You can be whatever you want to be."

I swallow hard. It's impossible to laugh this one off.

"I just don't want to feel stupid," I admit.

Harper clears her throat. "You know that I believe, above all other universal truths, that men are garbage," she says. "And I think Nina and I will both respect it if you tell us that you don't think Vincent is a good guy. If that's the case, then it's over. Done. No questions asked."

"Oh, one hundred percent," Nina adds. "But, with all the love and support in the world, I *really* don't think Vincent is the bad guy here. I don't get those vibes."

I swallow hard. "I know."

"Except the hair, maybe. It's very *sexy villain* of him. And while we're on the subject of golden retriever boys with nice hair . . ." Nina turns to Harper. "Jabari Henderson was utterly whipped for you. I know I said men are garbage, and I stand by that. But I simply refuse to believe he could switch up on you that fast."

Harper folds her arms across her chest.

"I'm not chasing after a boy," she says on a sniffle.

Nina looks like she wants to argue, but nods. "Fine. I accept that. Because I'm working on not meddling and pushing my friends' boundaries so much. What about you, Kenny? What do you wanna do?"

"I don't think it matters what I want," I admit, and voicing it out loud makes the fear I've been trying to stifle all week wash over me like a tsunami. "Even if I was wrong about everything, and he really did just like me and all his friends were just trying to support him"—the words make so much sense out loud that it physically hurts to hear them—"I still told him to fuck off and leave me alone. I mean, you saw his face, Nina. He was . . ." I shake my head. "I really hurt him. I don't know how we come back from that."

"You could start with an apology?"

I scrub at my eyes and groan. "I want to know what he's thinking without having to put myself out in the open. This is terrifying."

Nina reaches out to pinch my cheek. "It's never going to be a dual point of view novel, Kenny. You just have to talk to him and sort it out. That's all you can do. Try not to overthink it this time, all right? You get *way* too in your head about everything."

I sigh then, abruptly, snort.

"What?" Nina asks.

"I'm trying really hard to think of a good joke about head."

She shrugs. "It's not too hard once you open your mouth."

"Fuck. How are you so good at this?"

"It's a skill. Much like—"

"All right, all right," Harper shouts. "We get it!"

• • •

We end the night on the couch, all tangled limbs used as makeshift pillows and hair in one another's faces, with *Pride & Prejudice* on the TV. It's Harper's request this time. She figures we could use a little bit of comfortable, predictable, satisfying romance. She claims she just wants something to put her to sleep so she's well-rested for her flight tomorrow, but I catch the flicker of bittersweet emotion cross her face at Elizabeth and Mr. Darcy's first meeting.

I let my eyelids flutter shut sometime after the disastrous

first proposal, when Elizabeth is left alone in the gardens, rain-damp and utterly distraught. I'm too tired to stay awake, and I don't need to worry about how it'll turn out.

I know they get a happy ending.

Twenty-three

Our apartment looks like a thrift store ransacked by influencers. Nina's clothes and toiletries and textbooks and electronics are everywhere. I stand in the kitchen, clutching my coffee, and watch her try to shove an inflatable dinosaur costume (which she's assured me is an improv party thing and not a sex thing) into her carry-on.

Harper left early this morning. She landed safe and sent us a selfie from her childhood bedroom, with its pink curtains, glittery butterfly stickers pasted directly onto the wall, and faded poster of Harry Styles in his One Direction era.

This never leaves this chat, she captioned the shot.

"You can FaceTime me if you get lonely," Nina tells me as she stands on top of her suitcase, using her body weight to crush the contents down so I can tug the zipper shut. "I sent you the festival schedule. Seriously, any time we're not onstage, you can call."

"I'll be fine," I grunt. "I have my shift at the library tonight. I'll pick up some new books to get me through the weekend."

Nina jumps off her bursting suitcase and smiles sadly.

"I know I said I'd respect your choices and stay out of this—"

"But you won't."

She shakes her head. "You owe it to yourself to talk to Vincent. You're a storyteller, Kendall. You need the closure."

I pull her into a hug—the kind that's so tight it almost hurts.

"I hate when you're right," I mumble into her hair.

Nina squeezes me tight. "Now, as your whore best friend, I'm ordering you to go get your happy ending."

• • •

My lecture on Shakespeare is long and offensively dry—to the point where I stop listening to the professor and start making a bullet point list in my head about why this class is a waste of my tuition dollars and no one should ever be required to study Shakespeare to get a bachelor's degree ever again. But eventually I run out of reasons to be mad about Anglocentrism and androcentrism, and I start a new list in my head: ways to apologize to Vincent Knight.

When class lets out, I join the herd of tired students migrating outside. It should, in theory, be golden hour. Campus should be kissed purple and orange. But instead, the skies overhead are heavy and gray, and everything is dim and dark and moody.

I love it.

I have an entire Spotify playlist dedicated to this kind of weather. I pull it up on my phone and reach one arm around to fish my headphones out of my backpack.

After a few moments of awkward grasping at the outer pocket, I accept that my headphones aren't where I usually shove them. I stop at a bench along the path and plop down with a heavy sigh, annoyed with myself for letting my backpack become such a disordered mess—which feels like an on-the-nose metaphor for the rest of my life right now. If I've lost them, I'm either going to have to fork over the money for another pair or I'm going to have to join Harper and Nina and the rest of this godforsaken country in buying AirPods, which are completely out of my budget and which I will inevitably lose within a week.

"Fuck you, Steve Jobs," I mutter.

The wooden planks underneath me creak and dip. I still, lift my head, and find Jabari Henderson sitting on the other end of the bench.

"Hey, Kendall."

I'm immediately on guard.

"Can I help you?"

He lets out a low whistle. "God, you and Vincent are alike."

It aches like a prodded bruise. I narrow my eyes at Jabari—because glaring feels way more badass than turning into a puddle of tears—and yank at the zippers of my backpack, abandoning the search for my headphones in favor of getting out of here as quickly as possible.

"I have to be somewhere. Sorry. You'll have to let Vincent know you failed . . . whatever you were trying to do here."

There's a dare in my voice. *Own up*, it says. *Tell me this is all a scheme, or a joke, or a bet. Tell me I'm not the villain in my own story.* But Jabari flinches too, and the showmanship of his smile falls into a solemn frown.

"He doesn't know I'm here."

I arch an eyebrow.

"I'm sorry," he says. "Just—please, hear me out. I really fucked this up."

Jabari has brown eyes, like Vincent. They're wide and honest and imploring. It's sobering, and maybe a little disconcerting, to see someone who's always laughing and smiling look so serious.

"Five minutes," I relent.

Jabari nods and wipes his palms on the front of his jeans like he's readying himself. I brace myself for hard truths, reality checks, and some point-blank shots at my pride.

Instead, Jabari says, "Vincent's never had a girlfriend."

"I know." My face flushes. "I wasn't expecting him to commit to me or anything—"

"No, no. I don't think you understand me. It's not that he doesn't want to date you. It's that he has no fucking clue how to."

"But he's been with girls, though? Right?" It's a silly question. There's no way a boy would know how to eat a girl out like that without some prior experience. I wince at the thought.

"Sleeping with someone is different from dating them," Jabari says.

"What's his problem, then?"

"He's . . . shy."

I laugh in his face. "Fuck off."

"I'm serious," Jabari says, laughing a little too. "He knows how to be an asshole when he needs to show out on the court, but listen—I've *never* seen him like this. We had to hype him up the morning before he met with you at Starbucks. The kid was so fucking nervous. I don't know how he sat through class. And then I got a call from him while he was running across campus—"

"He was late."

"I know. That's why he called. He was worried he fucked it up. Wanted to know if he was supposed to get you flowers or not, or if that was coming on too strong."

The mental image of Vincent sprinting across campus, phone to his ear as he frantically consults his friends on how to woo a girl—how to woo *me*—hits me like a punch to the sternum. It leaves me winded. It *ruins* me.

"So, the whole thing about getting him laid for his birthday?" I ask, voice hoarse. "That was just some wholesome fun, then? A little team bonding?"

Jabari winces.

"That one's on me," he admits, fidgeting with an elastic bracelet on his wrist. "I was just excited for him. He's been so miserable this season, with his wrist and everything, and he's always had our backs . . ." Jabari pauses, and we're both thinking of the point guard Vincent knocked out in the middle of a game. "I thought all of us should have his back for once. He always does shit for us. I wanted to return the favor. Help him be selfish for once."

I think of what Vincent said in his bedroom, about being bad at asking for what he wants.

"By getting him laid?" I ask.

"By getting him the girl."

"*The* girl, or *a* girl?" It's my insecurity talking. The words taste sour and shriveled in my mouth, but it feels good to get them out, even if Jabari will think less of me.

He shakes his head. "You were it, Kendall. You're the only one."

Past tense. Present tense. Which is it?

"Is he . . ." I swallow hard. "Is he mad at me?"

I hate that those words actually left my mouth. They're so immature. So *middle school*. But then Jabari shakes his head again, and the tightest of the knots that have been in my chest all week finally tugs free. I'm glad I asked. Communication is brutal, and maybe I'm worse at it than I thought I was, but God, it's worth it.

"He's mad at what went down," Jabari says, "but I don't think he's mad at *you*. If that makes sense. He told me what you said after he asked you to come to the bar with us. First off—brutal. But personally, I thought you caught on to the fact that we were all trying to get him alone with you all night and it creeped you out. But Vinny took it a little more personal than that. Said something about knowing he wouldn't be good enough for you."

All the talk about romance novels, dukes and billionaires, and my high expectations. Vincent wasn't teasing me for the fun of getting me flustered and outraged. He was genuinely concerned he wouldn't measure up for me.

"That's quite literally the most ridiculous thing I've ever heard," I say.

Jabari nods. "I told you. He's new to this. And he's a sensitive little shit."

I groan and slump back on the bench. Campus is growing darker and grayer. I feel a tiny, cold drop of misty rain land on my cheek but don't make a move to wipe it away.

"Why does he think he wouldn't be good enough?" I ask.

Because, contrary to what Nina said, I know I'm exactly like other girls—just on the introverted and anxious end of the spectrum. It's not like I'm extraordinary.

Jabari shrugs. "Ask him. I mean, I could tell you he hasn't fucking shut up about you and your damn poetry, but you probably want to hear all that from him. Besides, it's not my job to win you back. That's on Vincent. I'm just here to tell you I'm sorry, and that I really like you and your roommates"—he almost stumbles over that last word—"and that I'll hate myself for the rest of my life if I'm part of the reason you guys didn't work. I scared you off. I know I did. I got too excited, and I was only thinking about my boy, and I didn't let you know what was up."

"I get that, though," I say very quietly. "My friends were doing the same thing."

"I still can't stand that I fucked it up, though. *Vincent's* the one who usually kills the vibe. Not me. I'm the life of the fucking party, okay?"

I croak out a laugh.

"He didn't hook up with anyone at the bar, then?" I ask, picking at a hangnail and refusing to meet Jabari's eyes. "I was the only birthday action he got?"

Jabari's quiet for a moment.

When I glance up, he's staring at me with wide eyes.

"Y'all hooked up?"

The surprise on his face is so genuine that I have to admit that maybe—just maybe—I was wrong. Maybe Vincent didn't tell anyone about what happened in his bedroom. Maybe he kept his promise to me.

"Shit," Jabari says, voicing my exact thoughts as we look

out across the park. Then, louder: "Shit. Well, *that* explains why he was such a fucking bummer after—wait, wait. Hold up. When we came up to his room to get him, were you . . ."

I clear my throat and suck my lips together.

"*Shit.* No wonder he was so calm."

"Calm?"

"Yeah. I mean, all night, it was like he was a nervous wreck, and then suddenly he's kicking back a tequila shot and he just says, *I'm gonna ask her to come to the bar.* No hesitation."

I laugh weakly, because the alternative is crying on campus.

"That birthday party really crashed and burned, huh?" I ask.

Jabari hesitates. "Is Harper—"

"Okay?" I finish for him, my tone sharp again. "Not really. Thanks for that, by the way."

He looks pained. "I don't want you to have to be the middleman or anything," he says, "but can I at least get a hint? She disappeared on me Thursday night. And she unmatched me, and she blocked my number. I know I can be a lot sometimes, but I really thought it was going well, so can you at least help me figure out where I might've fucked it up? She say anything to you?"

I want to tear him apart. I want to eviscerate him. But I decide to extend a small measure of patience to him in repayment for what he's told me about Vincent.

"She told me you ditched her to be with another girl."

Jabari rears back. "She what?"

"She saw you hanging out with another girl at Vincent's birthday party. A blond."

"My cousin?"

I arch an eyebrow.

"My dad's side of the family is white as hell," Jabari says. "Makayla's a senior at UCLA, but they had the week off because they're on the quarter system. She came up to visit."

I scoff in disbelief.

"I'm not even playing. Hold on."

Jabari tugs his phone out of his pocket. I watch a few droplets of rain land on the screen as he taps open his photos, pulling up a group shot of at least twenty people. He points out himself, his mother, his father, and then his father's sister and her tall, blond daughter—who fits the description Nina gave me right down to the vague *Speak Now*–era Taylor Swift resemblance.

His cousin.

I sigh, scrub a hand over my face, and groan. "Fucking *miscommunication*."

"What?"

"Look," I say, turning on the bench to face Jabari, "Harper likes you. A lot. But she's never going to chase a man down. She'll never admit she's got a sappy bone in her body, but I know she does—way down deep. So, you need to show her this family photo, and then you need to tell her how you feel. And you need to do it *big*. Flowers. Violins. Diamonds, if you've got that kind of budget. But if you're not ready for that, then you should probably fuck off and leave her alone, because she's way out of your league as it is."

"I know."

"Good."

Jabari shakes his head. "You and Vincent are *really* fucking alike, you know that?"

"Yeah," I grumble. "I'm beginning to see that."

"All right," Jabari says, holding his hands up in surrender as he stands up. "I said my piece. Don't tell Vincent I spoke to you, okay? Unless it goes well. Then I'll take the credit."

Unless it goes well.

My heart flutters. He wouldn't say that unless there was a chance. Right?

"Harper's out of town, just so you know," I call out. "She'll be back Monday."

Jabari salutes me. "Perfect. Gives me some time to find a violinist."

I watch him turn and jog off, jacket braced over his head to protect his hair from the steadily growing drizzle, and I realize that maybe I was wrong about Jabari Henderson.

Because I was definitely wrong about Vincent.

I've spent an entire week trying to talk myself out of him. Trying to convince myself that our time together really was just a bet, some similarly gross and misogynistic pursuit, or otherwise a big performance. Maybe I've been doing this whole red flag scavenger hunt even longer, because from the moment we first kissed, I think I've been looking for even the tiniest sign that he's not what he seems to be. Because if Vincent is for real, then he's . . . he's everything.

He's smart, handsome as hell, and quick-witted in a way that sometimes makes me want to throttle him and sometimes makes me want to jump his bones. He's got friends and team-mates who are completely and utterly devoted to him. He's softhearted, beneath the cold and aloof shield he puts up, and he's always patient with me. Always listening. Always gentle with me when I need a hand, and firm when I need to get over myself.

I was so worried about this thing between us blowing up, I detonated it myself just so I wouldn't be blindsided. Nina was right. I construct my own narratives.

But maybe there's still some strength in that, because in romance novels, there's always a dark point before the climax. A breakup. A misunderstanding. A fundamental clash in values or beliefs. And then the character who messed up harder has to pull themselves together, confront their heroic flaw, and make amends.

"Fuck," I say out loud.

It's me. I have to make the grand gesture.

Twenty-four

I sprint back to the apartment.

It's not cute or dignified. I'm panting, pink-faced, and my backpack bounces and rustles so loudly that people actually turn over their shoulders to make sure they're not about to be run down by some kind of street sweeper. By the time I reach our building, it's pouring. I scrape mud and dead leaves off on the welcome mat before I step into the apartment.

With Harper and Nina gone for the weekend, the place is weirdly cavernous and echoey.

The gentle but insistent patter of rain on the windows reminds me that if Jabari hadn't caught me after my class, I probably would've come home, stripped off my wet clothes, put on my ugliest and comfiest sweats, and settled in for a few hours of me-time before my Friday-night shift at the library. A hot mug of tea. A scented candle. Fuzzy socks. Some scrolling through my phone to pick out more romance novels to add to the list of books I want to buy. A slouchy, no-judgment, self-care kind of vibe.

But I can't sit down. I can't settle in.

Not when I have something very important to figure out.

I've never performed a grand gesture before, but I've read and watched thousands of them since I was a little girl. They all seem to be blurred together and tangled into one big ball right now. Airport chases and kisses in the pouring rain, thrown rocks and boom boxes held up outside windows, popping out of cakes and riding up on a brilliant white horse to propose marriage. I could build him a house, *The Notebook* style— except that's a bit impractical, because I have no construction experience and I *definitely* don't have the funds to invest in real estate. I need something more practical.

Maybe I should do something at one of Vincent's basketball games. Coordinate a flash mob, bribe someone to put the kiss cam on me at halftime, hold up some sort of embarrassing and self-deprecating sign.

I wince and scrub my hands over my rain-dampened face.

None of these ideas feel right. None of them feel like they're honest to me or to Vincent. I don't know how to express myself in a big, theatrical, public way. That's not me. The *me* thing to do would be to chicken out and write a letter—

I go still.

Vincent wrote me a note the night we met, and I still don't know what it said.

Nina's bedroom door is unlocked. I burst into her room, tripping over a small pile of sweaters that didn't make the cut for her trip this weekend, and make my way to the built-in bookshelves over her desk. I need to find *The Mafia's Princess*. I want Vincent's first note more than anything I've ever wanted before. But as I work my way down the line of books, my heart sinks.

It's not here.

I don't want to reduce Nina to my wing-woman best friend who only exists to fuel my romantic arc, because she's so much more than that. But I call her anyway.

"Don't tell me you're lonely already," Nina answers after the third ring, her voice crackly through the phone. There's singing in the background—something very chipper and distinctly *Mamma Mia*. Theater kids are so predictable.

"Do you still have *The Mafia's Princess*?" I demand.

"That one you didn't finish? No, I never started it."

"But do you remember where it is?"

There's a burst of sound in the background—someone has joined in with a guitar.

"Uh, I'm pretty sure I put it in the donation box at the bookstore downtown," Nina shouts over the acoustic butchering of ABBA.

My heart drops into my stomach. I lurch upright, abandoning my search.

"You're kidding."

"I thought you said you weren't going to finish it!" Nina cries. "I'm sorry, Kenny. I'll order you a new copy on Amazon right now. I have Prime! It'll get there before Harper and I get home, so you can thoroughly enjoy your alone time—"

"No, it's okay," I tell her. "It's fine. Forget it."

"Are you sure?"

"I'm sure. Look, I'll call you back tonight. I want to hear all about the festival. I just need to . . . um . . . take care of something."

I hang up and step out into the living room again. The glass doors out to our tiny balcony, all cluttered with plants and a folding pool chair Harper nicked from the rec center, are streaked with rain. It's pouring now—really and truly storming. Which means that I have a choice. I can either stay dry but spend the whole evening spiraling about what Vincent's first note said and if someone else is going to get their hands on *The Mafia's Princess* before I can retrieve it, or I can do what a main character would do: run through a torrential downpour to go after what she wants.

"Fuck it," I grumble.

This is what I get for rating so many books three stars on Goodreads for not having a thrilling enough third act. Someone all-powerful and all-knowing (maybe God, maybe Jeff Bezos) is definitely laughing at me right now.

Here's your grand finale, Holiday.

Eat your heart out.

● ● ●

I pass the basketball house on my way downtown. My heart's in my throat the whole time. I refuse to look up and search each window for signs of life, because the last thing I need right now is to make eye contact with Vincent while I'm half jogging past his house in the rain.

Luckily, the bad weather seems to have made everyone at Clement University disappear. I only pass two other students on my journey through the grid of off-campus student housing that eventually gives way to local neighborhoods and then, at last, the quaint little downtown dotted with a mix of mom-and-pop shops and beloved college staples like Chipotle and CVS. The Trader Joe's on the corner has buckets of sunflowers out front, each one a stroke of bright yellow against the moody gray of this rain-soaked town.

Flowers. I should get Vincent flowers.

It only occurs to me after I leave the store, a newspaper-wrapped bouquet tucked under my arm, that sunflowers aren't exactly the most romantic of flowers. Roses would've been a better move. And I don't know when I'm actually going to see Vincent again—the basketball team might have an away game somewhere out of state for all I know, since I've been studiously avoiding any sports news on social media—so there's a very real possibility that all these petals will shrivel up and go brown before I'm able to deliver them.

I grumble expletives under my breath as I hustle the last block to my destination.

The bookstore is housed in an old, rambling Victorian with two stories and an attic up in the eaves. It might be my favorite building in the world. Today, it's blessedly quiet, save for a well-dressed couple perusing the art history section and an old man sitting in the worn armchair over by the science fiction. I'm sure there are some stragglers on the second floor too, but once you get up into the eaves, it's all old poetry and novels nobody ever buys. It's a little dark if you're not sitting right under a window, but the attic is hands down the best place in town to spend eight hours straight reading without interruption. Especially on a day like this.

The woman behind the front counter welcomes me in with a sympathetic smile. I can't tell if it's because I'm panting and carrying flowers or because I'm *soaked*. My favorite over-sized cardigan was no match for the downpour, and my jeans are plastered to my legs. I don't want to *know* what my hair looks like.

But there's no time for vanity. I'm on a mission.

I head straight to the back of the first floor. There's a table tucked in the corner with six enormous cardboard boxes stacked under it and on top of it, all of them overflowing with books. The sign hanging on the wall above them reads: GENTLY LOVED BOOKS, IN NEED OF A HOME. $1 EACH.

My heart hammers as I start the hunt for something I have never looked for in a bookstore ever before: abs. I end up setting the sunflowers down on the table so I can drop to my knees and use both hands to dig through the seemingly endless pile of everything from children's picture books to dog-eared high fantasy tomes thicker than my wrist. There's no sign of *The Mafia's Princess* in the first box I go through, so I move on to the next. And then the next. And the next, before I stand up on stiff knees to tackle the ones on the table.

By the time I'm halfway through the fifth box, my stomach is in knots.

What if it's gone? What if someone else already found it and took it home? What if they found Vincent's note and mistook it for a receipt or a shoddy bookmark? What if they tossed it out?

I swallow back the thought and keep digging.

Maybe I'm too sentimental. Maybe I care too much about narratives. Maybe I shouldn't be here, soaking wet and frantically digging through boxes of books that are collecting dust, instead of tackling my problems more head-on. But I need this. I need this little piece of reassurance, this little piece of Vincent, this little piece of our story. I need his note.

I reach into the last box and shove stacks of miscellaneous paperbacks to the sides, letting them topple out onto the floor with heavy thuds.

And there, at the very bottom, is *The Mafia's Princess*.

I've never been so happy to see a naked male torso on a cover. With a sigh of relief and glee, I shove my hand deep into the treacherous pit of books and grip the corner of *The Mafia's Princess* between my fingers. It takes a great deal of tugging to get the thing free, and when I do, I stumble back a few steps.

A little scrap of something—the pale-pink lined paper I recognize from the notepad Margie keeps on the circulation desk—flutters out from the pages and drifts down to the floor. It lands face up. I recognize the neat block letters with a sharp pang of endearment.

It's Vincent's handwriting.

I'M NOT POETIC
BUT CALL ME FOR A GOOD TIME
(I REALLY LIKE YOU)

Printed beneath this is a phone number. *His* phone number. My eyes trace over the note three more times before it hits me. Three lines. Five, seven, five syllables.

He wrote me a haiku.

I bark out a laugh even as tears spring to my eyes. It's self-deprecating and tongue-in-cheek and so utterly *him*. The mental image of Vincent hunched over the circulation desk—maybe still trying to hide his boner, or maybe shielding this scrap of paper from Margie's prying eyes—and counting out syllables on his fingers is the nail in the coffin. I'm fucked. So utterly fucked. Maybe I should be mad at the cruel irony of it all, that this silly little book with a naked man on the cover is our Chekhov's gun, but all I can bring myself to do is pick up the note and read it again and again until I think the words might actually be seared into my brain forever.

And then, with my bouquet of sunflowers and my smutty romance novel cradled in one arm, I reach for my phone. I'm trembling a little because I'm so fucking cold and hopped up on adrenaline, but I manage to pull the keypad up so I can dial the number on the note. Just to check. Just to hear his voice (whether I get his voicemail or he says hello and I have to hang up like a complete stalker) so I can't talk myself back into doubt.

I lift my phone to my ear.

A moment later, I hear ringing—both against my ear and somewhere in the store.

And surely it must be a coincidence that someone a few aisles over is getting a call right now. Surely real life can't be so cinematic. It's too convenient. Too contrived. My English professors would rip it apart. But I grab my sunflowers, and my feet carry me around the corner and down the rows until I'm standing at the end of an aisle that I'm all too familiar with.

Vincent Knight stands in the middle of it, a romance novel in one hand and his ringing phone in the other.

Twenty-five

Vincent's hair is windblown, his black Clement Athletics jacket is speckled with rain, and his nose is a little bit pink from the cold. He's utterly and devastatingly beautiful. And for one brief but magical moment while he's frowning down at the ringing phone in his hand like he's debating whether or not to take a chance on an unknown number, I get to absorb the full weight of how badly I've missed him.

Then he looks up, and his dark eyes land on me like I've shouted his name.

My stomach drops into my feet. I want to run. It takes everything in me to fight that gut instinct, even though I'm really not ready for this. I'm dripping wet, my hands are full, and I still don't have a grand gesture planned. But I'm fresh out of time to brainstorm, because Vincent is straightening his spine and squaring up to face me. His expression is equal parts dutiful—like he sort of saw this coming—and pained—like he'd really rather not.

And his phone is still ringing.

"Oh, shit," I blurt. "Sorry. Hold on."

I fumble with my sunflowers and Vincent's note and *The Mafia's Princess*, nearly dropping all three in the process, before I manage to tap the button on my screen to end the call. Vincent looks between me and his (now-silent) phone like he's just now connecting the dots.

"Hi," I say, taking a cautious step into the aisle.

"Hi," he says back, and *fuck*, I've missed the deep timbre of his voice.

But he doesn't exactly sound thrilled to see me. Not that I can blame him. The last time we saw each other, at his birthday party, I told him to fuck off and leave me alone.

"Hi." *Fuck, I already said that.* "I, um, come in peace."

I offer him the brightest smile I can muster and hope he doesn't notice that I'm shaking. This is the worst. I hate being brave. I hate being perceived. Most of all, I hate this weird *distance* between us. Not the literal one—it would only take another five or six steps forward to get to him—but the metaphorical one. Vincent's not smiling back at me. I want him to. I want him to crack a joke about if I come here often, and I want him to call me by my last name and make a double entendre about the fact that I'm dripping wet.

I want us back the way we were.

But I broke it, so now I have to fix it.

"What are *you* doing here, Kendall?" Vincent asks on a weary sigh. "It's Friday. You're supposed to be at the library."

I shouldn't be so touched that he remembers my work schedule.

The bar really is too low for men.

"My shift doesn't start until ten," I say. Then, because I'm genuinely stumped: "What are you doing here?"

Vincent freezes up like he's suddenly remembered that he's holding a romance novel in one hand. Before he can either hide it behind his back or lob it over the stacks and into the next aisle, I tip my head to the side to read the title on the cover.

"Oh, ew. Don't get that one. It was published, like, a decade ago. There's tons of unchecked sexism and homophobia." I pause and then add, a bit sheepishly, "The main character is the worst too. She always says the wrong thing at the wrong time. It's infuriating."

I worry I'm being too subtle.

But then Vincent arches one eyebrow, as if to point out the irony of my critique, and it's such a familiar expression of his that I could cry. I'll gladly take his snark, his passive-aggressiveness, his scathing commentary on my high expectations and romance novel obsession. *That* I can handle. What I don't think I could handle is if he treats me like a stranger. But before I can latch on to the little spark of hope, he slides the book back on to the nearest shelf, shoves both his hands into the front pockets of his jacket, and fixes his gaze on a spot somewhere over my right shoulder.

It doesn't take a PhD in psychology to read the closed-off body language and scattered eye contact. He's got his guard up.

"I got your note," I blurt, lifting the slip of paper up as proof. "Nina donated my stupid Mafia book, so I had to come here to find it. And I did. Obviously. Finally, I . . . got your note."

I don't know what reaction I was expecting, but it certainly wasn't Vincent balling his hands into fists at his sides and biting down so hard a muscle in his jaw ticks. At first, I think he's mad. But then I catch the blush crawling up the column of his neck and painting the tips of his ears, and I realize that he's embarrassed. This note was him putting himself out there, and now he thinks I've come back to rub it in his face.

Fuck. How am I messing this up so fast?

"These are for you," I announce, thrusting the bouquet of sunflowers at his chest.

Vincent doesn't take his hands out of his pockets. "What are they?"

"Sunflowers."

"I know that," he huffs. "I meant what are they for?"

"Because I was going to look for roses, but I think the sororities are doing their recruitment or something, so this was all Trader Joe's had, and I—yeah. I got them for you. Because you deserve flowers."

Vincent's fully blushing now, but his eyes are narrowed.

"Is this another poetry thing?"

"What?"

He looks down at the bouquet, then up at me, and then the bouquet again.

"Beloved, thou hast brought me many flowers," he grumbles. "It's an Elizabeth Barrett Browning poem. You know it, right?"

"I don't think so," I admit. "What's the—oh, wait."

I tuck the sunflowers and the romance novel up under my arm and use one thumb to pull up a new browser tab on my phone. Vincent twitches like he wants to step forward and take something out of my hands before it all goes tumbling to the floor, but instead he folds his arms tight across his chest and watches me struggle to type out the aggressively long title into the search bar. The poem is public domain, so it's easy to find. I recognize it by the third line. I have read it before—we covered it in one of my freshman-year English lit classes.

The narrator's lover brings her flowers, and she cherishes them—really, she does—but the gifts she prefers to give and receive are far less ephemeral.

So, in the like name of that love of ours, Take back these thoughts which here unfolded too, And which on warm and cold days I withdrew From my heart's ground.

Poems.

Her love language is poems.

It hits me then that Vincent and I don't need enormous public displays of affection. We need words of affirmation, and eye contact, and a quiet moment to shed our armor and face each other with honesty and vulnerability—things an airport or a crowded stadium can't afford us.

Most importantly, I need to use my own words right now.

I owe it to Vincent to be brave. I owe it to *myself.*

I close my phone, hold my chin high, and ask, as seriously as one can: "Did you take my underwear?"

Vincent is, understandably, bewildered. "Did I *what?*"

"It's a yes-or-no question. On your birthday. After—*everything.* I really don't think you did, but I need to ask, even if it's completely idiotic, because I'm trying to prove something to myself. So. Did you take my underwear?"

He slowly blinks at me.

And then he asks, "Why the fuck would I take your underwear?"

There it is. The simple absurdity of my fear, laid out in plain English. I know that a question in response to a question can be a deflection tactic, but this doesn't feel like that kind of a situation. This feels like Vincent has no fucking clue why the girl who told him to fuck off on his birthday is at the bookstore, dripping wet and bearing flowers, asking him if he stole her underpants.

Because it's silly. I'm silly—and I've read the whole situation wrong.

"Well, that answers that," I say with a weak laugh.

Vincent's still frowning. "Hold on. You thought I took your underwear?"

I laugh again, because the truth is far worse.

"I thought it was a *bet*," I admit.

"What? Me stealing your underwear?"

"No—me. Us. The whole thing." I gesture sweepingly with the sunflowers. The newspaper they're wrapped in rustles violently. "When I saw all your teammates watching us when you asked me to the bar, I assumed there was some kind of big team joke about us hooking up, and you were just going to parade me or my missing underwear around like some kind of trophy. So, I ran."

"You thought . . ." Vincent's face twists like I've hit him. "That's—"

"Gross! I know. But I was scared, and I assumed the worst of you, and you didn't deserve it. So, this is me trying to tell you that I'm sorry."

I hold the flowers out again. But Vincent doesn't move to accept them. He's staring at me, something like horror written across his face, and then his expression sinks into something much worse. Hurt. He's hurt that I'd think so little of him. And when he exhales a little scoff and shakes his head, I feel it like a punch to the stomach. He's not laughing. I really wish he would laugh. Because if we can't laugh about this—if he can't forgive me for this—then I don't know what I'm supposed to do.

"But I realize, now, that I was wrong," I barrel on. "Because you're a good person." My throat gets tight when I look at him. I swallow and push through it. "You're *so* good, Vincent."

His face scrunches.

"Not good enough, though, huh?"

He says it like it's meant to be some kind of barbed joke, but we both wince when it lands with unexpected vulnerability. There's a tiny crack in Vincent's walls, and some of the hurt has managed to trickle through.

"You don't believe that, do you?" I ask softly.

Vincent shifts his weight back and forth between his feet, visibly uncomfortable with the direction this conversation is taking. I watch him fidget. He realizes I'm watching and tugs his hands out of his pockets to shake them out and scrub his hair back, leaving it even wilder and messier than before.

"Look, Kendall, we're good," he says, even though we are very much *not* good. "You don't have to nurse my wounded ego or whatever. I'm fine. I'm a big boy. I can handle a little bit of rejection."

He smiles, then, and there's some honesty in it. He's not saying this all for sympathy. He's genuinely convinced I'm here for some kind of closure, and he's willing to give it.

Unbelievable.

He really doesn't get it.

"You are . . ." I trail off, shaking my head. "You're so fucking handsome."

Vincent barks out a laugh, and it's half startled and half bitter. I take another step toward him and press on without a shred of humor.

"And you're better at interpreting poetry than you give yourself credit for."

"Thanks, Holiday," he says coolly.

One more step. "And you've been playing basketball since elementary school, so you're disciplined and you appreciate the value of hard work. You've been team captain, so you're good with leadership and responsibility. And you're going to graduate magna cum laude."

One more step, and Vincent swallows hard.

Almost like me being this close makes him nervous.

Almost like he's finally catching on.

"Is there a reason you're giving me my own résumé?" he asks, voice a little bit hoarse.

He's close enough now that I could reach out and touch him. And *fuck*, do I want to touch him. But grabbing Vincent by the shirt and kissing him won't solve our problems right now. So, I just clutch the flowers tight and refuse to break our eye contact, hoping that my words mean as much to him as they do to me.

"I like you," I admit, my face so hot it almost hurts. "A lot. I like that we can talk about anything, and I like that we have the same sense of humor, and I like that you understand me when I snap at you, and I—I like that you call me out when I'm being stupid."

Vincent snorts. I take it like a champ.

"Even though I hate feeling stupid," I press on. "It's probably my biggest fear. Maybe it's the dyslexia thing, or the introvert thing—I don't know. I guess I have a massive ego. We can psychoanalyze me later." I can't look into his eyes for this part, so I stare fixedly into the spiraling seeds of one of the sunflowers. "But at your birthday party, I—I just felt like if I ignored all the red flags, I'd be stupid for walking right into trouble despite all the warning signs. So, I tried listening to my gut, and now I feel stupid for overreacting and not giving you the benefit of the doubt. I don't know how to win here. I don't think I can. But I don't think I care anymore, because I'd rather be stupid than hurt you again. Because I really fucking like you."

Twenty-six

Vincent doesn't say anything right away, so my words settle heavily in the silence.

I've never told anyone I like them before.

It's terrifying.

It genuinely feels like I've handed him my heart—the literal internal organ imperative to my survival—and given him the choice to either accept it or drop-kick it across the bookstore. I can't look him in the eyes. If I do, I'm going to burst into tears. And I'm trying to hold it together and give him the time he needs to digest what I've just dumped on him, but *fuck*, I wish I had a free hand so I could fidget with my hair or pick at my nails or do *something* other than stand in front of him and hold my breath, waiting for him to slam-dunk me and my miserable, sloppy, unrehearsed excuse for a grand gesture in the nearest trash can.

Instead, he says, very gently, "You're not stupid, Kendall."

I scoff.

"Okay, you're a little stupid," he amends with the faintest twitch of his lips. "But I could've handled everything better.

You told me you weren't comfortable having all my friends involved and feeling like you had an audience, and I still asked you out in front of all of them. I crossed one of your boundaries, and I'm sorry for that. For disrespecting you."

It takes me a solid six seconds to register that he's apologizing too.

He's offering an olive branch. He's leading us to the middle ground. He wants to rebuild what we broke too. It feels like the sun breaking through the clouds after a long week of bleak, ice-cold darkness, and I want nothing more than to tip my head back and bask in the warmth his words bring—the *relief*—but then I realize that he's doing it again.

He's giving me exactly what he thinks I want.

"Oh my God," I say. "Stop. Please. You have to stop being so—so *nice* to me."

Vincent lets out a startled laugh. "What are you talking about?"

"I ruined your birthday! I essentially accused you of hooking up with me as part of some shitty misogynistic pact with your friends. I messed up, so I'm the one who's supposed to make a grand gesture and grovel and humiliate myself publicly or whatever. So, will you stop being so fucking selfless for, like, *five minutes* and let yourself be pissed off? Why is that so hard, to think about yourself first? Huh? You tell me I can *practice* on you, and you memorize poems for me, and you eat me out on your own fucking birthday, and I have no real clue what *you* want because it's always about *me*. What's up with that?"

I prod his chest with the bouquet of sunflowers for emphasis.

At last, I see the first real spark of anger in Vincent.

"You don't know what I want?" he demands, low and rough. "Seriously?"

When he looks me up and down in one slow stroke, it's not just indignation and frustration burning in his eyes. It's blatant, unapologetic hunger. It's the mirror image of my own desire, and beneath that, a tiny pinch of something bittersweet—something suspiciously like longing—that tells me this week has been just as painful for him as it's been for me.

It knocks the breath out of my lungs.

I clutch his note tighter in my hand and remember his haiku.

"Well, I do *now*," I say miserably.

Vincent isn't done. He takes a step toward me, so we're toe to toe and he's towering over me with every inch of his (absurd, unnecessary, honestly excessive) height.

"I kissed you because I wanted to kiss you," he says. "I memorized poems for you because I wanted to be able to talk to you about the shit you like." He lowers his voice. "And I ate you out because it was my birthday, and all I wanted was to make you come. That was for me, Kendall. All of that was for me. I didn't do it just to be *nice*. I did it because I. Like. You."

I'm light-headed.

My brain is legitimately short-circuiting. All I can do is stand there with my mouth hanging open, swaying and clutching the sunflowers like a life raft, as I stare up into Vincent Knight's enormous brown eyes and my cerebral cortex tries to fuck me over. But there's no evidence that this is a joke or a lie, or that I've somehow misinterpreted his words. There's no room for error. There's no room for me to overthink it.

I. Like. You.

"But aren't you mad?" I croak.

Vincent holds his arms out wide, palms up. "Of course I'm mad. You're telling me you ran out on me because you assumed I only hooked up with you to impress my friends. I'm mad you thought I would do that. I'm mad I didn't take the time to introduce you to everyone on the team so you wouldn't feel so nervous and weirded out. I rushed this—right from the fucking start—and I don't know how to take it slow with you, and it makes me feel stupid and selfish and out of my goddamned mind. So yeah. I'm fucking *furious*, Holiday. But none of that changes how I feel about you."

I really need to sit down, I think numbly. But we're in the middle of the aisle, and the nearest chairs are all the way at the front of the bookstore by the magazines, and oh my God, I think I'm in shock or something?

"I'm supposed to be the one grand gesturing you," I argue weakly.

Vincent folds his arms across his chest. "You're not grand gesturing me, Holiday. Not on my watch."

I hold his note up. "I'm literally grand gesturing you right now."

"Well, knock it off. Maybe I want to be the hero for once, even though my dad's not a billionaire and I'm not in the fucking Mafia—"

"Okay, first off," I interrupt, "sports romance is a thing. You're a Division I basketball player with pretty eyes and floppy hair. You're not exactly an underrepresented population in the genre." I would stop to appreciate how utterly endearing it is when Vincent blushes, but I'm on a roll. "And secondly, I've had enough of you talking about me and my *standards*. What

I want to read about in books isn't necessarily what I want in a boyfriend. And you've never been anyone's boyfriend anyway, so I don't know why you think you wouldn't be—"

It's Vincent's turn to interrupt me. "How did you know I've never dated anyone?"

"Jabari. He found me on campus today. We talked."

"I told him to leave you alone."

"Well, he put in a really good word for you."

"I'm still going to kill him."

I roll my eyes.

"Look," I say, "all I'm trying to say is that I'm not expecting you to be a character straight out of a romance novel. You're not fictional. You're not *perfect*. But I don't want you to be, because I'm not perfect either, and it would really suck if I'm the only one who ever puts my foot in my mouth and—"

"We have to learn each other's language," Vincent blurts.

I frown.

"It's like you said about poetry," he presses on. "We have to learn to speak each other's language. Get to know each other, so we can pick up all the subtext and shit."

"I'm pretty sure I never used the phrase *subtext and shit*."

"I'm paraphrasing. Sue me."

But he still makes a compelling point.

We haven't known each other very long, even though it sometimes feels like it's been decades since we first kissed in the library during my night shift. Maybe if Vincent and I can start handing each other the puzzle pieces, I'll stop trying to fill in the gaps myself. And maybe I need to get comfortable with the idea that it'll take time for us to get there—to a place where we have a full picture of each other.

I should probably start enjoying the process instead of letting the unknown torture me.

"I want to meet all your friends," I tell him.

Vincent nods immediately. "Good. I want you to."

"And I'd really like to hear about your family, and what you were like in middle school, and what you want to do after graduation, and—and I want you to teach me everything you know about basketball. Because you don't get to quote Elizabeth Barrett Browning to me if I can't talk to you about why the fuck the Clippers traded their first-round draft pick to the Cavs and let them scoop up Kyrie Irving."

"That was a shit trade in retrospect, but they couldn't have known—" Vincent begins, then narrows his eyes. "I thought you didn't know anything about basketball."

I shuffle the flowers and book and note around in my arms, suddenly shy.

"Well, I didn't. But then I met you, and I stopped scrolling past the articles and the videos on social media and started paying attention. Also, I read the Coach K autobiography you checked out from the library. It's actually kind of a fun sport to watch. I'm sorry I talked shit, okay? I care about it now. Because I care about you. I want to know your opinions and the teams you like and which players you'd want to be stranded on an island with."

Vincent arches an eyebrow. "You're genuinely interested?"

"Of course I am. It's part of you. And I'm interested in all of you, not just how good you are at reading me poetry and"—I stop short and blush—"*other stuff*."

Vincent blinks at me with those absurdly thick eyelashes of his, and then a slow smile breaks across his face.

"I'm good at *other stuff*, am I?"

There he is.

My Vincent.

I feel my whole body unwind and sag with relief. I want to reach out and touch him, somehow, but my arms are still full between the sunflowers and the romance novel and the note. All I can do is smile at him, even as my eyes start to sting and the built-up anxiety of the last week drains out of my body and leaves me feeling utterly exhausted.

"I'm sorry I ruined your birthday," I whisper.

Vincent runs his tongue over his teeth and shakes his head.

"You ruined my whole fucking week, Holiday."

Again, he tries to make it a joke.

Again, he's an open book.

"Vincent," I say miserably.

He takes the sunflowers and the novel from my arms and turns to set them, very gently, on a display shelf of erotic romance proudly labeled SPICY BOOKTOK READS. And then he turns back to me, loops an arm over my shoulders, and pulls me into his chest. The warmth of his body seeps right through my rain-damp clothes. I press my nose into the collar of his sweater and will myself not to make any audible crying noises as I clutch fistfuls of his jacket. But his stupidly large hand is flat against my back, bridging my shoulder blades, so I know he feels it when my breath catches as I inhale.

"I think that's enough groveling," he says above me.

"Are you sure? I can go bigger, I think."

The words are muffled by his chest, but he must hear me, because he sighs and squeezes me just a little bit tighter. I try to breathe steadily and focus on the steady thump of his heart-beat against my cheek so I won't lose it.

"Maybe another day," he says. And then he mumbles into my hair, so quietly I almost miss it, "Nobody's ever given me flowers before."

I push back so I can look him in the eyes.

"I can get you more," I tell him, forgetting to be embarrassed when a tear spills out and dribbles down my cheek. "Seriously, I'll give you fucking fields of them. Whatever it takes to let you know how into you I actually am. I just—I think, for now, I need you to give me aggressively straightforward statements of intent. Constantly. Otherwise, I'll run circles in my head trying to interpret things."

I step back fully, so I can discreetly run a fingertip under my eyes.

Vincent watches me with an odd expression on his face.

"Shit," he finally says, scrubbing his hand over his face. "Guess I'm a coward too. All right. Um." He rolls his shoulders back in a move I recognize: he's hyping himself up the way he does before a basketball game. "I've never dated anyone before. I mean, I've gone on dates, but I've never actually been in a situation where I wanted to keep seeing a girl after we hooked up once or twice. And that's not me being a dick—it's always been mutual. I genuinely thought I just preferred keeping everything casual. And then I met you, and you—" He breaks off.

"I what?" I press.

"You . . . intimidate me."

A burst of shocked laughter breaks through my tears. "Oh, fuck off."

Vincent lifts an arm to rake his fingers through his hair. There's a little tremble in his hand that tells me he's serious.

"You're scary smart," he says, "and you're so fucking pretty it hurts to look at you sometimes. I'm just—I'm *fucked*. I want to text you every time I see something funny, and I want to get coffee with you between classes so we can complain to each other. And I want you to know all my friends, and I want to know yours, and I don't know what I'm doing, and I feel like you want—like you *deserve* more than, I don't know, getting coffee on campus and hanging out at house parties and driving around in my car. That's so boring compared to the shit you read."

"You don't even know what I read," I protest half-heartedly.

Vincent shakes his head.

"I've gone through, like, ten of these this week," he admits, gesturing to the shelf of romance novels next to us. "I know I gave you a lot of shit, but I'm trying to work on unpacking that, so . . . Look, I still have my complaints. But I get it. I get why you like them. And I was wrong to say that your expectations are too high. They're not. You deserve to have this."

My eyes sting all over again.

I don't know if he'll ever understand how much those words mean to me.

"Well, you haven't dated anyone before, and I am"—I snort—"obviously not good at this either. So maybe we should just figure it out together."

Vincent nods.

And then he takes my hands in his and brings them up to his lips, one at a time, to press two soft kisses to my knuckles. It feels so utterly Jane Austen that I think I might cry.

"Your fingers," he says very seriously, "are fucking freezing."

"It's raining. I walked here. Sue me."

Vincent laughs a little too loudly. I can tell he's nervous—that he's trying to push through it, for my sake—so I squeeze his hands in encouragement.

"I want you so bad it hurts sometimes," he admits quietly, a little wrinkle between his brows as he stares down at my hands around his, one of his thumbs tracing laps back and forth across my knuckles. "I don't know if I like feeling this way. I don't want to be one of those guys who goes all caveman on the girl he likes, but I feel . . . *greedy* with you."

And there it is. My own feelings in his words.

"Be greedy, then."

Vincent blinks at me like he doesn't understand.

I shrug. "If you feel the same way I do, then I don't get what the problem is. I've been greedy. You can be greedy too. Ask for what you want."

He clears his throat and says, "I want to kiss you."

My heart hiccups.

I whisper, "Prove it."

Twenty-seven

The first time I kissed Vincent, I acted on instinct.

This feels a lot like that first kiss.

And maybe it's the fact that we already know how good it feels to have our mouths on each other, or maybe we're just too relieved and too excited to be patient any longer. Because one moment, Vincent is holding my hands in his with tender reverence, and the next, he's crushing me to his chest with one arm wrapped around my waist. I grab two fistfuls of his black Clement Athletics jacket and arch up onto my toes, determined to meet him halfway. He returns the favor by twisting his hand into my rain-damp hair and giving it a tug—too gentle to really hurt, but firm enough that I gasp as my chin tips back.

He kisses me. *Hard*.

Like he means it.

Like he's starving.

I kiss him back and hope he doesn't mind that my eyes are wet again.

All week, I've been shaken up like champagne. Now Vincent's uncorked me, and all the feelings I bottled up are bubbling to the surface so fast that there's no way for me to stop the messy overflow.

I really fucking missed him. His smile. His voice. The heat of his body, so big and solid against mine. The soft scrape of his barely there stubble against my skin. The way he *smells*—laundry detergent and that familiar undercurrent of something warm and spiced that makes me dizzy. The way he grasps at my head and my hips like he won't be satisfied until he feels every inch of my body against his. We're kissing like we're lovers reunited after one of them returned from war or something, which is probably overkill considering we're just a pair of students standing in the romance aisle of our college town's local bookstore.

But up until all of ten seconds ago, I really thought I'd ruined everything and let this boy slip through my fingers. So, I think I deserve to be a little dramatic. Just this once.

I'm so lost in Vincent that I don't hear the footsteps approaching.

But I do hear a scandalized gasp, followed by, *"Oop."*

Our mouths break apart in surprise.

There are two girls standing at the end of the aisle, both wearing Clement sweatshirts and both staring at us with wide eyes. They've got their phones in their hands in what I recognize as the trademark stance of avid readers who've been hunting for recommendations all week and have come to the store armed and ready for battle.

Right. Because it's Friday night.

And this is a bookstore.

And we can't catch a fucking break, apparently.

"I'm so sorry," one of the girls stammers. "We just need to get to the, um . . ."

She trails off, clears her throat, and points to the SPICY BOOKTOK READS shelf behind us like she can't stomach the thought of saying it out loud. I feel immediate kinship with this girl. Which is probably the only reason that I don't tell her and her friend to pretty please take a fucking hike.

"Yeah, no, of course," I squeak, releasing my white-knuckled grip on the front of Vincent's jacket and clearing my throat. "Excuse us."

Vincent doesn't budge. It takes a few encouraging pats to his shoulder before he relents and untangles himself from me with a tortured groan. I smooth down the back of my hair, which is thoroughly rumpled, and then shake out the wrinkles in my oversized cardigan. Vincent watches me with a look I haven't seen on his face since Jabari Henderson interrupted our birthday festivities in his bedroom.

Sorry, I mouth.

The look he shoots me back says, *Please end my suffering*.

Vincent reaches around me to grab his sunflowers off the shelf—and I'm glad for the reminder, because I momentarily forgot about the existence of literally everything except for Vincent. I would've been so upset if I lost his note. I snatch it off the shelf and tuck it into the safest part of my wallet, right between my student ID (which I can't afford to lose) and a gift card to a sporting goods store (which I haven't touched since it fell out of a card on my seventeenth birthday). I go to reach for *The Mafia's Princess* too, but hesitate when a wonderful thought occurs to me.

I won't need a romance novel to get me through this weekend.

I turn back to the pair of girls at the end of the aisle.

"This one," I say, tapping the naked abdominals on the cover, "is *really* good. She's a lawyer. He's an ex–hit man. There's an elevator scene in chapter three where he—yeah. I haven't gotten to finish it yet, but the dialogue is . . . five stars."

Vincent's lips twitch when I turn to face him again.

"Shall we?" he asks, offering me his arm.

I loop my hand around his forearm and give it a squeeze as we begin our walk of shame out of the romance aisle. Behind us, in the least discreet whisper I've ever heard, one of the girls says, "This is the most embarrassing cover I've ever seen."

"The sticker says it's only a dollar," her friend points out.

"Yeah, because it's garbage."

"So, you're not getting it?"

"Of course I'm getting it."

The worn-down original wood floors creak under our feet as Vincent and I march to the front of the store. Everything is just as it was when I rushed in here: the well-dressed couple perusing the art history section are still flicking through architecture books, and the old man posted up in the armchair over by science fiction is still deep in what looks like a Tolkien book. The woman behind the front desk is arranging a display of female-led crime thrillers. It's bizarre. Everyone's going about their business like I didn't just have a life-altering experience three aisles over.

Vincent and I slow to a stop by the door. The rain is coming down in torrents, the trees lining the street outside nothing but dark blurs swaying in the howling wind.

"My car's a few blocks away," Vincent says. "You wanna wait here, and I'll come pick you up?"

His chivalrous offer, while appreciated, is a little too late.

"I'm already wet," I point out.

Vincent lets his eyes take a pointed lap down my body and back up again. I want to laugh. I do. Instead, I sway on my feet, unsteady from the force of how much I like it when he looks at me like he's just as affected as I am right now.

"Should we make a run for it?" he asks, low and rumbling.

I shake my head and tighten my grip on his arm.

I have a better idea.

Vincent's face scrunches up in an adorably confused frown as I steer him down the science fiction aisle toward the far side of the bookstore, where a narrow staircase with a wrought iron banister curves up to the floor above us. We have to climb in single file, so I drop my hold on Vincent's arm. He makes a tiny sound of displeasure. I reach back and let him hook his pinkie finger around mine as we ascend to the second floor.

It's a barren maze of nonfiction. Nobody in Clement has the motivation to drag themselves through the pouring rain just to browse this section of the store. Cookbooks, health and wellness, philosophy, religion, travel—every aisle we pass is empty.

Vincent gives my hand a gentle tug, urging me to stop here.

I tug back. *Not yet.*

He huffs but follows without complaint. We weave through the stacks until we reach another set of stairs—narrower and darker and tucked way back in the corner. At the top of them is the attic. It's my favorite part of this bookstore. There's a little window bench tucked in the eaves where no one bothers you; you have to time it just right because, without some decent sunlight, it's far too dark to read without annihilating your eyesight.

I've always thought of it as a calm place.

But today, with Vincent behind me, I'm not calm. My whole body is humming with anticipation. I feel electric, like I'm one good spark away from combustion.

"Sometimes I come up here to read," I explain, feeling suddenly embarrassed as I stop in front of the window bracketed by shelves crammed with battered old paperbacks. This was a stupid idea. It's not romantic, and it's not very practical. We'd probably be way better off in Vincent's car. "It's a little dusty and, like, aggressively dark academia, but I feel weird sitting downstairs where the staff can see me. It always feels like they're mad at me for reading for hours without buying something. Which is stupid, because they're really nice here. But they never come up here. Nobody does. So, it's . . . private."

Vincent doesn't make fun of me or the weird little attic that I haunt.

Instead, he sets his sunflowers down on the bench under the window and advances toward me until my shoulders hit the shelf behind me. He crowds me in, blocking out the cool draft from the old, rain-streaked window and casting us both in soft shadows.

"Please tell me that you didn't bring me up here to read poetry," he says.

I feign a frown. "What else would we do?"

Vincent takes my face in his hands, but he doesn't kiss me right away. Not as urgently as I need to be kissed. He holds me so we're nose to nose, his warm breath coming in slow, steady puffs against my face while mine gets stuck somewhere in my chest. And, yeah, all right. I totally brought this upon myself by choosing the wrong moment to give him cheek. But this is just cruel.

"So *mean*," I whine.

"I thought you said I was too nice to you," Vincent counters. Then, after a moment of silence that tells me he's replaying our conversation, he asks, "Could you touch my hair again?"

I open my mouth to tease him, because I'm sure he's teasing me, but then I catch the little glint of self-consciousness in his face and remember when I ran my hands through his hair on his birthday. Vincent likes his hair played with. I don't have to be asked twice to indulge him: I reach up, thrust my fingers into the soft thicket of his hair, and graze my nails back and forth across his scalp, tugging softly and then soothing with gentle presses of my fingertips.

I watch, entranced, as his eyelids flutter and his throat bobs.

"How's that?"

He hums. And then he melts, exhaling a long and heavy breath like he's finally shrugged some unbearable weight off his shoulders. Seeing him so vulnerable and so relaxed makes me want to say things that I don't think I'm entirely ready to say.

So, I roll up onto my toes and kiss what I can reach. His chin. His jaw. The corner of his mouth.

"I missed you," I admit in a whisper. And then, because I'm nothing if not horrible at dealing with my emotions: "See what happens when you ask nicely?"

Vincent ducks his head and catches my lips with his.

And this time, it's not nice. Not at all.

Twenty-eight

I didn't realize Vincent was being gentle with me downstairs.

Not until right now.

Because there's nothing gentle about the scrape of his teeth against my bottom lip or the press of his thumb against my jaw, urging me to open wider for him. Downstairs, our kiss was all relief and elation and tender longing. I thought it might take the edge off. It hasn't. All we've done is broken the seal, and now when Vincent's tongue strokes into my mouth, it's like a gallon of gasoline tossed right into my bonfire.

Boom.

My hands fly up to grip Vincent's broad shoulders, white-knuckled as my nails dig into the slick fabric of his jacket. His hands slip inside the front of my cardigan and bracket my hips briefly, in a way that feels like we're at a middle school dance.

I giggle. And then he's smoothing his palms down over the curve of my ass and gripping me through my jeans so tightly that my giggle breaks off into a gasp.

I have the strangest sense that Vincent is thinking about

lifting me up against this bookshelf the way he did the night we first met. I'd let him. Happily. I'd love nothing more than to let my thighs fall open, hook my heels around the back of his legs, and have him press into me where I ache the worst. But it appears Vincent has other plans—plans that include sliding his hands up under the hem of my shirt and tracing a path from the hollow of my back to my stomach and then up over my ticklish rib cage.

The warm, rough drag of his touch against my bare skin makes me a fluttery, squirming mess of goose bumps and hitched breaths.

And then his fingertips brush the underwire of my bra, and I've never hated a piece of clothing so badly in my life. I want it gone. Burned. Buried. Out of the fucking way, so there's not a single thing blocking Vincent from doing whatever he so chooses.

All week, I've been haunted by the fact that he didn't touch my tits on his birthday. I saw the hunger in his eyes when he traced the neckline of my borrowed bodysuit. I heard the wobble in his voice when he complimented my tits, half teasing and half serious. But he was too worried about getting everything else right—figuring out the snaps on my bodysuit, making sure I was comfortable and slack-limbed, asking if he should stretch me out with one finger or two—and my poor breasts got the short end of the stick.

I arch against him, blindly hoping that he gets the message and won't step back to make some kind of smart-mouthed comment about *being greedy*, because we're well past that. I'm fucking desperate.

But he does step back.

Except, instead of tormenting me, he looks me up and down like he's trying to commit the sight of me to memory. It's too much. Like direct sunlight in my eyes or the blast of music through my headphones when I forget I had the volume all the way up.

"What?" I demand self-consciously.

Vincent squeezes hard against my ribs.

"I'm still so mad at you," he whispers, bending to catch my lips with his. "Can't fucking believe you thought I didn't want you."

I rake my fingers through his hair and pull him closer, trying to kiss him hard enough that he'll know how sorry I am. That he'll know I'll never doubt him again. I loop my arms tight around his neck and push off the bookshelf behind me, plastering myself against him so our knees knock and my tits are pancaked against his hard chest.

Vincent briefly tenses up at the contact, and then—with a low, primal rumble somewhere in the pit of his chest—he drops his hands back to my ass and grinds his hips into me.

Oh my God, he's hard.

I actually *whimper* against his mouth.

It must startle Vincent as much as it startles me, because he tears himself away.

"Sorry," he says. Then he laughs in that breathless, self-deprecating way and angles his hips toward the shadows like he could possibly hide the tent he's pitching in his jeans. "I got carried away. I like kissing you a little too much. We can slow down. Just give me a second."

I can't believe he's apologizing for getting an erection.

There's so much that I missed about Vincent—so much I

had to mourn when I thought I'd never see him again—that I'd sort of forgotten how close I'd come to getting my hands on his dick during his birthday party. I'm still bitter about that, I think, because my first thought is: *I'm going to help Vincent commit premeditated murder.*

My second thought is: *I'm not letting this opportunity pass me by twice.*

Despite the fact that Vincent has just gallantly proposed that we pump the brakes, I choose to floor it by reaching between us and palming the hard length of him through strained denim.

Vincent's eyes flash, and his breath catches.

"I thought of something else I want," he croaks.

God, I hope we're thinking the same thing.

"Tell me."

The words come out like I'm some kind of 1950s movie star who's taken a break from her hundredth cigarette of the day to goad her lover into confessing his feelings. Splotches of pink appear high on Vincent's cheeks. He blinks like he's coming out of a daze and cuts a look up and down the aisle, checking if the coast is clear. But even the confirmation that we're alone up here doesn't stop him from chewing on his kiss-swollen bottom lip.

"I feel like I shouldn't say it."

"Oh, come on. Don't tease me."

"Forget it, Kendall," he says on a groan, pitching forward and burying his face against my neck like he wants to hide. "Please forget it. I just want to kiss you. Kissing you is more than enough."

He tries to catch my mouth again.

I grab the collar of his jacket and twist it around my fist.

"*Vincent*. What do you want?"

"You. On your knees."

The admission, delivered in the ragged voice of a man fighting for his life, sends a shot of heat straight between my legs.

Giving a guy a blow job always seemed like something I'd eventually have to learn how to do—sort of like how I knew I'd eventually go to the DMV to get my driver's license, or eventually take a nice piece of clothing to a dry cleaner, or eventually file federal and state taxes. A rite of passage. A chore. Something adults just did because they had to. But I'd be lying if I said that I hadn't thought about it since meeting Vincent. Not my taxes—a blow job. I've wondered how he would taste. How he would feel in my mouth. What he'd look like standing above me and if he'd ask nicely or grip my hair and take what he wanted.

So, yes. I've thought about it. In great detail.

And as I let my eyes drop down to the erection straining against his fly, I realize I'm about to do something that will make Nina and Harper lose their fucking minds when they inevitably ask me how my weekend without them went.

Because yeah. I want me on my knees too.

I hook my fingers through Vincent's belt loops and twist us around until he's the one with his back to the bookshelves.

"Holiday," he says warily, "what are you . . ."

But he knows. He definitely knows, because when I reach up and start gathering my hair to twist it up in a low bun, he swallows hard and looks at me like he's been stranded in the desert for weeks and I'm an oasis. It's both deeply flattering and incredibly inconvenient, because I'm pretty sure the way my stomach just clenched means my underwear is going to be soaked.

"We're celebrating your birthday."

He lets out a strangled laugh. "Fuck off."

"That's my line. And keep your voice down."

Vincent watches with equal parts horror and wonder as I slide the hair tie off my wrist and then smooth my palm down the back of my head, checking that I haven't missed any pieces.

"I didn't mean *right now*, Kendall."

"Why not?" I challenge.

"This is a *bookstore*. People come here to *read*."

It's a bucket of ice water on my red-hot desire. Just because I let him eat me out at a party doesn't mean Vincent is totally cool with the threat of accidental exhibitionism. He's right. Our local bookstore definitely isn't the place for me to be so overcome with lust that I throw common sense to the wind. I need to respect his boundaries—and not wanting to get arrested for public indecency is a pretty reasonable one.

I won't take it personally if Vincent turns me down right now. I won't.

"Do you want me to stop? Or do you want—" I gesture vaguely at his crotch.

"No."

Brutal.

"That's fine!" I hold my palms up in concession. "Completely understandable. Yeah, no, I totally get it. Sorry, I just got a little carried away with—"

Vincent catches my chin between his thumb and forefinger.

"Holiday," he says very slowly. "*No*, I don't want you to stop." The naked desire in his eyes is enough to end me—because he wants this, wants my lips wrapped around his cock—but what really does me in is when he adds, solemnly, "But only if you want to."

I laugh in his face.

And then I drop to my knees.

"Tell me what to do."

Vincent blinks down at me with the kind of baffled expression I'm pretty sure he'd be sporting if I started reciting Chaucer in the original Middle English. I wait for him to catch up, fidgeting with one of the buttons on my cardigan impatiently, but it's like he's stuck, buffering, staring down at me with a half-open mouth and wide eyes. I sigh. It would appear that I'm on my own down here. That's fine. I can definitely get his jeans unbuttoned without a user manual. After that, we'll just have to take it one step at a time.

The sight of my hand approaching his crotch seems to jolt Vincent back to reality.

Lightning quick, he catches my wrist.

"Wait."

I'm fully convinced he's about to drag me back up to my feet and tell me he's changed his mind about the whole thing, but then he drops my hand and shrugs off his jacket. I wait patiently as he folds it up, crouches in front of me, and offers me his shoulders for balance while he tucks the makeshift pillow under my knees one at a time. They'll probably bruise anyway. I don't really care—but I'm touched that he does.

"Such a gentleman."

Vincent shakes his head as he stands to his full height again. "I'm not thinking like a gentleman right now."

"Tell me what you're thinking, then. What do you like? What feels good?"

A weak laugh rips out of his chest. "You could literally just look at me and I think I'd come in my pants, Holiday."

This earns him a blush and an eye roll.

"Seriously, though," I say, wiggling into a comfortable kneeling position, "give me some tips. I want to be your best."

"That . . . wouldn't be hard."

I look up at him, eyebrow arched in question. He looks down at me, fully blushing.

"I've only ever done this drunk," he admits. "It's usually not great."

"Like *this* specifically? A blow job?"

I'm proud of myself for saying the word in an even voice.

"Yeah," he says. Then, quieter: "But also . . . the rest of it."

I keep staring at him.

Vincent groans and scrubs his hands over his face, like he can't believe I'm making him say it.

"I've only had sex drunk, Kendall."

Unbelievable. For the better part of a month, I've agonized over the fact that I told him (in a horrible burst of panic-fueled oversharing after mauling him in the library) that I'd never kissed anyone sober. I still have to fight back a full-body cringe every time I think about the breathy, nervous pitch of my voice.

"And you decide to tell me this *now*?" I demand, thoroughly offended.

Vincent's lips twitch. "Well, it feels relevant."

"It was relevant a while ago!"

But even as I say that, I realize I'm not upset he hasn't told me until now. Not really.

"Hey, I wasn't totally sober on my birthday," Vincent says, echoing the argument I've already made for him in my head. "I had two shots before you got there. I might not have been *drunk*, but I wasn't technically sober, either, so what was I supposed to do? Tell you it was my first time eating pussy while slightly tipsy?"

I will not laugh.

And I will not be distracted by the way the word *pussy* out of his mouth makes me want to do unspeakable things to him.

"Well, I told you I'd never kissed anyone sober within, like, fifteen minutes of meeting you."

I don't mean to sound so petulant. I really don't. But I'm a little bit furious that I've spent so long beating myself up for another thing that—*surprise*—was only an issue in my own head. Once again, Vincent and I are more alike than I realized. And the way he's looking down at me, half amused and half affectionate, makes me feel stubbornly disgruntled about it.

"You also kissed me sober within fifteen minutes of meeting me," Vincent points out.

I try to frown. His lips twitch. Mine follow suit. Now he's full-on grinning.

Before I can crack, I say, "Fuck off."

And then I reach for the button of his jeans.

Twenty-nine

It's unspeakably satisfying to watch the smug smile get wiped clean off Vincent's face, but I only get a moment to soak in my victory.

Because after I unbutton his jeans, drag his zipper over the impressive curve of his erection, and tug his black boxers down, Vincent's dick springs free—and it's simultaneously the most glorious and most intimidating thing I've ever seen. Longer than my hand, nearly as thick as my wrist, pink at the tip and darker at the base, standing proudly at attention. I don't know why I didn't see this coming. I don't know why I wasn't mentally and emotionally prepared for the fact that *of course* this particular part of Vincent is just as big and beautiful as the rest of him.

Don't say it, I think. *Don't say it, don't say—*

"You have a ridiculously pretty dick, Vincent."

He makes a choked sound that I think is supposed to be a scoff.

"Shut up," he says. "Dicks are *not* pretty."

They're really not. Harper's been on Bumble since freshman year, so she's forwarded an extensive collection of unsolicited dick pics to our apartment group chat. I think she enjoys terrorizing us. She always waits and sends them when we're sitting in the same room as her, so she can watch our faces contort in horror and—sometimes—laughter, because dicks aren't exactly one of nature's most aesthetically pleasing creations.

But Vincent's is.

"I take back what I said before," I tell him. "You are perfect. And so is your dick."

Vincent doesn't have a comeback this time. He just hums in that *yeah, okay* way that tells me he thinks I'm full of shit. I think he's just being humble, but there's a blush crawling up the column of his neck that makes me wonder if he's genuinely flustered by the praise. I know how much courage it can take to let someone put their mouth on you like this. I remember how nervous I was for him to eat me out—to taste me, to smell me, to see everything up close. For all the bravado and big talk Vincent can throw around, he's also human, and he's never done this sober.

To break the ice, I ask, "Is this what you meant when you said you'd tutor me in human biology? Because if there's a pop quiz at the end of this—"

Vincent pinches his eyes closed. "Don't make me laugh right now, Kendall."

"—with one of those anatomical diagrams—"

"I'll be so mad at you."

"—and fill-in-the-blanks—"

"All right. You're done."

Vincent reaches for the front of his jeans to tuck himself back into his boxers.

"No, wait!" I grab his wrists. "I'm sorry, I'll stop. I promise."

Vincent is obviously strong enough to shake me off, but he lets me push his arms back to his sides. I offer him an apologetic smile. Then, still clasping his wrists, I lean in and bestow a soft, chaste kiss to the tip of his beautiful cock. I'm not expecting much as far as a reaction, but Vincent surprises me: his breath hitches. His thighs tense. His dick twitches. My jaw drops, because *holy shit, I did that*. When my eyes flicker up to Vincent's face, he smooths his expression over and tries to play it off like I didn't just make his whole body shudder with one little touch.

"You good?" I ask, so smug I sort of hate myself for it.

"I'm fantastic," he deadpans.

But when I reach out and rub the pad of my index finger over the head of his dick, featherlight and exploratory, Vincent drops the cool and collected facade, hissing like he's been burned.

"I barely touched you that time!"

"I'm *very* aware," he says through gritted teeth. "Forget foreplay, all right? I'm already so hard it hurts. You can just . . ."

He gestures meaningfully at his erection.

Because I sort of enjoy watching him squirm, I ask, "Just what?"

His eyes flash.

"Get it wet."

There's a slight edge to the command—a hint of snapped

patience—that makes me clench down on nothing. But I'm not about to let Vincent see just how much I liked that, because I know it'll go straight to his head. I'm trying to humble him here. So, I lean forward and lick one quick, gentle stripe up the length of him, from the root to the head. Above me, Vincent lets out a soft grunt but holds perfectly still. I lick another stripe, a little slower and with a little more pressure this time, cataloguing the feel of his hot skin against my tongue and praying my long-term memory stores this one safely.

And then, at last, I build up the nerve to wrap my hand around his shaft.

Immediately, I feel like a kid at a petting zoo. It's an utterly absurd metaphor that I will *not* think about right now, because the last thing I want to do to this sweet boy is laugh into his crotch while I'm holding his dick. Vincent covers my hand with his. I'm convinced he's read my mind and decided playtime is over, but then I realize he's not trying to stop me. He's showing me exactly how tight he wants me to grip him. It's tight. Really tight. And when he uses my hand to pump up and down his spit-slicked shaft in one slow stroke, it's rougher than I would've dared to.

I look up at him, wide-eyed. "Really?"

His lips twitch. "You won't break it, Holiday."

He says my last name like it's a term of endearment, and there—in the eaves of my favorite bookstore, with Vincent Knight's dick in my hand—I have a major life revelation.

I'm done being afraid of asking dumb questions or making a fool of myself. I refuse to let my fear of embarrassment cause me to miss out on something I really want to do, like getting white girl wasted with Nina and Harper, or writing my own romance novel, or giving the boy I'm completely obsessed with a blow job. This is me letting go of my nerves. This is me learning to put my pride aside, for both our sakes, and reminding myself that this is *Vincent*. He's frustratingly good at calling me out on my shit and pressing my buttons, but he's not going to purposefully make me feel ashamed for doing anything weird or wrong.

So, I grip him tight and pump my hand once, like he showed me.

Vincent's chest rumbles with a hum of approval.

"Attagirl."

When I cast a glance up, I find him watching me through heavy lashes with desire-drunk eyes. The unabashed appreciation on his face hits me like a shot of Nina's top-shelf tequila sliding down my throat and pooling low in my belly—all heat.

"I've thought about this a lot," I admit in a whisper. "About you."

"I think about you all the fucking time," Vincent says. "I had a chem exam yesterday, Kendall. I didn't even study. I couldn't. I kept thinking about how your voice gets all serious when you read poetry and how your nose scrunches up when you're mad at me and how you *taste*."

Something tightens in my chest.

It makes me bolder. I let my hand wander to the solid muscle of his thighs; to the tensed muscles of his abdominals; to the delicate trail of dark hair that starts just below his belly button and becomes a soft thicket around the base of his cock. He inhales sharply when my knuckles brush his balls. I'm briefly mortified that I've hurt him—because all I know about testicles is that you're not supposed to go around smacking them—but Vincent reaches out to stroke my hair.

"You're fine," he says. "Sorry. Just surprised me."

There's a vaguely pleading look in his eyes that compels me to reach my hand up again and, very gingerly, cup his balls in my palm. I roll them a little, testing their weight, and the muscles in Vincent's thighs and belly tighten up.

I didn't realize how responsive male anatomy could be. It's really feeding my ego.

"Is this okay?" I ask.

"It's so fucking good," Vincent says hoarsely. I think he realizes that I wasn't kidding about wanting some directions, because he adds, "Keep touching them just like that, or you can—you can put your mouth on them—"

"Like this?"

I lean in and swipe my tongue over his hot skin.

Vincent sucks in a sharp breath through his teeth.

"Okay, that's—that's a little too good."

He takes himself in one enormous hand, all golden tan and flushed pink skin and *veins*, and reaches out with the other to catch a piece of hair that's fallen out of my bun. He tucks it safely behind the shell of my ear, fingertips lingering for a moment. He's just . . . staring at me.

"What?" I demand.

He shakes his head. "You're so fucking beautiful."

My whole body warms with something decidedly different from lust. I'm pretty sure I'm blushing. I don't know what it says about me or how badly I'm down for Vincent that one compliment is capable of reducing me to a puddle of feelings.

"Less sweet talk, more action," I grumble.

Vincent arches an eyebrow and pumps himself with one slow stroke of his hand.

"You gonna give me somewhere to put this?"

Wherever you want to put it.

What I actually say is a very soft: "Uh-huh."

"Open your mouth for me, Holiday," Vincent whispers.

I don't have to be told twice. I brace both my palms flat against Vincent's thighs and tip my chin up so he can guide the head of his cock between my parted lips. His other hand cups my jaw like I'm made of glass as he rolls his hips forward, slow and careful, until he's filling my mouth. It's all so gentle, so fucking *nice*, that it makes me wild and needy and impatient. I take the initiative and press my head forward. His cock slides right over my tongue, just as hot and hard as the velvet-wrapped steel romance novels have always told me to expect—but nothing prepares me for how quickly I feel the weight of him hit the back of my throat or how sharply my body convulses at the intrusion.

I jerk back, Vincent's cock slipping out of my mouth, and splutter out a cough.

"Shit," he curses above me. "Don't hurt yourself."

He says it with more concern than genuine reprimand, but my face still heats.

"Didn't hurt," I grumble.

I clear my throat and scoot forward, determined to prove that I'm capable of doing this. I'm capable of being the heroine who drops to her knees, all wanton and seductive, and makes a man beg for relief. But Vincent palms the back of my head and knots his fingers into my hair, like he's prepared to pull me back as soon as I do something stupid again, and the fact that he's still sane enough right now to worry about me burns far worse than my gag reflex.

"I can do it," I snap. "I can. Just let me practice."

"I don't want to hurt you," Vincent snaps back.

"You won't."

The words come out easily because they're the truth. I trust him. But as Vincent shakes his head, I notice the persistent tremble of his abs and the sweat beading on his forehead. He's a rubber band pulled taut, ready to snap—and he'd choose to deprive himself of relief if it meant making sure I was comfortable.

"I'm not doing this for you," I blurt, throwing his words from earlier right back at him.

"Kendall—"

"I meant what I said. I've thought about this. About making you come. Like, a *lot*. I've wanted to do it for weeks. So let me. *Please*."

Vincent swallows hard and eases his grip on my hair.

"You're in charge, Holiday."

My heart hiccups.

"I'll go slow," I promise.

This time, I try to be patient and enjoy the process. I brace one hand on the back of Vincent's knee, denim rough against the hypersensitive pads of my fingers, and place open-mouthed kisses down the length of his cock. I try to make a mental note of the places where his breath catches or his knee buckles against my hand when I touch him.

When my tongue flicks over the tip, Vincent lets out a soft grunt.

"S'good right there," he says.

It feels natural—instinctual, really—to pop my thumb in my mouth before I reach for him again and trace slow, wet circles against the head of his cock. Vincent's eyes flutter shut, and his head falls back against the shelves behind him. I watch his face for a moment, appreciating the column of his throat, the sharp angles of his jaw, the way his face scrunches up in a way that walks the line between ecstasy and agony.

"Please," he rasps.

He's *begging*.

Apparently, this is a turn-on for me. I'm learning a lot about myself today.

Luckily for Vincent, I'm not about to deny him when he asks nicely.

Thirty

I blame the fact that we're hidden in the shadows and sur-rounded by stacks of books, only the patter of rain and Vin-cent's heavy pants to break up the silence. It's public, yes, but it's insulated. Intimate. Quiet and cozy and magical. There's really no other explanation for how bravely I tuck the head of his cock between my lips and suck.

Vincent's body arches, his eyelids fluttering and breath hitching.

"Kendall," he groans. Then, again: *"Please."*

I pull back. "I want to try again. Can I?"

Vincent needs no further elaboration or convincing. He immediately presses back against the bookshelf, bracing himself.

"Stick your tongue out for me, Holiday," he says. "Keep one hand around it—yeah, just like that—and put the rest in your mouth, okay? You can take it. I know you can. Show me."

I know it might just be wishful thinking on his part, but something about Vincent's confidence in me makes me feel like I've got this. It also makes the muscles in my lower abdomen tighten and tremble, but that's a me problem. We can sort out how needy and damp I am later.

This is about Vincent.

I keep one hand wrapped around the root as I take him into my mouth again, my tongue pressed flat to my bottom lip. This time, I'm prepared for the size of him. The easy slide, the slow stretch of my jaw, the sensation of being stuffed. My throat spasms a little, but I force myself to stay calm and hold still. To wait until the need for air outweighs the satisfaction I feel from listening to the noises Vincent is trying to stifle as he lets me do what I want to him.

Because I might be the one on my knees, but what Vincent said holds true.

I'm in charge.

"Good girl," Vincent whispers. "Knew you could do it. Holy shit."

When I reach up blindly to grip his hip, he responds obediently.

Vincent moves in shallow, tentative thrusts at first. He's still scared to hurt me, I think, and I can only take about half of him before it's too much—but we find a rhythm. He keeps his pace predictable, and I time my breathing. He gets a little more confident with each punch of his hips when he sees I can take what he's giving. I get more confident too, because he never gives me more than I've shown him I can handle. His fingers tighten in my hair again, but this time, he's not pulling me away. He's holding me steady. The surrender of control gives me the chance to slide my hands up his legs, over his thighs, and under the hem of his sweater. I'm a little bit obsessed with the way his stomach tenses and flexes under my palms.

I hum around him, just to test a theory, and his cock twitches hard in my mouth.

"Do that again," he rasps. "Fuck, Kendall. Exactly like that."

The praise, delivered with such raw and strangled reverence, makes me ache. I hum again, and it sort of dissolves into half-maniacal laughter, because *holy shit* I did not realize that I would enjoy this so much.

"You're evil," Vincent accuses, breathless but smiling.

I pull back, catching his cock in my hand when it slips out from between my lips.

"Do you want me to stop?" I ask.

"Don't you fucking dare."

With a deep breath, I take half of him into my mouth again and moan. Vincent's hips instinctively hitch forward to meet me, stuffing another inch of him down my throat, and I think he tries to apologize but it's a string of unintelligible words punctuated with an equal mix of curses and praise. My eyes water up like crazy, but it's worth it.

I do, tragically, still have to breathe. I tap Vincent's thigh twice to let him know. Tapping out is a pretty universal sign, but emotion still flares up in me when he immediately pulls back and gives me the space I need to gasp in air.

I lavish him with grateful kisses and sloppy strokes of my hand.

"We're such a good team," I say, my voice a little hoarse.

Vincent laughs weakly. "I think you're getting MVP."

"Ha! Most valuable player. See, I know sports stuff."

Vincent laughs.

I take him into my mouth again, and his laugh dovetails into a groan.

My knees are killing me, and my jaw is starting to ache, but there's something addictive about making him lose his composure. I realize now that maybe he wasn't lying when he said eating me out was a birthday gift. Because this? This is glorious—watching Vincent's flushed face crunch up with pleasure, a few pieces of his disheveled hair sticking to his sweat-damp forehead. Feeling his body twitch and writhe each time my thumb presses that spot on the underside of his shaft that makes his abdominals clench, one hand still resting on the back of my head perfectly still but the other hand clawing at the bookshelf behind him for dear life. Hearing his breath catch when I swallow around him or swipe my tongue over the delicate head of his cock.

"Holiday," he rasps.

It's a warning.

I make the executive decision to ignore it.

Vincent catches on to my intentions immediately. There's a shift in him. His hand tightens in my hair. His breathing becomes rougher. His thrusts get sloppier and harder, the rhythm stuttered and harder to predict. He gets a little bit selfish.

I'm going to make him come.

The realization makes me giddy—and a little bit greedy.

I hollow my cheeks and dig my nails into the muscular curve of his perfect butt. With a low and brutal groan, Vincent explodes in my mouth, hot and salty and slick against my tongue. It's new, for sure, but not unpleasant. Definitely not as gross as I always assumed it would be. But maybe that's because it's Vincent, and the satisfaction of making him come undone like this totally outweighs any squeamishness I have about bodily fluids.

I swallow what he's given me, sit back on my heels, and wipe the back of my hand across my mouth before I beam up at him with triumph.

"Told you I could do it," I say.

Maybe I'm a bit of a people pleaser too.

Vincent, still red-faced and breathing hard, shakes his head in disbelief.

"How was it?" I press. "Ten out of ten? Five stars?"

"Does a June wedding work for you?" he asks hoarsely.

I know he's joking. I totally know that. Also, I'm still not entirely convinced that the patriarchal, capitalist scam that is heterosexual marriage is for me. But that doesn't stop my stupid heart from lighting up like New Year's fireworks.

"I'll have to text my parents," I say more seriously than I mean to.

Vincent reaches down, hooks his hands under my armpits, and drags me up to my feet with the casually impressive strength of a Division I athlete. I'm glad for the assistance. Both of my feet have fallen asleep. Vincent swaps places with me, so I can lean back against the wall of bookshelves, and braces his hands on either side of me so I can clutch his forearms as I shift my weight back and forth from one leg to the other and try to get the blood flow back.

"How fucked are your knees?" he asks, assessing me for any damage.

"Surprisingly not too bad. Your jacket definitely helped."

He ducks in and kisses every inch of my face. Forehead. Cheeks. Chin. When his lips connect with the corner of my mouth, I turn away—because I imagine he'd rather not taste himself on me—but he lets out a low grunt of frustration, cups his hand around the back of my neck, and kisses me open-mouthed and insistent.

Because of course he does.

"Thank you," Vincent murmurs against my lips. "That was . . . yeah. Holy shit. Thank you."

"You're welcome," I snort. "And, um, happy belated birthday."

I smile at him, and he smiles at me, and then I glance down between us.

"You can probably put your dick away now," I add.

Vincent nods. "Good call."

He steps back to tuck himself into his pants. Then he reaches down to retrieve his black jacket, which is thoroughly wrinkled and smooshed down with two distinctly knee-shaped imprints. I have to clap a hand over my mouth so I don't laugh so loud the people down on the first floor of the bookstore hear me. Still, a snort manages to escape, and Vincent's head snaps up.

"I can't believe I did that," I whisper.

"I can't believe you did that either," he whispers back, the corner of his mouth quirking.

"In *public*. Like, I'm sorry, *what*? Who *am* I?"

Vincent shrugs on his jacket.

"My girl."

He says it like it's obvious. Like there's no other acceptable answer.

"Your girl?" I repeat, clearing my throat when my voice comes out a few octaves too high. "You haven't even taken me out on a date yet. What if I show up three hours late? Or chew with my mouth open? Or order the most expensive thing on the menu and bail before the check comes? Or talk about Maya Angelou the whole time?"

Vincent sees right through my deflection attempts.

"Then I'll learn to appreciate Maya Angelou. Besides, I like to think Starbucks was our first date, so we've already gotten that disaster out of the way."

"Oh, absolutely not," I say. "That can't be our first date."

"Why not? Because it went so badly?"

"Well, yeah. But also because it's *deeply* unromantic. I'm supposed to tell people that we had our first date at *Starbucks*? I'm sorry, that's so embarrassing."

"Would you rather tell people our first date was you attacking me in the library?"

My mouth falls open.

Vincent bites back a laugh.

"Oh, now *I* was the aggressor?" I demand. "That's funny— because I distinctly remember *someone* goading me to *prove it* and telling me he was all mine to practice on."

"And you *still* somehow missed the hint that I was into you."

My cheeks are on fire. I make a big show of turning around and huffing like I'm done with his shit and fully intend to leave him here in the attic of the bookstore while his dick softens. Vincent hooks his arm around my shoulder and tugs me into his chest, so I can press my nose into the soft cotton of his sweater and hide properly.

"Sorry," he says, sounding not at all sorry.

"Jerk," I grumble into his chest.

I wrap my arms around his middle. For the first time, the heat between us isn't the wildfire burn of lust. It's a little different. It's a slower and steadier kind of warmth. I hum. Vincent squeezes me a little tighter. It feels like he's acknowledging that he feels it too.

"I would invite you back to the house to hang out," he says, his voice hoarse in a way that tugs at my heartstrings, "but the whole team's coming over to watch the Lakers game, and I know I said I want to introduce you to everybody, and I *do*, but I'd really rather have you to myself right now. I just—" He exhales. "I really missed you."

I know exactly what he means. I want him all to myself right now.

And, by some great stroke of fate, I have that option. Harper and Nina couldn't have known that leaving me alone for three days would end up like this. They're going to lose their collective shit when they get back on Sunday afternoon and I sit them down for a PowerPoint presentation entitled *So You Left Your Roommate Unchaperoned*. Slide one: *I Borrowed Your Mug, Harper*. Slide two: *I Gave Vincent a Blow Job in Public (Oops?)*.

I press my face into the crook of Vincent's shoulder to muffle a giggle, but he definitely hears.

"You wanna share what's so funny?"

"I really do," I admit. "I think you're gonna appreciate this one."

He raises an eyebrow in challenge. "Hit me."

"My roommates are out of town this weekend."

Vincent's face splits into a grin. "Are you serious?"

I bite down on my bottom lip and nod. I want to grab him by his shirt and kiss him until both our legs give out and we're a tangle of limbs on the floor, fully desecrating this bookstore, but I think we've been pushed far enough out of our comfort zones today.

Instead, I say, "Take me home, Vincent."

Thirty-one

Vincent is parked four blocks from the bookstore, which is unfortunate, because it's still pouring rain when we make our walk of shame down to the first floor.

"You sure you don't want me to bring the car around?" he asks as I follow him to the front of the shop, studiously avoiding eye contact with the woman behind the cash register (because despite the fact that there's no way she heard what we were doing up in the attic, I have the horrible feeling that she'll see our rumpled hair and just *know*).

"We'll just walk fast," I say.

Vincent hums. "Someone's impatient."

My cheeks are warm when I shoot him a warning glare. Then he offers me his jacket as we pause just inside the door to brace ourselves, and now I'm fully blushing, because five minutes ago I was kneeling on that jacket and doing unspeakable things.

"I'll be fine," I insist. "It's just a little rain."

We make it a solid ten steps down the sidewalk before a particularly fat and heavy drop rolls off a window awning and smacks me straight in the eye. I gasp, swear like a sailor, and then huff in resignation. Vincent refrains from saying *I told you so* as he hands me his sunflowers to hold, shrugs off his jacket, and pulls me close to his side so he can drape it over both our heads.

By the time we get to his car—an unpretentious but very large SUV—we're both half soaked and breathless from giggling every time our hips bump.

Vincent holds the passenger door open until I've climbed in and folded my knees out of the way so he can shut it for me, then tucks his bouquet of sunflowers carefully on the back seat. While he waits for traffic to pass so he can duck around to the driver's side, I rub my frozen hands up and down my thighs to try to get some feeling back in my fingers. I scan the interior of the car. It's comfortably clean, just like Vincent's room . . . and now I'm thinking about what we did in his bed, which makes me think about what we just did in the bookstore, and suddenly I'm not cold anymore.

Vincent gets into the car, starts the engine, taps the button to turn my seat-heater on, and meets my eyes over the center console.

"Don't look at me like that, Holiday."

"Like what?" I ask.

"Like you want me to fuck you in my back seat."

I choke on a startled laugh. "I—that's—"

Exactly what I was thinking about.

"Look, Holiday, you know I'm down," he says, his smile just this side of cocky. "But do me a favor and let me make your first time a little more special than that."

I could tell Vincent about my teenage obsession with

Titanic, and that I'd be more than happy for him to play the young Leo DiCaprio to my Kate Winslet and fog up the windows of his car. I could tell him that my imagination can't decide if I want to straddle his lap and use his shoulders and my knees for leverage, or if I want him to move his sunflowers out of the way so he can drape me over the length of the seats and slot himself between my open thighs to use his weight to pin me down.

Instead of saying any of that, I fold my hands neatly in my lap.

"Fine," I say. "I'll behave."

Vincent looks like he doesn't believe me for a second, but he concedes by putting the car in Drive and pulling away from the curb.

Tragically, there's no third-act montage to get us to our long-awaited denouement as quickly as I'd like to. It's seven o'clock and pouring rain, so the downtown traffic is stop-and-go. It's torture. But Vincent connects his phone to the speakers and tells me to open a Spotify playlist Jabari made for him as a joke (it's just forty duplicates of "Kiss the Girl" from *The Little Mermaid* and one lone Frank Ocean song) and suddenly I don't mind that we can't cut right to the chase.

The worst thing about romance novels is that they always end.

There's a declaration, a kiss or a sex scene, and maybe—if I'm lucky—an epilogue that doesn't automatically relegate the female lead to the role of stay-at-home mom, even if she spent the whole novel pursuing other goals. Right now, it may feel like Vincent and I are driving off into the sunset, but there are no credits to roll and no curtains to close.

We still have so much ahead of us.

We have *everything* ahead of us.

It won't always be big moments between us. It'll be little ones, like this—the two of us in his car, passionately debating which route will get us to my apartment the quickest while Jabari's joke of a playlist loops in the background. And I want them. All the little moments. All the unimportant stuff suddenly feels so important.

"What are your parents like?" I blurt, mid–Frank Ocean.

Vincent casts me a quick glance, and it occurs to me that he probably didn't anticipate seeing me today, much less getting head in the back corner of a bookstore and being grilled on his family ten minutes later.

But then he answers, very confidently, "They're the best. Kind. Supportive. Just, like, ridiculously good human beings. My dad's in biomedical engineering—like surgical implants and prosthetics and stuff—and my mom used to teach fifth grade, but she started a ceramics studio with some friends a few years ago, so now they all make pottery full-time. They've got a whole business going."

Something in my chest tugs at the way his eyes light up.

"How'd they meet?" I ask.

"Basketball."

I arch an eyebrow. "They're both really fucking tall, aren't they?"

Vincent nods. "*Very*. You'll like them. And my mom will love you—not just because you're tall, I mean. You're just more artistic than me and my dad. She'll appreciate having someone on her team." His eyes cut over to me. "They're coming up here for our next home game, actually. You can meet them."

He adds, a beat later, "If you want to. We don't have to do a whole meet-the-family thing so soon—"

I cut in before he can overthink it. "I want to."

Because I do. Even though I know I'll be a nervous wreck and I'll probably humiliate myself trying to impress the wonderful people who gave Vincent life, I want to meet them, and I want to tell them, to their faces, what a good job they've done of raising their son.

Vincent beams at me and reaches across the console to grab my hand.

He keeps hold of it as we sit through the rain-soaked traffic, and as we circle my block for ages waiting for street parking to open up, and as I slide my key into the door and lead him into my dark apartment. It isn't until I trip over my backpack, which is still sitting where I shrugged it off in the front hall before I ran out to do my whole grand gesture thing, that Vincent lets go of my hand so I can smack on some lights.

And then it's just the two of us, standing there.

In my apartment.

Where I *live*.

Whatever sex goddess possessed me in the bookstore has been replaced by the spirit of a middle schooler at her first co-ed dance.

"Can I take your jacket?" I ask, because that seems like something a good host would do. It's not until I have it hooked over my arm that I remember the front hall closet is packed tight with women's outerwear and Nina's overflow collection of costumes she's stolen from theatrical productions. I shuffle back and forth for a moment before draping Vincent's jacket over the back of one of the kitchen stools. Vincent's lips twitch, but he refrains from commenting on my hospitality.

"Wanna give me the tour?" he suggests as we kick off our wet shoes.

"Sure. This is, um, the kitchen." I gesture toward what is very obviously a kitchen. "And this is our living room. Sorry about the mess. Nina was packing for this improv festival. Um. That's her room. And there's Harper's. And mine is—mine is over here."

"Lead the way," Vincent says with a nod.

I wish I'd cleaned up a little before I ran to the bookstore. My bed is made, and my floor was vacuumed in the last few days, but my desk is a certifiable disaster. The entire surface is covered in stacks of notebooks, loose pens, scented candles, skincare products, makeup, and one individually wrapped tampon that I want to drop-kick into orbit. The IKEA bookshelf wedged into the corner beside it is overflowing with an unholy mix of old YA, English literature from all centuries and genres, and romance novels with varying degrees of heat. Even the corkboard hung on the wall is littered with photos and ticket stubs and business cards.

Naturally, Vincent heads right for the mess.

I'm immediately self-conscious. It's only fair that he gets to snoop. I've used his bathroom. I've orgasmed in his bed. I can bite my tongue and let the boy look through my stuff. But that doesn't mean I'm not dying inside.

I peel off my rain-damp cardigan to deposit it in my laundry basket, dart over to my bed to fluff the pillows and pat down the lumps in my duvet, then shift my weight between my feet and search the room for something else to fuss with.

My eyes land on Vincent. His broad shoulders are bent over and his head is tilted to the side to read the spines of the books on my shelf. The sight of him like this—in my room, in a sweater and rain-speckled jeans and just his socks—is so domestic that it makes my heart clench. I want to wrap him up in a blanket and keep him here forever.

I wonder if he felt the same way when he had me in his room.

"Would you sit down?" Vincent says. "You're giving me secondhand anxiety."

I huff and sink into my desk chair, tucking my hands under my thighs so I can't fidget with them anymore. Vincent raises an eyebrow as if to ask, *You okay?*

"I've never had a boy over before," I admit. "Well, Perry Young came over to my house, but that was freshman year of high school, and my parents were there the whole time, so that doesn't really count."

Vincent snorts. "They chaperoned your date? Brutal."

"It wasn't a *date*. We were partners on a project for honors English. And I was a solid ten inches taller than him, so there was zero romantic interest from either end. There's a picture of us at senior prom up there—top left corner." I pop up to my feet and point it out on the corkboard. "We didn't go together. It was a group picture. But, look, I'm not even wearing heels."

Vincent brushes his fingertip over the toe of my ballet flat where it's peeking out from under my dark-blue dress, then taps the side of the picture with the boys in it.

"Which one was your date?" he asks.

I pick at an imaginary hangnail on my thumb. "I didn't have one."

It's like bumping an old bruise that I was sure had healed. But it hasn't. The girl in the picture might be smiling, but I know how miserable she was that night. I know the hunch of her shoulders, her ballet flats, her simple navy-blue dress— floor-length, sleeves, no sequins—were all to not draw any attention to herself. To make herself smaller. And I know college has changed me for the better, but it still aches when I look at pictures of that girl and wonder how much of her fear and pain still lingers with me. Sometimes I wonder if I'll ever get over the need to fade into the background.

"I wish we'd gone to high school together," Vincent says suddenly.

I don't know why that makes my chest squeeze and my eyes sting, but it does. *Me too*, I think. But then I try to conjure up the mental image of teenage Vincent, and all I'm getting is Troy Bolton gallivanting around the halls of East High in a well-choreographed musical number with a basketball under one arm.

"I bet you would've bullied me," I blurt. Vincent looks genuinely offended, so I add, "Not because you were a meat-head asshole jock or anything. I was an insufferable English nerd with, like, two friends."

"You still are, but I'm not bullying you for that, am I?"

He dodges my punch to his shoulder.

"All right, all right," he says. "Here. We'll make it even."

He reaches into the pocket of his jeans and pulls out his phone. Some scrolling and a few taps later, he's holding the screen up in my face. It's teenaged Vincent, his hair longer and his body about thirty pounds leaner. His tux is just a little too small for him too. But the boy in the photo is definitely a heartbreaker.

"Fuck off," I grumble. "That doesn't make me feel better."

"What do you mean? Look at my sleeves, Holiday. They don't even hit my wrists."

He's right. It's weirdly endearing.

"This is from your senior prom?" I ask.

"I was a sophomore, actually. I got asked by my team-mate's sister."

The girl in the photo next to him has braces and curled hair that looks like it's seen a little bit too much hairspray, but she's got the confident posture and pretty bone structure of a girl who probably enjoyed high school. I sort of hate her for it. And then I feel bad, because she's literally a child. Despite the definitely-borrowed-from-Mom stiletto heels she's wearing in the picture, she barely comes to Vincent's armpit.

"How tall were you?" I ask.

"In this picture? No idea. I hit six-four freshman year, though. Great for my basketball career. Horrible for clothing."

I nod solemnly. "Pants were a nightmare."

"See?" Vincent says, tucking his phone away. "We proba-bly would've been friends."

I shake my head. "No way. That hair and those puppy dog eyes? *And* you were taller than me? You would've ruined my life, Vincent."

He stares at me a moment, his eyes twinkling like he wants to say something, but he just shakes his head and turns back to my bookshelf. He slides a paperback off my shelf to examine the cover. It's an Oscar Wilde play. If Vincent noticed that it was sandwiched next to a battered copy of *Twilight*, he doesn't comment on it.

"You're not going to start reading that to me, are you?" I ask.

"You'd like that, wouldn't you?" Vincent murmurs. He slides the book back onto my shelf before tossing me a look. "I could whip out the Shel Silverstein for you, if you're still interested."

"Did you really memorize one of his poems?"

"No."

"Oh."

"I memorized three."

I let out a bark of shocked laughter. "Why would you do that?"

He smiles. "Because I knew you'd laugh just like that."

I'm going to say absolutely ridiculous things—mushy, sentimental things that will probably terrify him—so instead of letting myself open my stupid mouth, I step forward and cup Vincent's face in my hands. He stands still and lets me. His eyelids flutter shut as I run my thumbs up and down, tracing from his chin to the corners of his mouth to the faintly freckled skin over his nose and cheekbones. There's some dark scruff on his jaw. I wonder what it would feel like against the insides of my thighs.

I drop my arms to my sides. Vincent takes a breath before he opens his eyes.

"My shift at the library starts in three hours," I blurt.

He arches an eyebrow. "You're seriously still thinking about going?"

"No. I just—" I say. "I'm trying to figure out what I'm supposed to tell my supervisor."

"That you're busy making out with me," Vincent says, like it's obvious.

"Oh? Is that all we're doing?"

Vincent's eyes flash with surprise, and then his tongue darts out to wet his bottom lip. The step he takes toward me is hungry. Primal. I'm suddenly and violently reminded of how much I enjoyed having his cock in my mouth.

"I thought you said you wanted to take it slow," I croak.

Vincent smiles and shakes his head. "I can't move slow with you, Holiday. But we don't have to do anything else tonight. We can go to the house and you can meet my team-mates, if you want. Or we could go to dinner just the two of us, and we can talk about our parents and our favorite songs and whatever else we want to."

There he goes again, being nice.

But I don't want to move slow—not when I've spent my whole life moving slow. I know everyone runs the marathon that is life at their own pace, and there's nothing wrong with the fact that I've needed a longer warm-up than a lot of people my age . . . or that I'm about to take off sprinting when there are women a decade older than me who are still stretching. It's not a race. It's just a circular track we all get to share. I won't regret listening to my gut and waiting to feel ready.

I'm ready now. Too ready, perhaps.

I grab the hem of my shirt and peel it up and over my head.

Thirty-two

In my head, taking off my shirt was a smooth and seductive move.

In practice, the collar catches on my nose, and my right elbow flails and knocks into something very solid. I let out a sharp curse as a dull tingle shoots up and down my arm—*funny bone*—and Vincent grunts, because the hard object I just elbowed was definitely his chin.

"Sorry! Oh my God, I'm *so* sorry."

Vincent lets out a slightly pained laugh.

"Are you okay?" I ask, still stuck inside my upturned shirt.

"I'm fine. You've got a killer right hook, though."

This is humiliating. I don't think I want to take my shirt off anymore, because I'm pretty sure I can't look Vincent in the eye, but I also don't want to put it back on, because that means I'll have to admit that I really suck at this whole romance thing.

Maybe, if I'm lucky, I think, *I'll just die right now.*

Vincent sighs. "Come out of there, Holiday."

He grabs my shirt and helps me wrangle it off. My hair crackles with static and goes everywhere. I brush it back into place, take a bolstering breath, and look up to find Vincent staring at my chest with that same frozen expression I've decided to call his buffering face. I can't tell if this is a good or a bad thing. My bra is beige. No lace. No nonsense. I also have lines across my stomach where my jeans were cutting into me earlier, but I'm not worried about any of that. Vincent isn't going to change his mind about me because of some boring underwear and weird jeans indents.

Still, I wish he'd stop *staring*.

"What?" I snap.

"Your tits look fucking phenomenal."

I'm so mad that I laugh. "You're never going to let me live that down, are you?"

"Absolutely not."

"Any other compliments you want to shower me with before I kick you out?"

Vincent frowns pensively and reaches a hand out to stroke his fingers through my tangled hair. His palm settles flat against the side of my neck. The touch sends a bolt of electricity down my body—sort of like hitting a funny bone, but in a good way.

"You're beautiful," Vincent tells me. "You have the best laugh. You're one of the smartest people I've ever met. And you smell so *good*. Why do you always smell this good?"

"It's probably my three-in-one soap."

"Shut up."

With his hand still anchored against my neck, Vincent pulls me close and brings his smiling mouth down to meet mine. He kisses me slowly. Lazily. Like we have all the time in the world. And I appreciate the tenderness—I really do—but the second I taste him, everything I felt in the attic of the bookstore comes rushing back to knock me off my feet like a fifteen-foot wave.

I pull back to say, with feeling, "I am *so* sorry I elbowed you."

Vincent shakes his head. "It's fine."

"Are you sure I didn't break your jaw or something?"

"Does my jaw feel broken to you?"

He slots his mouth over mine again, and no, it's definitely not the kiss of an injured man. I let out a sound that *might* be a moan and flatten my chest against his. Vincent's sweater is impossibly soft against the bare skin of my stomach, which just confirms that my kink for men in sweaters is still very much alive and kicking.

I pull back and blink at him, dazed.

"Please." I'm not even sure what I'm begging for.

"Patience." Vincent kisses the tip of my nose.

Maybe he has a point. This isn't something to rush. I should probably savor it, and then I take a deep breath and try to enjoy the slow burn of his mouth tracing over the curve of my jaw, down the column of my neck, and across my collarbone. His hands slide up the sides of my rib cage, calluses tickling places that never get touched, until he reaches the underwire of my stupid, inconvenient bra. Before I can offer to burn it, Vincent hooks two fingers into one cup, tugs it down over my tit, and ducks his head to take my nipple into his mouth.

"Yeah," I gasp. "I'm definitely missing my shift."

Vincent hums in a way I take to mean, *You think?* The vibration against my breast sends goose bumps up and down my arms. I laugh, a bit erratically, as my brain—without prompting—composes a draft of the email I could send my supervisor.

Dear Margie, I won't be able to come to work tonight. Vincent Knight has my tit in his mouth. Sincere apologies! Best, Kendall.

"What's so funny?" Vincent asks.

"It tickles when you do that."

He hums again, drawing a high-pitched squeal out of me, then stands up straight with a triumphant smile that knocks the breath out of me.

"Can I take this off?" he asks, tugging my bra strap.

"You don't want me to do it? I could aim for your nose this time."

"I'll pass, thanks."

I concede and hold my arms out at my sides. Vincent reaches around my back, unclasps my bra, and lets it fall to the floor between us. I'm naked from the waist up. It's *weird*. All I can do is hold my breath and watch Vincent's dark eyes roam my bare skin like he's trying to memorize the sight of me. It's suddenly too bright in my room. And too cold—my nipples are, like, *aggressively* hard.

"What's wrong?" Vincent asks.

"It's just . . ." *It's weird*, I think. What I say is, "It's just scary."

His face goes soft. *"Kendall."*

"What?" I demand, folding my arms over my chest and then dropping them when Vincent's eyes go wide at the sight of my pushed-up breasts. "It is! Not like *scary* scary, but . . . I don't know. It's *intimidating*, okay? Nobody ever sees my boobs."

"Well, that's a travesty. You're a work of art."

I roll my eyes.

"Holiday," Vincent says, voice low, "I mean what I say to you."

Elizabeth Barrett Browning taught me that actions are louder than words.

When Vincent's wide palms smooth over my breasts to cup them and test their weight, I think I finally agree with her, because Vincent touches me like he means it. Like the invitation to touch me is a fucking honor, and he's prepared to do whatever I ask of him for the privilege to *keep* touching me. I shiver when Vincent brushes his thumbs over my nipples, dark eyes lifting to watch my face as he pinches them into tight peaks—softly, first, and then just enough to draw a keening whine out of my lips.

"Too much?" he asks.

I shake my head feverishly. *Not enough*.

Vincent takes his sweet time with his hands and his mouth, dancing back and forth between being cautiously delicate, like I'm a glass artifact he can't afford to break, and rough, like he's a little bit mad that the universe has kept my tits from him for this long.

"Okay," I squeak. "That's—that's good."

Vincent has mercy on me. "Bed?"

"Yes, please."

He grabs my hips and lifts me, like I weigh nothing, up onto the edge of my mattress. I have one of those semilofted beds you sort of have to hop up and launch yourself onto—standard college furniture—but Vincent is tall enough that when he stands between my knees, our hips are perfectly lined up. I look up at him, my mouth open to point out how well we always fit together, but he's already smiling at me like he knows exactly what I'm thinking.

We're the perfect size for each other.

"I really, really want you," I whisper.

"Good," he whispers back. "Because I'm all yours."

I really do love when we're on the same page.

Vincent's hands settle on my thighs and give them a squeeze.

"You're in charge, Holiday. What's next?"

"Take this off," I say, plucking at the front of his sweater.

Vincent's lips twitch. "Yes, ma'am."

He reaches one hand behind his back, grabs a fistful of buttery-soft material between his shoulder blades, and pulls the whole thing up and over his head in one swift tug. I don't have time to brood about how much smoother that was than my attempt at undressing because the sight of his naked chest knocks my train of thought right off the rails.

I've never seen him shirtless before. Not in person, at least. There's a video of Vincent taking his jersey off to swap it out with another one right before one of last season's games (a video that I may or may not have saved to a private YouTube playlist that I will take to my grave). He was sweat-soaked and pale under the harsh arena lights, and he was magnificent. It was horrible. This is somehow worse, because all that beautifully carved torso is now standing between my legs while I'm sitting on my bed, and my little overloaded brain can't decide what it wants to do with him first.

I settle for pressing my palms flat against his pectorals.

Vincent shudders.

"Sorry," I blurt. "Are my hands cold?"

"No, you're good. It feels nice to have them on me."

His quiet admission makes me lean forward and press my lips to his sternum. That familiar scent of him—warmth, spice, laundry detergent undercut with deodorant—tickles my nose. My hands slide down to his hips to tug him a little bit closer, so I can kiss looping trails up to his collarbone and over his broad shoulders. *Trapezius*, I think as I press my open mouth to the crook of his shoulder and drag my tongue over his skin.

"Are you trying to give me hickeys, Holiday?" Vincent rasps.

"Maybe," I murmur. "You want one?"

He lets out a sound that's half groan and half laugh.

"I thought you said you'd behave."

"Yeah, but it's really not fair, is it?" I sit back. "You've had your fun. I'm dying over here."

He offers me a mock-sympathetic pout. "Poor thing."

My only comeback is to shove my hand into his jeans and beneath the waistband of his boxers. He's already hard, but when I wrap my hand around him, he twitches and swells in my palm.

"All right, joke's over," Vincent croaks. "I need to be inside you."

"Thank you." *About fucking time.*

Vincent steps back to push his jeans and black boxers down his hips. His phone tumbles out of his pocket and lands on my carpeted floor with a muted thud, followed by the second, softer thud of a slim black leather wallet. Vincent sighs, bends down to retrieve his fallen phone, and sets it on my bedside table. Then he reaches for his wallet.

His face suddenly falls. *"Shit."*

"What?"

Vincent shakes his head in disbelief and devastation. "I don't have a condom. *Please* tell me you have one somewhere in this apartment, Kendall, because I can't walk into CVS like this. I mean, I will if I have to, but—*shit*. I really didn't expect this. I had no idea I'd even *see* you today—"

Later, I'll let myself laugh at the mental image of Vincent Knight sporting the most glaringly obvious erection that the CVS on the corner of campus has ever seen while he shoots death glares at everyone else using self-checkout. But right now, my brain is a little too preoccupied with the realization that Nina is the greatest whore best friend a girl could ask for.

"My bookshelf. Check my bookshelf. There's a paperback on the second shelf from the top. Black spine with the red cursive. No, to the right—that one!"

Vincent plucks the book off the shelf and examines the cover.

"Bedding His Secretary?" he reads in a monotone.

"Don't. Say. Anything."

Vincent looks back and forth between me and my porn.

"Do you want me to read it to you?" His smile is teasing, but there's an acceptance in his eyes that tells me he's very much down.

I tuck the idea away for later.

"Just toss it to me," I say, clapping my hands out in front of me.

Vincent lobs the book to me underhanded. It soars across my bedroom in the gentlest and most graceful arc, perfectly aimed into my waiting hands. I somehow manage to let it slip through my fingers. It lands hard against the side of my knee.

"Ow. Jesus."

"You going out for the softball team?"

"Fuck off," I grumble, gripping the paperback by its spine and shaking it over my duvet.

Out tumbles the "bookmark" that Nina gave me for my birthday last year: a row of condoms in leopard print foil. I pluck them up and examine the back of the packets.

"We're good," I announce, holding them aloft like I've got a winning lottery ticket. "We're fine. They don't expire for another two years."

Vincent snatches them out of my hand, rips one off the end of the row, and tears open the corner of the packet with his teeth.

"We'll be lucky if these last us two days," he says. "You want me to put this on myself?"

It's less of a challenge and more of an open invitation. I hold out a hand, and he passes me the opened packet and sits back on his heels so I can demonstrate how much I remember from high school sex ed. The condom is neon pink, because of course Nina would give me neon pink condoms in leopard print foil. I pinch the tip. Roll it down. Make absolutely certain my fingernails don't puncture the ultrathin latex.

"Ta-da," I announce with a proud flourish.

"Nicely done, Holiday."

"All that human biology tutoring really paid off."

He rolls his eyes. "Get on your back."

My head hits my stack of decorative pillows with a soft whoosh. As soon as I'm sprawled across the duvet, I become hyperaware of the fact that I'm completely topless and Vincent's got nothing but a neon pink condom on. My heart kicks hard against my rib cage. I briefly consider how embarrassing it would be to go into cardiac arrest right now.

"Is this a pop quiz?" I ask.

It's a joke, of course, but my voice comes out all wobbly and high-pitched. Vincent must realize that I'm using humor as a defense mechanism again because he shakes his head solemnly.

"No pop quiz. No test. No games."

"Oh." I swallow. "Good."

He pats my hip. "Lift up for me."

I press my knees into the mattress and push myself into a half-bridge. Vincent peels my jeans down over my thighs. I flop back down and let him guide one ankle and then the other out of my pants legs. I open my mouth to ask if he's forgotten my underwear, but then he runs his hands back up the length of my legs—his palms mapping every curve, freckle, patch of cellulite, stretch mark, and spot I missed shaving—before he hooks his fingers around the waistband of my panties and pulls them off.

And then, *finally*, we're both naked.

Took us long enough.

Thirty-three

Vincent makes a point of setting my underwear on my bed-side table—where we won't lose it this time around—before he climbs up onto my mattress with me.

The rustle of my duvet, the creak of the bed frame, and the patter of the rain on my windows are *almost* loud enough to drown out my heavy breathing. Almost. I swallow hard as I let my thighs fall open so Vincent can slot himself between them, his hands braced against the mattress on either side of my shoulders. My skin sparks with electricity everywhere our skin brushes, his body radiating warmth that melts right through me. And as I stare up at Vincent, our faces close enough that I could count the faint freckles across the bridge of his nose if he had the patience for it, the gravity of the situation settles heavy on my shoulders.

Virginity is a social construct.

I know that. I know that nothing about a boy putting his penis inside me is going to fundamentally alter me as a person. It's *really* not a big deal.

But, to me, it kind of is.

I'm soft. I'm sentimental. I'm a romantic. And I want to hate myself for it, but then I remember what Nina told me: I'm allowed to feel this way. I'm allowed to be shaky with nerves and giddy with excitement in equal measures, and I'm allowed to feel the weight of this moment with my whole chest.

"I don't really know what I'm doing," I warn Vincent, "so please don't roast me if I do something weird."

"No promises."

I smack his bicep. His lovely, sculpted bicep.

He arches an eyebrow. "Is that the hardest you can hit?"

"Keep making fun of me and you'll find out, Knight."

Vincent brings his mouth to my ear and whispers, "Joke's on you. I like it rough."

But he's not rough. He's heartbreakingly gentle as he rocks forward, the muscle in his forearms flexing like a live-action sculpture out of Greek antiquity. My eyes lock on his left wrist—the one that was in a brace and a sling the night we met—and my heart hiccups. *This is it.*

My little moment to myself is interrupted when Vincent shifts his arms again, trying to find better purchase on my too-soft mattress, and catches a strand of my hair where it's splayed out around my head.

"Ow," I hiss. "Hair, hair, hair."

"Shit, sorry."

Vincent quickly lifts the offending hand and presses it flat against the wall above me instead. We lock eyes. We're both a little bit mortified, but as soon as we see it's mutual, we're snorting and smothering our laughter like kids in the back of a classroom.

"I swear I know what I'm doing," Vincent says.

"Sure, sure. You seem like you're a real—"

He pulls his hand off the wall, reaches down between us, and plunges two fingers inside me.

"Cheap," I gasp.

I think Vincent tries to give me that smug smile he always wears when he manages to prove me wrong, but his eyelids flutter as he wiggles his fingers against tensed muscles and then works them in and out in slow, seeking strokes.

"Fuck, Kendall," he curses. "How are you this wet?"

"Now you're fishing for compliments," I say hoarsely.

Vincent keeps his eyes on my face as he withdraws his fingers, leaving me suddenly and achingly empty. Thankfully, he's quick to wrap one hand around his erection and line our hips up. I feel the gentle but insistent nudge of him between my legs. And then it happens: the head of Vincent's cock nudges just inside me.

My face scrunches up against my will.

"Give me a status update, Holiday."

My only response is a very earnest, *"Oof."*

Vincent winces. "You're too tight. I should've warmed you up."

"I don't think I can get much more warmed up," I admit with a pinched laugh. "Really. I promise. It's just—it's just, like, the initial nerves. I'll get over it." That's how it always works in romance novels, at least. An initial burn that fades. A pain that becomes pleasure. God, I really hope that's not just another trope that doesn't apply to real life. "You can keep going. Seriously. I want to know what it feels like when you're all the way in."

Vincent doesn't look totally sold.

"Stop me if it's too much?"

"All right, big boy," I say with a roll of my eyes, "you're not *that* massive."

But he kind of is, and my attitude gets a swift adjustment when he accepts the gauntlet I've thrown down and sinks another two inches inside me. I hiss in a breath through my teeth and clutch blindly at my sheets.

"Breathe, Kendall."

I meet his eyes and do as I'm told. Two deep, slow, measured breaths. In, out. And again.

He nods. "Good girl."

Vincent knows what that does to me—and he must feel the way my abdomen tightens up, because his eyelids flutter again and color appears high on his cheeks. He looks feverish. Wild. I brace my hands on his shoulders and give them a squeeze, urging him on, and Vincent resumes his slow push inside me, filling me until I'm sure I can't take anymore—but I do. With one last press of his hips, Vincent sinks inside me right to the hilt. We both groan. My muscles flutter and contract, trying to adjust to the stretch of him. Vincent lets out a ragged laugh.

"Don't do that," he says under his breath. "Please. I won't last long."

"M'sorry. Not doing it on purpose."

I'm really not. I've never felt so full. It's a new sensation, but it's not *painful*. Not like one of those scenes in a historical romance where the wedding night ends in tears and blood-speckled bedsheets. I'm a modern woman, thank fuck, and I've had fingers (my own and Vincent's) inside me. But when he moves—just one slow, experimental thrust—there's way too much friction. Maybe he really is too big. Maybe I'm just too tensed up. Whatever the cause, there's a sharp sting where our bodies are joined. My entire body goes rigid with panic.

What if I can't do this? What if, even though my brain is fully ready for this, my body hasn't gotten the memo? What if I've somehow ruined everything?

"Wait," I gasp. "It's—it's too much."

Vincent goes still. I'm briefly horrified that he's going to do what he did back at the bookstore and shut this down at the first sign of even the slightest bit of discomfort on my part, so I dig my fingernails into his shoulders until his skin goes white.

"Kendall," he says very calmly, "I'm not going anywhere."

"Okay," I squeak.

"What do you need?"

"Huh?"

"What can I do? Can I touch you?"

"Y-yeah, of course."

"I'm gonna rub your clit, okay?"

"Mm-hmm."

Vincent shifts his weight onto one arm and reaches the other down between us to trace two fingertips in exploratory circles—slower and softer at first and then in faster and steadier strokes when I hum to let him know he's found the perfect spot. And *oh*, that's nice. I sigh beneath him, my limbs slowly going slack and a content sigh leaving my body. I squeeze my eyes shut (because sometimes, when I'm trying to get myself off, it helps me concentrate) but then I think better of it. I want to stay present. I want to remember that I'm not doing this alone. Vincent is better than any fantasy I'd be able to conjure up in my head.

"Talk to me," I plead.

Vincent's eyebrows pinch, and for a moment I'm worried I'm going to have to explain myself, but then he says, "I'm assuming now is a bad time to recite that Shel Silverstein?"

I can't help it. I toss my head back and laugh.

The movement makes my muscles clamp down around his cock, and it's still a little too much, but it doesn't sting this time. Vincent grins, then takes advantage of my bared neck and kisses a line from my collarbone to my jaw and back down again.

"I don't think I can remember the words right now, actually," he admits against my shoulder. "I'm pretty sure I'm blacking out. You feel so fucking good, Kendall. I'm so sorry I'm hurting you. We can take as much time as you need, okay? Don't worry about me. It'll probably take a lot more for me to come the second time, anyway, so all that matters is making it good for you."

The words melt me.

And he means them, too, because they're not delivered like some big chivalrous speech. He's trembling over me, his left arm and abs straining with the effort to hold still while his right hand rubs steady patterns against my clit. His expression is one of intense and single-minded focus. Like this is the most important task in the world. Like his greatest—and perhaps only—aspiration in life is to get me off so I can enjoy this too.

There's an odd twist in the pit of my stomach that has nothing to do with the joining of our bodies. I'm not entirely sure how to process it, so I do something a little silly: I push up off the bed just enough to press a soft kiss to the tip of his nose.

"You're doing great," I tell him.

Vincent ducks his head and laughs like a man in pain.

The movement makes him rock against me. This time, it's less of a sting and more of a blunt ache. I think I might like it. I think I might want a little bit more of it.

"You can move now," I whisper.

Vincent lifts his head and searches my face. "Yeah?"

"Oh, yeah."

He gives me the gentlest rock of his hips, at first. I hum in encouragement, but his strokes remain shallow and tentative.

"Is it okay for you?" I blurt.

Vincent immediately loses his rhythm. "What?"

"Does it feel good? For you, I mean."

Just because I'm the one losing my virginity doesn't mean I've forgotten that Vincent told me he's never done this sober. He deserves to be checked in with too.

"How do you *think* it feels?" he asks.

My eyes narrow. "Is that a rhetorical question?"

Vincent pulls almost all the way out of me, the head of his cock tugging at my entrance, before plunging in again. *Yep. Okay. Rhetorical question.* We both groan. Vincent repeats the motion for a second time, then a third. On the fourth thrust, I lift my head off my pillows to watch his cock disappear inside me and almost choke on my own breath at the sight.

I reach out to touch the place where we're joined. Vincent looks down too and groans. I can't tell if it's because my fingertips brush his cock or if he's just as turned on by the sight of us as I am. Everything feels hot and swollen and slick. At first, I think Nina's hot pink condom must be lubricated or something, but then I realize it's not the condom. It's *me*. Vincent wasn't kidding: I'm soaking wet. It makes me strangely proud of myself.

I just needed to relax. I just needed to take my time. Vincent and I will figure this thing out together, even if we have to stumble and laugh our way through it.

At the thought, I feel myself loosen up.

I think I get why Vincent is a human biology major now. Shit's cool.

"Little bit harder," I request.

Vincent arches an eyebrow and snaps his hips once, roughly.

He's joking. I'm not.

"That," I gasp. "Fuck. Do that."

Vincent ducks his head into the crook of my neck and takes a deep breath, like he's trying to collect himself. Then he starts pumping into me, bottoming out on each stroke and stretching me until I'm *full*. So full it brings tears to my eyes. When his rhythm picks up speed, it's all I can do to hold my thighs wide apart and clutch at his shoulders, his waist, his stupidly muscular ass, and try to keep my eyes from rolling back into my head.

"More," I urge, tilting my hips up to meet each thrust.

I know I'm whining. I can't help it.

"Jesus Christ, Holiday," he groans. "You're out of your mind."

I manage a laugh. "Thought you—liked it—rough."

Vincent hooks one hand under my knee, wraps my leg

around his waist, and drives into me like a man with a point to make.

And it's so good. It's *so* fucking good. Better than I thought it would be, because I've fantasized about this. About Vincent. I've spent a solid month imagining him and myself as the stars of every romance novel I could get my hands on—soft and sweet, hot and heavy, dark and deliciously depraved. Every dynamic. Every trope. Every position. But this is different. This is *more*. My imagination couldn't make a composite picture: the heat of his breath on my forehead; the warm, slick slide of our thighs; the familiar hum of his voice, his grunts and muttered curses reverberating in my bones and drawing the muscles in my stomach tighter and tighter.

Oh, I am in trouble.

I'm going to say ridiculous things.

Things like *harder* or *more* or *literally just crush me, Vincent*.

"You're making faces," he tells me. "Talk to me."

"You can't make fun of me," I mutter.

"I won't." Vincent's pace slows. "I promise. Give me your worst."

He shifts his weight onto one arm. The new angle makes me squeeze my eyes shut. It's *glorious*. So glorious that it takes me a second to register his lips on my cheek, my nose, my eyelids. I tilt my head up blindly, and Vincent puts his lips on mine without being asked to. It gives me a burst of courage.

"You're so big," I groan against his mouth.

"You're so warm," he shoots back. "And so fucking wet."

"Wet for you. Oh my God, I'm sorry. That was so bad."

"You're a bad girl, huh?"

A laugh rips out of my mouth. "What was *that*?"

Vincent laughs, too, his eyes twinkling with self-deprecation and affection.

"I don't know. Not very poetic of me, huh? Maybe I need some more tutoring."

"I'm not sure if I'll be much help. I mean, fuck, I'm in the honors English program—I'm supposed to be the articulate one here—and I'm like ten seconds away from going, *Oh, Vincent, hold me down and make me take it.*" Vincent makes a choked sound. I power on. "See? *Batshit.* People don't really talk like this during sex, do they? That's just in bad erotica."

I'm joking, of course.

But then Vincent's hand comes down on my shoulder, his thumb pressing hard against my collarbone and effectively pinning me to the bed, and it's not a joke anymore.

"Be a good girl for me, Kendall," he says without a drop of humor, "and take it."

Thirty-four

I try to laugh.

Really, that's what I intend to do. But somehow the sound that bubbles up in my throat is the lowest and loudest moan I've ever uttered. Vincent doesn't tease me. His eyes stay on mine, patient and dark with hunger, as he gives me a moment to get over my embarrassment. I wrap a hand around his wrist—the one pinning me to the mattress—and nod.

When he moves again, it's not slow, or shallow, or gentle.

"Look at you," Vincent murmurs. "So good for me. Taking all of it. Knew you could."

Maybe if he weren't buried inside me to the hilt, and maybe if he were laughing at me, I'd have the strength to remind him how cheap I find dirty talk. But I must be off my game, because everything coming out of Vincent's mouth is starting to sound like poetry.

More, I think deliriously. *Say more.*

Vincent reads me like an open book.

"Messy girl," he says. "Who made you this wet? Who's this for?"

"You," I gasp.

"Whose pussy is this, huh?"

I sob out a laugh. "Mine."

Vincent's hand leaves my shoulder to grip my chin, squeezing my cheeks just hard enough that my lips are forced into an open-mouthed pout.

There's laughter in his eyes. He looks utterly furious about it.

"You and your smart—fucking—mouth." He punctuates each word with a snap of his hips that makes my eyelids flutter and my breath catch. Then he ducks his head and kisses me so hard I see stars. "I set myself up for that one. But nicely played."

"Thank you," I squeak. "Could you please—"

I don't have to finish the thought.

Vincent shifts his weight on one arm again and reaches down between us. He presses his palm down just below the soft curve of my lower stomach and grinds the pad of his thumb on my clit. I return the favor by clenching in that way that made him gasp earlier, and I'm rewarded with the brief stutter of his hips before he finds his rhythm again.

It's too good. Too much. The pressure is unbearable and glorious, and, when he tunnels into me, I can feel every single inch of his perfect cock drag against the tender spot inside me. My thighs are tensed and trembling, my toes curled, one hand grasping hard around his wrist—entranced by the way I can feel his muscles and tendons work under his skin as he plays with my clit—and the other hand clutching frantically at his bicep, his shoulder, his dark, disheveled hair. Anywhere to hold on while the tide rises higher and higher.

"Please, please, please—"

"Come on," he says. "You can do it. I've got you."

My back arches. My abs contract. My fingernails carve into his skin.

"Vincent," I gasp.

It's the eye contact that does it.

His hands and his dick and his encouraging words have dragged me to the point of no return, but I am, as I've established, a soft and sentimental bitch. So, it's the sucker punch of Vincent's pretty brown eyes, heavy-lidded with lust and bright with affection, locking with mine that shoves me over the edge.

The aching pressure low in my belly coils tight and then, abruptly, explodes.

My eyelids flutter and threaten to slam shut, but I force them to stay open. I need to see Vincent. I need the tether of him watching me while I come undone. And Vincent—my rock, my anchor, the boy who always keeps the door open for me and gives me more than I've ever thought I deserve—holds me as I come apart and back together again, the aftermath of my orgasm leaving me limp and gasping.

But he doesn't stop thrusting.

Stupid, unselfish, people-pleasing bastard. He's going to kill me.

I groan and lift my head to tell him that there's really no need to be such an overachiever, but then I notice the little wrinkle of distress between his eyebrows. He keeps glancing down where our bodies are joined like he's trying to calculate something, to time it just right. I hate it. I hate that he's preoccupied with anything other than enjoying himself.

Also, I think he's planning to pull out, and *fuck that.*

"*Don't,*" I say.

Vincent blinks up at me, dazed but determined. I want to remember him like this forever.

"I'll pull out," he tells me. "It's okay. I'm close. I'll pull out—"

There's the tiniest twist of reluctance in his voice. He tries to hide it, but I hear it.

It's sweet that he's trying to be so considerate, but if he thinks I'm about to let him sacrifice this because he feels guilty asking me for what he really wants, I'll kill him. He's wearing a condom. Nina and Harper will gladly pay for my Plan B out of their sheer hatred of the surprise pregnancy trope. Vincent and I are being responsible adults, and responsible adults get to live a little. So, I hook my arms under his, reach across the broad expanse of his sculpted upper back, and grip his shoulders. The move forces him to hunch in on me, pressing our bodies closer and letting me use his impressively solid core strength for leverage to angle my hips up.

I meet him on his next thrust with such force that it rattles my bones.

"Don't," I say again.

Vincent's eyes flash with understanding. He sucks in a ragged breath.

"Holiday."

It's another warning. Once again, I choose to ignore it. I cross my ankles over the back of Vincent's thighs, wrap myself tight around his waist, and look him straight in the eyes as I flex my tired muscles with all the strength I have left.

"Inside me. Come inside me, Knight."

"Holy shit," he says, breathless, and starts to thrust. He repeats those two words over and over again, like a mantra, as his forehead drops to rest against mine. And then he's kissing me—sloppy, scattered presses of his lips over my sweat-damp skin and then a hungry swipe of his tongue into my gasping mouth—as I rake my fingernails through his hair with encouragement and affection and . . . something I can't name yet.

"It's yours," I whisper. "It's yours, it's yours."

I'm yours.

Vincent wraps a hand around one of my thighs and hikes it farther up against his waist. On the next thrust, I realize, with aching clarity, that the pressure is building all over again. It's different now—less sharp, but dull and deep in a way that sort of scares me. It's always taken me ages to chase down a second orgasm. I almost always call it a night after one, because getting to the next one is just too much commitment and ends up in sweat-drenched pajamas and a cramped wrist.

But this is different. I think I might actually come again.

Vincent must see it on my face, because his eyes light up.

"One more," he tells me, keeping his pace steady. "Give me one more, Holiday."

"I can't—"

"Yes, you can."

His blind confidence in his ability to make me orgasm might be infuriating if it weren't so fucking hot. I reach up to pinch his nipple. Vincent easily catches my hand and drags it down between us, pressing my palm flat against my lower abdomen so I can feel him inside me while he strums my oversensitive clit with the pad of his thumb.

I can't move. I'm pinned beneath a sweaty, flushed, panting

boy who is apparently going for an Olympic gold medal in making me orgasm, and I'm helpless to stop him.

I really, *really* don't want him to stop.

"Wait," I sob, even as I arch into his touch. "Vincent—"

"Let it happen," he says. "I told you, Kendall. I love when you're a mess."

"Fuck off—"

And then I come. Again. Just like he told me I would.

If the first one was a lightning bolt, this one's the thunder. There's no quick burst or sudden snap of release. The rolling pressure climbs and climbs and then, almost *gently*, spills over some unmarked tipping point. But the resulting flood that ripples through my body is anything but gentle. It's so intense, so deep, that I briefly lose all control of my body. I think I sob. I think there's a rush of warmth and slickness between my legs. I think I clamp down so tight around Vincent that he barks out my name like an invocation. With stuttering hips and a low roar, he follows me over the edge, the cradle of his hips grinding flush against mine as his cock pulses and throbs, before collapsing on top of me.

Vincent gives me only a moment to appreciate the full brunt of his weight (crushing) before he loops one arm around the small of my back and rolls us over so I'm sprawled across his sweat-damp chest. His heartbeat hammers against my cheek. I feel the echo of my own heartbeat thudding between my legs.

For a very long moment, we're both too spent to do anything but try to catch our breath.

And then, slowly, my brain starts to reboot.

Holy shit.

I try to press my lips together and keep quiet, because it seems rude to start full-on laughing after sex, but Vincent must feel me shaking on top of him.

"Shit." He tries to sit up. "Did I hurt you?"

I lift my head to look at him, equal parts exasperated and elated.

"Oh my *God*, Vincent! I'm fine. Holy *shit*. Why didn't we do that weeks ago?"

The pinched concern on his face immediately dissolves.

"That good, huh?" he asks with a smug grin.

"It was . . ." I trail off, shaking my head in disbelief. "Perfect. It was perfect."

I've thought a lot about how I'd lose my virginity.

Worst-case scenario, I knew it could involve either a complete lack of enjoyment or—and this was something that I'd tried not to think about—a lack of consent. Best-case scenario, I figured Harry Styles would notice me at the back of one of his concerts and whisk me to an unspecified European city to do adorably artsy date activities before we eventually made love, by candlelight, on a bed of rose petals (a girl can have her dreams, and this was one I'd nursed since high school and gradually tacked more plot points onto over the years).

But this? This was better.

It was clumsy and frantic and messy and *perfect*. Vincent and I communicated—even when it was more practical than provocative—and we laughed—even when we were making complete fools of ourselves—and we both came so hard I think it's going to take us a solid half hour to come back down to reality, so I'm chalking this one up as a big fat win.

All the romance novels I've read and the wildest fantasies I've entertained can kiss my ass.

They don't measure up to this. To me and Vincent.

"It was perfect," he agrees.

I beam at him. And then I say, very quietly, "I'm really glad I waited for you."

Vincent's face scrunches up.

"Shit, Holiday. Don't get soft on me."

His voice is tender, and his eyes are suspiciously shimmery. I think maybe what I just said means more to him than he's entirely ready to admit. I cup my hands on either side of his face and scoot up to kiss him, gently but firmly enough that I hope he can feel what I'm not ready to admit either. When we pull back and look at each other, I have the unshakable sense that we're thinking the same thing: it's half terrifying and half exhilarating to realize you're falling for someone, but it's a little bit easier when you know you aren't alone.

"That was really fun," I whisper.

Vincent nods. "Yeah, we're definitely doing that again. But you're gonna have to give me some time to recover. That was . . . a lot. I really didn't plan to be that rough with you."

I push up onto my elbows.

"Hey," I say, fingertip pressed to his sternum, "I asked you to be."

There's no way I'm letting him beat himself up and play martyr for something I very expressly requested. If anything, I'm the one who's going to apologize for not warning him, in advance, that he was opening up a can of tightly pent-up sexual tension.

But Vincent just snorts. "I know you did. I was there."

I press my lips together and tuck my chin against his bare chest sheepishly. In retrospect, it probably wasn't my *brightest* idea to ask for it hard and fast when my body isn't used to the impact. I'm going to be sore. Probably not as sore as I was the last time I tried to keep up with Harper at the gym, but there's definitely going to be ibuprofen and a lot of groaning involved.

Vincent looks a little worse for wear too. Hair dark with sweat and sticking out in every direction. Tiny pink scratches and half-moon divots peppering his chest and arms where I clung a little too tightly. Body flushed and sweat-damp and shaky. He looks like he's just won a brutally competitive championship game in overtime.

"I *might* have been a little overambitious," I concede.

"No shit," Vincent says. "I'm gonna need to wash your sheets."

My face heats. "You don't have to do that—"

"Shut up and let me take care of you, Holiday."

I roll off Vincent so he can dart into my bathroom to take the condom off. He only leaves me sprawled out alone on my mattress for about fifteen seconds before he returns with one of my hand towels, soaked and wrung out so it doesn't drip all over my floor. With one dry corner, he blots sweat and a little bit of foundation off my forehead, and then he wipes between my legs with a few gentle passes of the wet side of the towel. He used warm water. That was nice.

But Vincent's always nice.

Well. *Almost* always.

Vincent tosses the towel in my half-full laundry basket, then comes back to the bed. But rather than sit on the perfectly open stretch of mattress next to me, he throws the entire length of his enormous body directly on top of me, like he's my own personal weighted blanket.

Air leaves my lungs in a whoosh.

"Hey," he says into my neck.

"Hey," I grunt back.

"You wanna grab dinner or something?"

I laugh breathlessly. "Like, right now?"

He shakes his head against the crook of my shoulder. "No. For now, we're just going to do this, so you know I'm not going anywhere this time."

My eyes feel tight and wet.

For a long moment, we stay like that. Sandwiched together. Vincent hums in contentment when I stroke my nails over the back of his head through his sweat-damp hair.

"I mean, I am a little hungry," I finally murmur.

Vincent lifts himself up on his elbows. "We should probably put on some clothes first. And you should chug some water and take an Advil or something. But I meant what I said about going on a real date. There's this new Thai restaurant downtown that opened up over the summer. I've only had it through Postmates, but it looks nice online. It's probably nice and cozy in the rain. Wanna check it out?"

"I could definitely go for some Thai food."

Vincent nods, like it's settled. "C'mon. I'm taking you out."

He stands up from the bed and crosses my room in two easy strides to collect his shirt and jeans from the floor. Vincent frowns when he looks back and realizes I haven't moved.

"Or we could order delivery," he offers, sounding like he

might actually prefer the idea of staying here, just the two of us. He braces his hands against the mattress on either side of my waist and leans over me, smiling with such honest and uninhibited joy that it momentarily knocks the wind out of me. "You could still make it to your shift if you wanted to, Holiday. I'll walk you to the library. I'll even hang around and bug you for more reading recommendations until you kick me out. But I don't want you to feel like you have to give anything up for me. I'll have practices and games and stuff, and you'll have your time to do your thing too. You're still in charge."

My heart hiccups.

I'm done being afraid. No more hiding from my life. No more living every Friday night like it doesn't really belong to me, or like the only good adventure worth having is printed on pages. My TBR list isn't going anywhere, and I've only missed one other night shift this semester. Margie won't be too mad if I call in sick again.

"We're going out," I announce, hopping off my bed. "And I'm paying."

Vincent arches an eyebrow. "Your treat, huh?"

"Mm-hmm. This guy who's taking a poetry class Venmoed me a hundred bucks for a thirty-minute tutoring session. *Total* sucker."

He catches my wrist and pulls me in close.

"In his defense," he says, "he's shit at flirting."

I don't think either of us is entirely done exploring this new and wonderful world we've unlocked. Maybe he's not quite tired of playing with my phenomenal tits; maybe I'm still a little curious what his stubble would feel like against my thighs. But right now, going out to dinner sounds like a dream. To hold hands on the sidewalk, to sit side by side in a little booth by the window, to talk and laugh and exchange anecdotes and fun facts and secrets—one at a time, savoring each—until the restaurant closes and they kick us out. And then, if the rain has stopped, we can take a long walk around the moonlit campus, or we can come right back here, to my bed, and talk until we can't stay awake.

We don't have to choose right now. We get more than a few hundred pages of hand-selected moments together. There's no rush. No last page to turn to.

We have time.

All the time in the world.

Epilogue

The library is quiet.

Then again, it's always quiet on Friday nights.

Moonlight floods the atrium. The fake ferns rustle softly in the heat spilling from the air vents. Somewhere on the other side of the nearly empty first floor, the wheels of Margie's book cart are squeaking sporadically as she weaves up and down the stacks. It's all very routine, except for one minor detail: for the first time since I started working at the library, I'm not holed up behind the circulation desk with a romance novel in my hands.

Instead, I have my laptop propped open, a draft of the first chapter of my first novel staring back at me in full-screen mode to help fight the siren call of "just checking" Twitter.

Nobody warned me how hard writing would be.

It's brutal, and it's frustrating, and it's entirely worth the pain every time I manage to string the right words together to capture the image in my head or the feeling in my bones. There's something satisfying about creative endeavors. I think I finally understand why Shakespeare wrote all those love sonnets and Taylor Swift writes all those songs. I get it now—the inexplicable and inescapable need to untangle the garden of feelings growing inside you, leaf by leaf and vine by vine, to put them into words.

"Are you writing erotica about me again?"

My head snaps up.

Vincent stands above me, a teasing smile on his face and a cup of coffee in his hand. He sets it on the circulation desk. His name is printed on the side along with a tiny permanent marker doodle of a sunflower that I recognize as Vincent's handiwork.

"I thought you promised not to distract me during my shift," I say, snatching the cup up to take a sip.

Our arrangement is simple: every other Friday, I swap my night shift out for an afternoon shift so I can hang out with Vincent in the evenings. It's actually kind of fun now that I've gotten to know most of the guys on the team. We hang out at Vincent's place, or mine. We go on double dates with Jabari and Harper. We even go to the occasional party, where I'll let Vincent make me the weakest mixed drink known to man if he promises to dance with me, because I like when he's tipsy and loose and belts out glaringly incorrect lyrics to popular songs just to make me laugh.

In return for this small modification of my schedule, Vincent has agreed to give me my Friday-night shifts as a devoted time for peace, quiet, and my works in progress.

So, I tell him, "You're not allowed to be here."

"Oh, I'm not here for you," Vincent says.

I arch an eyebrow. "Really?"

"I can't believe you'd think that. For your information,

I'm here as a tuition-paying student, not your boyfriend. The coffee was just a nice gesture."

I clutch the warm cup to my chest and watch him through narrowed eyes.

"You're not going to distract me?"

"Wouldn't dream of it."

I purse my lips. "You didn't bring a backpack."

Without breaking eye contact, Vincent reaches over to grab the latest issue of Clement University's student-run newspaper off the wire rack beside the circulation desk. He holds it up so I can read the front-page headline (SEX, DRUGS, AND ROCK AND ROLL: NATIONAL COLLEGIATE IMPROV FESTIVAL BUSTED BY LOCAL LAW ENFORCEMENT), tucks it under one arm, and turns to stride across the atrium. He takes a seat at the closest table and makes himself comfortable.

Nobody should look this good reading the newspaper.

His hair is fluffy and disheveled in that way it gets when he sleeps on it wet, and his long-sleeved Clement basketball shirt is stretched tight across his chest. His face is a work of art, each sharp line and wicked curve of his profile enough for me to write entire essays on. Cast in the moonlight, he's magnificent. I could almost imagine he's a Mafia hit man on the job, a cutthroat billionaire in the boardroom, or a brooding duke poring over important letters from Parliament.

I can't decide if I want to write fiction about him or march across the library, drag him to the floor, and ravish him.

Then Vincent props his elbows on the table, biceps straining and bunching against the sleeves of his shirt, and I know without a doubt that he knows I'm watching and that he's flexing on purpose. To test me.

Well, joke's on him.

Two can play at that game.

I peel off the sweatshirt I'm wearing—a Clement basketball crew neck I stole from him the night we located my missing underwear where it'd landed on top of his wardrobe (turns out I'd chucked it pretty hard on his birthday, so my softball career may still have hope). I'm only wearing a thin cotton shirt underneath, and the library is chilly tonight, but freezing my nips off is a small price to pay for the win.

A covert sideways glance tells me I've pulled ahead.

Vincent is watching me, eyes on fire and a muscle in his clenched jaw ticking.

I go for the kill. Smoothing away a smug smile, I stretch my arms high up above my head, back arching off my chair and lips parting with a soft groan when the stiff muscles in my shoulders pull taut.

My phone vibrates in the back pocket of my jeans.

I half expect it to be a text from Vincent telling me to stop playing dirty, but instead it's a notification from the roommate group chat. Nina, who was both overjoyed and deeply moved when I informed her the birthday condoms she'd given me last year as a joke had actually saved the day ("Oh my God, Kendall, I can't believe I was there with you in spirit!"), has sent another picture of herself. This time, she's modeling her favorite light-wash jeans and a delicate pink sweater that I'm pretty sure she found in Harper's closet.

Her follow-up text reads: *Thoughts???*

She has a date tonight. And although Nina will never admit it, the steadily growing collection of mirror selfies in our chat tells me she's a little nervous for this one.

I text back: *Boo. Not hot enough. Wear the green dress with the spaghetti straps.*

I can't wear that one, Nina replies immediately. *It's fucking freezing out. She'll think I'm weird.*

Harper chimes in with: *Trench. Coat.*

Um??? I'll look like a hooker??? Nina shoots back.

I send: *And?*

It's radio silence for about thirty seconds, and then Nina sends another photo. Green dress. Camel trench coat. A crossbody bag she didn't have to ask to borrow from me because she already knows I'll let her use it anytime she needs to. She looks like the femme fatale in a 1950s French noir film. Harper and I immediately send lines upon lines of emojis—heart eyes, flamenco dancers, fireballs, shooting stars—that Nina responds to with a single middle finger emoji, followed reluctantly by a final message: *Thank you.*

I smile at my screen before I tuck my phone away.

It's fun to take over the role of whore best friend for the night.

As if summoned, a shadow falls over me.

The guy standing on the other side of the circulation desk is tall—really, really tall—and beautiful but not at all menacing. Not now that I know him so well. He's the star of Clement's basketball team. The one all the sports broadcasters and NBA fanatics predict is going to be a first-round draft pick. The one who got ejected from last year's big game for breaking the nose of a guy who totally deserved it. The one who recites poetry to me just to make me laugh and blush.

"Can I help you?" I ask, looking up at him through my eyelashes.

Vincent's frown is begrudgingly defeated.

"I'm looking for a book," he grumbles.

"Do you know the title and author name?" I ask, dragging the keyboard closer like I'm actually prepared to look up the ISBN for him.

"*The Giving Tree* by Shel Silverstein."

I just barely swallow my startled laugh.

"Right," I say, all business. "That's a tricky one. Very hard to find."

Vincent nods. "You'd better lead the way, then."

I shut my laptop, stow it safely under the desk, and prop up the little paper sign that tells people I'll be back in fifteen minutes (a blatant lie). Vincent doesn't step aside as I circle around the desk and slip past him. He lets our arms brush. But I'm nothing if not professional. I keep my chin high, pace brisk but casual as I glide across the atrium, weaving through the tables so quietly that none of the handful of yawning students scattered across the floor even look up.

Vincent follows so close behind me that I'm half expecting him to reach out, haul me back against him, and make me pay for teasing him. But he keeps his hands to himself. He's a perfect gentleman.

It makes me fucking feral.

I stop at the elevators and smack the call button.

"You don't want to take the stairs?" Vincent asks, jabbing his thumb in the direction of the staircase that's literally five steps to our left.

"Stairs are out of commission."

Vincent hums. I can't look him in the eyes.

The elevator arrives with a cheery ding. I dart through the

open doors. Vincent follows me inside, smacking the button for the second floor and then advancing toward me in a slow prowl. He crowds me into the corner with eyes so dark I can see myself reflected in them.

"You," he says, lowered voice echoing off the walls, "are a shitty actress."

"Stop talking."

He smiles wickedly. "Make me."

I wait until the doors slide shut before I grab his face and haul him down so I can kiss him. He meets me halfway, like he always does. We've kissed hundreds of times now, but somehow, we still come together with the primal force of two waves crashing against each other. I'll never get sick of it.

Distantly, I'm aware of the elevator stopping. The doors slide open, I guess, because Vincent's walking me backward and I hear carpet under our feet. Our movements are clumsy and slow, since we're grabbing at each other's shirts and giggling breathlessly as we try to keep our mouths locked. It's not until Vincent sets his hands on my shoulders and holds me at arm's length that I realize what section he's led me to.

British literature.

"You sentimental little shit," I accuse. And then, softer, I tell him, "I'm really glad you took that shitty poetry class."

"I'm glad I didn't *drop* that shitty poetry class."

"Is that shots fired at Professor Richard Wilson? I thought you were besties."

Vincent groans at his name.

"I still hate that fucker," he mutters. "He was such a dick about that first essay. I tried to tell him my wrist was fucked up and I needed an extension, but he shot me down. I was fucking miserable. All I wanted to do was sleep, but the team was throwing a party, so I had nowhere to go, and I figured I'd just power through. That was almost the worst week of my life."

"Almost?"

"Well, yeah. It sucked. But it was worth it, because I met you."

I reach up—without thought, just pure muscle memory—to thrust my fingers into his soft hair. Vincent's shoulders sag the way they always do when I play with his hair, and then he ducks down to kiss me.

"Pick me up," I demand.

Vincent nips at my bottom lip. "Ask nicely."

"I'm jumping. One, two, three—"

He catches me with a sigh that's both exasperated and affectionate. His wide, strong hands slide under my thighs, supporting my weight and pressing me close to him, so I can feel the hard wall of his abdominals in the cradle of my hips. I briefly forget where we are and let a content moan slip out.

Vincent gives my ass a tight squeeze. Not enough to hurt, but enough that I yelp.

"Greedy girl," he scolds, voice low and rough.

"Says the man with his hands on my ass."

"I need you to keep quiet," Vincent whispers against my parted lips, "because if we get caught, I'm not sure how the hell I'm supposed to stop kissing you."

The opening to be a smart-ass is just too appealing.

"You *don't* want me to recite any poetry?"

"Kendall, I swear to God—"

"If thou must love me, let it be for nought—"

Vincent growls but supplies the next line: "*Except for love's sake only*. Please don't quote Elizabeth Barrett Browning right now. You *know* what that does to me."

I bury my face in the crook of his neck to muffle my laugh. When I lean back again, eyes a little wet and cheeks sore from smiling, Vincent is watching me with a soft expression.

"I do, by the way," he says. "Just in case that wasn't obvious."

"You do what?" I ask, even though my heart gives a knowing kick.

Vincent smiles. "Love you."

It's the first time he's said it out loud, but it's not the first time I've heard it. It's in the way he holds my hand. The way he texts me when he's read a book he thinks I'll like. The way he comes with me to Harper's swim meets and Nina's improv shows, but insists on staying away on Thursdays so we can keep up our sacred roommate ritual of movie nights. The way he gifted me one of his old basketball jerseys to wear to his games. The way he introduced me to his very tall and very lovely parents approximately two weeks after we first had sex (I was a trembling, babbling mess when his angel of a mother invited me to visit her ceramics studio over the next school break). The way he leaves me notes covered in doodles of little sunflowers.

"I love you too," I tell him.

Vincent's smile isn't surprised. I haven't exactly been subtle either.

But it's still nice to say it out loud.

So much about our little love declarations would never make it into a romance novel. The rattle of air-conditioning.

The stained carpets. The faint dampness between my thighs that reminds me I'm about to have one hell of a time composing myself in the women's bathroom, followed by a very long and torturous shift before I can drag myself home and finally, *finally* climb into bed with Vincent to enjoy those gloriously lazy hours after I'm done with work and he's done with his Saturday-morning practice.

The thing is, I don't read romance novels for the realism. I read them because they make me feel seen and heard as a woman. They let me explore my desires—both the ones I'm proud of and the ones I clear from my search history—and they've taught me who I am and what I want.

I'm always going to be a reader. And I'm always going to be a romantic.

While Vincent and I might not have a high-stakes and cinematic love story (we're just two college kids getting handsy in the twenty-four-hour library), I choose to see the fantastical in us.

For one perfect, wondrous moment, the world stops spinning and the stars wink at us through the window. Vincent's heartbeat matches mine. His arms are solid and warm around me, and there's laughter on our lips as we kiss. The books around us are quiet, in the way inanimate objects are, but I can feel them around us—full of magic; full of possibility.

I've always loved libraries after dark.

Acknowledgments

My mom, for reading this book even though I politely asked you not to. Thank you for believing in me, fielding all my questions about taxes, and cheering me on, always, even when I'm a little bit mortified to tell you what I've been spending all my time on. I love you to the moon and back.

Simone, for being keeper of the shared brain cell and my twin in everything from birth month to favorite drink to neuro-divergent journey. Thank you for your skill, your courage, and your ability to always know exactly what I need to hear when I'm letting the imposter syndrome win. I hope we keep writing accidental companion books for decades.

The group chat, for making—and following through on—international travel plans with a bunch of strangers we met on a writing app when we were fifteen (bold of us). I love you guys, and I love that all the years and all the miles never keep us apart.

Deanna, my editor, for trusting me, seeing the vision, and holding my hand through this adventure.

Kiley and Avery, for being my publishing mentors and

answering even my silliest questions. Thank you for the insight, honesty, and your wealth of good vibes and teamwork. It's an honor and privilege to know such talented, lovely women.

Jenna, Deidre, and the very long list of readers who've championed this book: you all deserve the world. Thank you for your video and aesthetic-making skills, your keen understanding of the romance genre, and your enduring support of me, even through the posting hiatuses and the sleep-deprivation-triggered typos. I'm so lucky to have you in my corner.

BESTSELLERS ARE IN OUR BLOOD

Michael Joseph, our founder, was already a bestselling author before he turned publisher in 1935 – the same year Penguin paperbacks arrived. He loved authors. In particular, Michael Joseph loved guiding them towards commercial success, bringing their brilliant stories to the wider world. In 1985, exactly half a century after their mutual founding, Michael Joseph became the commercial imprint of Penguin Books. Our founder's legacy – the nurturing of writers and making of bestsellers – remains proudly in our blood to this day.

NURTURING WRITERS SINCE 1935

He just wanted a decent book to read ...

Not too much to ask, is it? It was in 1935 when Allen Lane, Managing Director of Bodley Head Publishers, stood on a platform at Exeter railway station looking for something good to read on his journey back to London. His choice was limited to popular magazines and poor-quality paperbacks – the same choice faced every day by the vast majority of readers, few of whom could afford hardbacks. Lane's disappointment and subsequent anger at the range of books generally available led him to found a company – and change the world.

'We believed in the existence in this country of a vast reading public for intelligent books at a low price, and staked everything on it'
Sir Allen Lane, 1902–1970, founder of Penguin Books

The quality paperback had arrived – and not just in bookshops. Lane was adamant that his Penguins should appear in chain stores and tobacconists, and should cost no more than a packet of cigarettes.

Reading habits (and cigarette prices) have changed since 1935, but Penguin still believes in publishing the best books for everybody to enjoy. We still believe that good design costs no more than bad design, and we still believe that quality books published passionately and responsibly make the world a better place.

So wherever you see the little bird – whether it's on a piece of prize-winning literary fiction or a celebrity autobiography, political tour de force or historical masterpiece, a serial-killer thriller, reference book, world classic or a piece of pure escapism – you can bet that it represents the very best that the genre has to offer.

Whatever you like to read – trust Penguin.